3/20

MW00380587

MEET ME AT THE MET

Marble Column from the Temple of Artemis at Sardis

Eric G. Müller

Plain View Press
P.O. 42255
Austin, TX 78704

plainviewpress.net
sb@plainviewpress.net
512-441-2452

Copyright © 2010 Eric G. Müller. All rights reserved under International and Pan-American Copyright Conventions. No part of this book may be reproduced or distributed in any form or by any means, or stored in a data base or retrieval system, without written permission from the author. All rights, including electronic, are reserved by the author and his publisher.

ISBN: 978-1-935514-49-7
Library of Congress Number: 2010924972

Cover and interior photos by Eric G. Müller.

Contents

for Tina

Acknowledgements

Having come to the end of this project my heartfelt gratitude and thanks go out to all the people who have assisted me in one way or another, who have shown an interest in my novel and encouraged me to see this book through to its completion. Foremostly, I'd like to thank my wife, Martina Angela Müller, whose artistic expertise, patience, scrutiny, advice, and multifaceted suggestions nudged me into directions I needed to go. I am especially indebted to Matthew Zanoni Müller for his thorough, relentless and perceptive editing. During our endless discussions over coffee he offered invaluable perspectives, and accompanied the book's gradual development with unwavering enthusiasm through to its final stages. Thanks are also due to Candace Bachrach for editorial assistance; Michael Thomas for support; Sidney Mackenzie for insightful comments; Thomas Locker for his kind words, helpful critique and spontaneous approval; Gertrude Reif Hughes for incisive pointers; and to Susan Bright, my unflappable publisher, who could identify with my vision and who understood what I was endeavoring to achieve. I would also like to give thanks to the innumerable people who have contributed to the existence of the Metropolitan Museum of Art, and to all those who continue to do so. And lastly, I feel moved to give humble thanks to that inscrutable personality who welcomed me so warmly each and every time I came to visit – the Met itself.

Preface

One quiet Sunday afternoon in the fall of 2002, after a pleasant stroll in the woods surrounding our home in rural Columbia County, I sat down to write a short story. I placed the protagonist in the Metropolitan Museum of Art with the intent of having him capture the essence of the world at the beginning of the new millennium. About an hour and a few pages into the story I became acutely aware that Clarence had graver and more personal issues to sort through, and that the museum was to play a central role in his coming to terms with himself and the world. Little did I know at the time that the initial story would expand into a full length book, and result in umpteen trips down to the Met!

The unfolding novel kept calling forth current themes, initiated by Clarence's divorce, which, most importantly, included women's issues (especially women's treatment by men) – set off against a backdrop of a world beset by war, natural catastrophes, and greed, in all of its multifaceted manifestations. The resultant struggle for inner peace, and for overcoming persistent feelings of guilt, formed the matrix of Clarence's self-confrontation and ultimate self-development. Having the novel set within the context of the Met facilitated a natural and unique connection to these disparate themes, both on a personal and general level.

Working on this project gave me a good excuse to visit the Met over and over again, and though I am no expert and never went beyond my one year of art history at university, I found myself forming a deep and very individual connection to a great variety of art, which, under different circumstances, I would have bypassed or not sought out.

Through Clarence's engaging and interacting with the museum's treasures, the novel has almost become a companion book of sorts for those seeking to find an intimate and personal relationship to the visual arts. It gives a vivid picture of how the Metropolitan Museum of Art can be a true friend to anyone who loves and appreciates art, regardless of age or education.

Eric G. Müller

PART ONE

Façade of the Metropolitan Museum of Art

Broken Hiatus

Great Hall

I want to find a place to write.

I enter the Metropolitan Museum of Art and pass by the upgraded scrutiny of the post 9/11 baggage-check. Hard to believe, but it's my first time back in a long while. Briefly I pause to scan across the human throng and up at the Great Hall's three cupolas, before letting my gaze settle for a few seconds on the fountains of radiant sun-drop forsythias in the five giant vases. In the spirit of reconnecting I send a ritual nod to the four corners of this 'grand central' of culture, upheld by the sovereign strength of the fluted, four times four Greek pillars. Briskly I walk over to the cashier, pay my pro forma dollar, fix the pink metal admission button onto my black coat-collar, step past the two chatting guards, and bound up the first twenty-three steps of the Grand Staircase to the first landing, where I stop short, turn around, and catch my breath. I look down and contain my impatience to find a place to write.

I breathe deeply. Through the gateway of the large glass doors I savor the late afternoon's Indian summer sun as it descends, covering the rest of Manhattan with its gallant vermillion glow. It is Saturday and strains of a Haydn string quartet, coming from the Balcony Bar above me, expand the moment, stroking and soothing my restive mood. How good it feels to breathe the air of my old stomping ground again.

I used to be a regular at the Met. I've drunk hundreds of cups of coffee here – the bitter juice that gets me going. Apart from paying homage to my favorite works in the permanent collection, I was constantly on the lookout for something new. I was an exhibit junkie, forever anticipating the next show to roll through the Met. Even just walking around in a desultory manner was satisfaction enough. I turned paintings and sculptures into poems, which are now piled up in pockets, boxes, drawers and on shelves – testimony to my erratic obsession with words and ideas. Maybe someday I'll find time to collate them, those tears of feeble and elusive truths. But writing ekphrastic poems is not my purpose today.

I turn abruptly and move on, springing up the next twenty-three steps of the wide central staircase to the top of the second floor, impulsively making for the Balcony Bar to catch the sounds of the alluring music more clearly. Now it's Brahms's Waltzes lusciously flowing through my ears. I sit down at one of the round tables, warmed by the soft light of the little white candle centered on the indigo tablecloth. Of all the times I have come to the Met I have only frequented the bar once. Arietta and I were celebrating our wedding anniversary, and I remember her ordering a martini (stirred). That was at least three years before the breakup. Soon I'm fondling a martini too, feeling carried by the cultured ambience. I rarely drink, but I need something to calm me down. Be that as it may, I've found my place to write. With hurried deliberation I take out and open my green, pocketsize notebook.

I click my ballpoint pen, ready to reexamine my forgotten resolution.

O

I turned forty on January 1st, 2000; never thought the day would come, and it's almost two years ago already. I shared my birthday with the world, and what a bash it was. I'd joined the other two million revelers in Time's Square to watch the mythic 1,070-pound crystal ball descend at midnight (surrogate fireworks), atomic time. I wasn't fazed one bit by the gross Y2K scare – ridiculous hype. And I was determined that Y2K was not going to ruin my birthday. Ever since I could remember I'd looked forward to that birthday, that long awaited number – 2000: a triptych of zeroes to peer through, windows into the future. My penchant for rituals made me want to honor and celebrate my birthday with appropriate ceremony. With that in mind, I absorbed the circus around me in mad Manhattan – the loud music and raving masses, caught up in torrents of confetti – and conceived of and clarified my new millennium's resolution: to do away with any kind of falsehood – to fight it, like I'd never fought anything in my life before! I thereby hoped to gain transparency, both in my personal life and in the workings of the world around me! Thus, in that momentous exploding midnight moment, I shouted my resolution out into the noisy neon blaze, while millions of throats cheered the birth of a new day, year, decade, century – millennium (albeit technically incorrect).

They were the words of a desperate man, of course, trying to get a handle on a life that had spun out of control, crashed, and left debris. '98 and '99 had been terrible years, driving me to the brink of suicide. However, the passion with which I screamed into the noisy night surprised me. I was like a little kid, exhilarated and carried away by the hoopla of the quasi ceremonial moment. Fact is, I just wanted to be utterly and unequivocally myself again, because the "little me" had made quite a mess of it all. But the truth is: I'm just as far from being myself again, and I'm still in a mess!

O

Now the musicians are playing Beethoven's first string quartet, immediately recognizable by the one-measure motif, driven forward by the emotionally powerful rhythmic quality. While listening I'm nostalgically reminded of my mother and the long evenings we spent listening to scratchy vinyl records. She'd sit reading a book (always alternating between a whodunit and a classic) while I'd be lost in play on the carpet. Intermittently she'd comment on the music and respective composers, pointing out, for instance, how effortlessly Mozart could shift between major and minor, that Wagner was the one responsible for the dissolution of tonality; or dour stories, like the surreptitious exhumation of Haydn's body by an amateur phrenologist who cut off the composer's head to determine whether he had fully developed 'bumps of music.'

I'm lost in reverie until someone asks for the vacant chair by my table. I smile and gesture "take it." The elderly Lincolnesque man gives me a kind "thank you" nod and I want to cry. I don't know why. Maybe it's because I'm lonely, or because Arietta left me. Since then the tears come too easily. Anything can get me watered up. But to cry, really cry? I wish I could. Something always gets in the way. Maybe I'm too proud to allow myself the luxury, or maybe I'm just in denial. By now the Balcony Bar is packed.

O

Except for a quick peak at the Rock Style exhibit in 2000 I haven't come to the Met since our separation. The place reminded me too much of Arietta and all the good times we had shared together. For years we'd come here, at times almost weekly. Arietta would impart her vast knowledge of art history, which generally evolved into stimulating conversations (our relationship was based on meaningful dialogue). We would roam the exhibits and she would stop to draw and sketch, while I wrote poetry. Later, over coffee we'd share the results. Ironically, it's partly because of her that I'm back here today.

Last night, after an unfortunate phone call that ended in us shouting obscenities at one another, I lay fuming in bed, tossing and turning, until I got up and wrote her a nasty letter – one long poison epistle. At least I could sleep after that (though it was shallow and dream infested). This morning when I woke up, emotionally sobered, I burnt the letter (which set off the fire alarm). At least I'd restored some smidgen of my soiled dignity. But God, how good it had felt to write! That's when I decided to come here again – *to write*. The desire overcame me like an innate, inexorable need. I chose the Met as my office because I knew that the world's greatest art can function as a triggering device for dormant ideas, while uplifting the broken spirit – anyway, that's how it used to be when I was a regular within these hallowed walls.

So now I'm here, scribbling down line after line in my notepad, to help me tap into various segments of my past, and, with a bit of luck, mend the future. I've broken my hiatus. I'm giving way to the moment, slowly opening the sluices of my pent up spirit, hoping to capture some essence of our present era and my place in it. I want to latch on to the New Year's resolution I made back in 2000, and I want to get to the core of what is bothering me. I know it's about Arietta – but to what extent? One thing is clear: when she left me, taking our daughter Alicia with her, I realized, like never before, that I had to change my life. It's what led to my new year's resolution. In that sense it is all about coming to terms with myself, and of dealing with the consequences of my blindness.

But then again, I just want to write, and see where it leads me. It's what I always tell my students in the creative writing classes: "Write, every chance you get. It's a means of self discovery. The act of writing will lead you as much as you lead it. Choose any form you want – journaling, poetry, short stories, essays, letters or just random notes. Anything! Persevere through the crap because epiphanies come unexpectedly. It's a means of gaining clarity and control of your life. At the very least it's therapy." So here I am, following up on my own advice.

But I'm driven by more than just a momentary whim. Though not revealed, I feel the purpose. I've got to figure something out. The end is not clear to me – yet…

So, how to proceed?

O

While caught up in my musings I become aware that the music has stopped and the Balcony Bar is closing. Looking at my watch I note it's past 8:30. I've sat, pondered and written for about three hours! I'm amazed how quickly the time has flown by. Though my hand is cramped and my left leg feels like a sack of pins and needles, my mind is cleared, and my body is finally a beating heart again. If nothing else, something has been set into motion.

Momentarily satisfied, I shake the limp from my leg and hobble out into the cool, crisp night. I didn't view much art – but I'd begun: I'd started a new writing project – maybe a memoir of sorts. Won't be able to stop – that much I know – till the end reveals itself.

Facing Page: *Two Tahitian Women (Femme aux Mangos)* dated 1899, Paul Gauguin

Her

Woman Drying her Foot, 1885/6, Edgar Degas

In the darkened room of Degas' pastels I find my medicinal dose of art for the day: a series of intimate, private moments of women, depicted in various poses of feminine toiletry – the archetype of womanhood captured in the simple act of bathing, washing and drying, of having their hair combed. They are fluid, natural, and fleetingly pure – away from the world of men, their nakedness given over to bodily care in almost ritualistic simplicity.

On my way out I'm stopped by Paul Gauguin, whose paintings evoke a contrasting mood. The sensual, exotic depiction of these far off Tahitian island women elicit a throbbing ache that I almost crave; an inexplicable instinctive pang that has accompanied me whenever I've fallen in love – secreting dream vapors within my psyche, beguiling like an hallucinogen. Images of carnal wonder seep through – primal as much as mythical, though the quintessential fulfillment is usually only found in the *meta*-physical.

I free myself from Gauguin's semiconscious grip and move on, with something stirred, disturbed. I find a seat close by, near the pensive Madame Ginoux from Van Gogh's Arles period, fumbling for my notebook and pen. My thoughts have already turned to Arietta.

O

I met her on an island – Greece, not Oceania. She helped me push-start the scooter I'd rented for the day on Naxos – the same shores on which Theseus had unfairly dumped Ariadne, leaving her a vulnerable victim for bliss driven Dionysus. "Where are you staying," I shouted above the buzzing rattle of my running motor.

"At the Alkion Hotel next door," she yelled back, pointing to the whitewashed building right by the ocean.

"Well, I hope to see you later… thanks for the push," I hollered, as I revved up and rode off. Straight away I wanted to kick myself for not having invited her to join me. The spontaneity with which she'd helped me, coupled with the image of her unassuming smile, long red hair and curvaceous, bikini clad body, stuck in my mind. After a few hours of randomly tooling around the island I turned back to track her down. I found her sunbathing between two olive trees in the secluded cove in front of her hotel. A book was lying open and face down on her belly. She was wearing sunglasses and I couldn't tell whether she was sleeping or not. Except for the trance inducing drone of the cicadas, everything was quiet, caught in the siesta's sacred spell, which I was hesitant to break. She lay there so perfectly still that I felt guilty just standing there, looking at her. I'd almost made up my mind to retreat and return later, not wanting to encroach on her privacy, but instead I said, "Hi, I'm Clarence from earlier," taking a few steps toward her. "You helped me with the scooter." She turned around, startled. The book slid off her belly into the sand. "Sorry, I didn't mean to sneak up on you like this." Quickly I bent down and retrieved Henry Miller's *The Colossus of Maroussi* and wiped the sand off it. "Here you go," I said, handing it back to her. "Great book, by the way." I was compensating for my nervousness and feeling bad about my sudden intrusion. "Funny, I just read it a few weeks ago. Have you already come to the part where he talks about the planet Saturn for about three pages? …"

For a while she listened to my awkward ramblings, until she took off her sunglasses, smiled and said, "So, what did you say your name was?"

That evening we dined in a restaurant right on the beach, our bare toes digging into the sand, as we drank ouzo, chewed souvlaki, and watched the wine red sun set over the Aegean Sea. We'd only known each other a few hours and already we were in love. Later, in the light of a waxing moon, we went skinny dipping, joined by the acting troupe she was traveling with. The beach became our bed on that inaugural and sultry night.

Right from the get-go I was struck by her unpredictable, mercurial personality. Her thoughts often surprised me and it was easy to misinterpret her moods and actions. I was also struck by her unusual physical appearance. The rare contrast between her syrupy soft skin – the color of pure, polished amber – and the thick, smooth waves of long, straight red hair that shone like bronze in the sun, and turned into undulating sheets of saffron in the shade, was just as extraordinary. At six feet, but appearing even taller due to her naturally upright and dignified bearing, she made for an uncommon sight wherever she went. And although I was a little taller, I often felt smaller due to my stooped posture. The thing I liked is that in her presence I automatically found myself standing straighter.

Arietta, who'd grown up in upstate New York, was a drama student in her senior year from Carnegie Mellon, and had come to Greece to perform Sophocles' *Antigone* in a newly excavated and restored amphitheatre on the island of Syracuse. She had played the part of Antigone – King Oedipus' daughter/sister – determined to preserve the will of the gods, albeit with fatal consequences. It didn't surprise me that she'd landed the part. Her bearing was naturally regal, and she had a disarming intensity that was deceptively veiled by her feline nonchalance. In my mind she completely embodied the tragic grandeur of the role.

We had much in common: both of us were avowed aficionados of art (though she was the undisputed expert), had an eclectic taste in music, and shared a profound love for the theater. Like her, I'd studied drama, having just graduated from the theatre program at NYU. And besides, we saw it as auspicious that we'd met in Greece, birthplace of drama. Given our compatibility, I had no intention of letting this bird fly – this red haired divinity with the unexpected anthracite eyes, flashing with every glance.

The entire cast was spending a few days of leisure on this, the largest, greenest, and to me, the most beautiful island of the Cyclades, before moving on to Athens and then back to America. I readily interrupted my island hopping and stayed with Arietta till her departure. During that exotic week I was transported into a dream that was more real than anything I'd experienced up till then.

One evening, a few days later, as we walked along the waterfront towards the Temple of Apollo, Arietta said, "I'm afraid to enjoy this… afraid that it's all an illusion, you know… afraid that all the joy I'm feeling now is going to be followed by pain – divine justice, or something."

"I know what you mean – some kind of payback time… it's almost too good to be true, isn't it? …us, meeting here, on this beautiful island."

"Yeah…" She paused, bit her lips and scanned the ocean. "What worries me, though, is that it's at one remove from normal life, and statistically, these vacation relationships have a slim chance of surviving. The daily grind busts the bubble." As she said those last words she turned abruptly and looked straight into my eyes, catching me off guard.

"Come on, don't jinx it! Besides, it was the scooter that got us together," I said laughing, trying to evade the intensity of her scrutiny for which I was totally unprepared. That was the moment I knew we'd stay together.

For a few more seconds she kept on looking at me, before she finally punched me on the arm and said, "Still, I prefer to see it as an act of divine intervention."

"What's with all this *divine* stuff?" I asked, laughing. "But hey, I agree. Maybe it is karma. The gods move and intervene in mysterious ways. The scooter merely served as the link to our Homeric moment."

"What the heck does that mean?"

"Homeric moment? Well, it's when something gets revealed – in this case, something about us. Our lives are sprinkled with Homeric moments, if we're awake to them.

"I kind of like that… come on, I'll race you up to Ariadne's Arch," she said, taking off and running up the promontory, dodging the fallen marble blocks of the ancient ruins. "If you catch me you can kiss me."

O

Looking up from my writing I'm locked into the dark, wistful eyes of Gauguin's *Tahitian Women with the Mango Blossoms*, gradually noticing the similarity of the left one with Arietta, except that Arietta's hair is red like the mango blossoms held below the beauty's naked breasts. From these 'noble savages' my gaze goes back up to pensive Madame Ginoux, and I think of Van Gogh and his desperate yearning to have a woman to love in his life, a family to live with in simple harmony – a desire tragically unfulfilled.

Feeling low, I start walking and make for the bathrooms above the restaurant, the memories of my Paradise Lost still clinging to me. As I pass through the Greek section I glance casually over at the fine exemplars of Cycladic art, when something catches my eye. I veer off and enter the Robert and Renée Belfer Court to take a closer look: there it is, the small marble sculpture of the *Seated Harp Player*, dating back to about 2800 – 2600 BCE. Another latent memory flashes up and finds its focus.

O

I can recapture the scene vividly, that very moment before she stepped onto the ferry boat back to Piraeus. We'd been standing on the pier waiting for the ferry to let the people board, talking and dreaming about starting a theater company in New York after her graduation and my return from Europe. The moment the jostling crowd began to move she drew me aside and said, "I have something for you." She opened up her bag, took out a small box and handed it to me. "Here," she whispered, "for you," kissing me fervently before turning her back and walking swiftly into the hull of the boat. At the last moment, just before she was lost to view, she turned around and glanced at me – she was crying, but smiling.

I sought refuge in the nearest taverna and opened the box to find a marble replica of the self same harpist. A little note in her beautiful script read: *Parting is such sweet sorrow, and, to quote the bard – 'If music be the food of love, play on' – yours, Arietta x x x x x x P.S. See you in New York!*

I cherished that figure of the seated harpist. Over the next six months, as I continued my extensive travels through Europe, I would always take it out and place it ceremoniously next to my bed. Unfortunately, just before my return to America, as I made my way across the Swiss Alps, part of the arms and harp broke off. I hadn't packed it carefully enough in my backpack, and it must have gotten bumped accidentally. I'd always meant to glue the pieces back together, but never got around to it. And now it wouldn't matter, even if I did find the broken sculpture again.

○

It's been fifteen years.

Seated Harp Player, Cycladic

Chaos

Front steps of the museum.

The morning was frazzled and chopped up; but now I'm on lunch break, sitting on the stairs outside the Met, fifth step from the top, left of the main entrance. From the high school where I teach on 79th, it's only a seven minute walk. I like the number seven and I monitor my pace accordingly. I've got to be back in half an hour, so it makes little sense to go inside.

I saw the news today, oh boy – and another war is in sight. At least the sun's shining and warding off the winter chill, though there's a halcyon crowd all around. I like it. I also like the word halcyon.

I've got my new, green, pocket-size, spiral-bound notepad, and a cheapo red ball point pen I found last night by the bus station on 82nd and Madison. I'm ready and alert, with not a clue of what to write. Everything about this project is vague; except for the existential notion that I want to uncover the reason behind my present condition and explore a segment of my life. I pause and empty myself, questioningly. Soon, three words come to mind: *periphery – center – chaos*.

I don't quite know what to do with these words. They most likely got subliminally stuck in my head after walking past the noisy ninth grade projective geometry class – with emphasis on chaos rather than point or circumference. But I like the words for their figurative value and I leave them on the page, trusting the process. Nothing cogent follows.

Again I cast my pen's red line into the page-pool, letting my thoughts slowly reel out into the center of possibilities. I'm a fisher waiting for a bite. I'm almost content. But my peripheral attention is caught by a young, spunky looking woman. Her thong is showing above her low-rider jeans. She's immersed in writing, face hidden beneath a heap of shaggy blonde hair. I wonder what she's writing about. She seems more inspired than I am. I want to touch her thick hair, run my hands through the locks. I feel a kinship through shared occupation. Silly and adolescent. I pull myself together and try to write something meaningful.

O

Chaos, the shaker and waker of our time. Chaos: Shiva's holy dance – visible polyrhythm, serving invisible melodies to form the future. All the world's a Chladny Plate, and we're the sacred grains, waiting to dance from chaos into harmony. The dance of the new world order – grain for grain, once the celestial tone has found its focus....

O

Sounds significant, but I'm just trying to impress the girl sitting two steps down from me. Mind fluff.

O

More papers arrived this morning. Signatures and sacrifice. I thought the divorce with Arietta would be over and done with by now. Will it ever? Right from the outset I'd decided not to ask for anything. I made no demands. I accepted everything, whatever deals the lawyers came up with. I did not want to contest anything. I wanted to avoid going to trial at all costs. Only in regard to visiting rights was I relatively firm. I missed my daughter Alicia, and wanted to see her on a regular basis. That too was fraught with complications. What a cumulative waste of time and money – not to mention the toll these endless proceedings take on the emotions. Yes, the chaos remains real, and is constantly updated. I've got to *understand* my chaos – only then can I grow beyond the current mess of my life, inner and outer. The real stuff.

○

What if that woman turns around? What if she looks at me? Smiles? What if she hits on me?

○

Chaos comes in many forms; often in disguise. Our age is propelled by chaos. There's a war on every front, and war is chaos. Still, we're sleeping. Alarms rang throughout the twentieth century – epitomized by the holocaust – and the sirens continue to wail ever more urgently – everywhere, now that we're beyond the turning point of the new millennium – even as we speak, as we sleep. We've failed the lesson of the century – F it! Study harder.

Now where am I going with all of this?

○

She lifts her head, sits up and throws her tresses back. She looks nothing like the way I envisioned her. The disappointment is almost physical. A crossword puzzle lies trapped between her knees, and after tapping her blue ball point pen against her fleshy nose for a couple of seconds she bends over again, scribbling away, her chunky hair falling back into a heap. Nope – no kinship here, and my interest is immediately stubbed. The desire she provoked was just a dull automatic reaction. I'm ashamed. She was just another rebound phantom.

○

The point is: I haven't found the connection between the center and the periphery for myself.

○

Enough, I'm late. Got to go.

The Thread

Steps leading down to the Robert Lehman Collection

I go down thirteen steps to the lower level of the Lehman collection; then pause to think how landings have the tendency to make me halt in my path. I empty my mind and give myself over to the senses, becoming a stock still pillar of attentiveness – *an echoic cough from the medieval section... hushed whispers fluttering like retreating bats along the walls... cupped, high-pitched kids' giggles from below... an admonishing bass voice silencing the mirthful eruption... faint smell of Old Spice mixed with some citrus detergent... ample ambient light, cool expansiveness....* After this moment of mindfulness I descend the next thirteen steps to the ground floor and enter the embrace of another peaceful courtyard. A further four steps and I'm level with the central 'Pazzi' fountain. I sit on one of the four benches around the beautiful marble vessel from 1470, and for a while it banishes my doomsday self. I'm grateful for the relative quietude, and my spirits rise. I've found my place to write for a while – a way of sprinkling water over my wilted soul.

No thoughts come. That's okay. I'm used to it. I'm enjoying the trees, plants and beauty around me. The fountain is empty, but imaginatively I fill it with the splish-splash of water. I'm resting, and rest is a rejuvenating force. Having just come from a class teaching Homer's *Odyssey* with a group of willing but chatty 10th graders, it feels good to simply sit here, quietly. I'm waiting to find out what's on my mind.

○

Pazzi Fountain, 1470

I know what's on my mind, but it takes will power and maybe a touch of courage to enter the labyrinth and kill the Minotaur, even with Ariadne's thread to possible freedom; because the path it describes is one of self confrontation. The monster is, after all, just a composite of my past actions, my inveterate doppelgänger. I see it all ahead of me: the Met, the maze through which I'll wander for a few weeks, months or even years, recording snippets of my story in little green notebooks; a different place and time for each new entry, my thoughts the thread I must unravel in order to face the beast and find my way back to the point of departure – liberated. I hope.

Lofty thoughts and obfuscations aside, all I really need to do is examine how I made such a mess of my relationship with Arietta. Again and again I've noticed how my entire life has depended on the way I've handled my most intimate relationships, so it stands to reason that I should follow that thread – just not quite now.

○

I get up and move on, back up the stairs. I count them all in my habitual manner – arithmomaniac that I am. With many stops and starts along the way I end up on the second floor, wandering among the European masters. As I'm strolling past the impressive selection of drawings and prints, the eerie etching of Francisco Goya's naked and monumental *Giant* demands my attention. He sits alone in the black, bitter night. A foil thin moon casts blunt light, lending the colossus of his sculpted body more bulk – offset by a baleful gaze, up into the empty firmament. I see in him the heavy embodiment of my own predicament. What's he waiting for? What am I?

I move on, troubled. A few galleries farther I find a bench to sit on. Something is preventing me from getting a firm grip on the stuff I want to deal with. I want to write, but after some false starts I realize it's not going to happen today.

I look up and am met with the knowing gaze of the aging Rembrandt. He nods and mouths some words I cannot catch, raises his eyebrows ever so slightly, and then retreats back to 1660.

Self-Portrait, Rembrandt, 1660

The Written Word

Coffee and Muffin

I'm standing in front of *Koran Leaf* in the Islamic Art section, admiring the Arabic cursive script from 1307-8. As I'm looking at it I reflect on how the viewing of art is in itself a creative act, which must be schooled like any other discipline. Observation is my starting point. It takes a certain amount of will force, though the question is always whether I want to exert my energy or not. Mostly I don't, but this beautiful script has caught my attention. I'm taken by it – the foreign, almost mystical characters, conjuring forth evocative images from the magical land that gave us Aladdin, Scheherazade and 999 other legendary tales. My eyes involuntarily follow the shapely lines – very satisfying.

I've found my spot, my office space for today. I pull up a comfortable wicker chair, secure my humble writing accoutrements, remove my jacket, hang it over the back of the chair, and begin.

O

Associative thinking leads me to the memory of the first two words I ever wrote – my name. It was a Friday afternoon, back in first grade, and I was standing alone by the blackboard, piece of white chalk in hand. I was the only one in my class who still couldn't write his name and I felt terribly ashamed. I stood there, perplexed, while everybody else was already dismissed. Sardonic Miss Flutsch was watching my every false move, rapping the desk with her wooden ruler every time I made a mistake – thwack... thwack... thwack. After an endless struggle I could at last write my name without any mess-ups: *Clarence Somerset*. Finally I'd signed my name to the unwritten biography of my first six years! It was a seminal moment. Since then I've been a writer. I wrote before I could read. I'd copy long passages from large, leather bound tomes that my mother had inherited from my grandfather, without knowing the meaning of a single word. I even developed my own script (reminiscent of Nordic runes), filling reams of paper, which I then stapled into crude homemade books, replete with pictures. The act of writing became my favorite pastime, on par with playing basketball. However, writing, as taught in school, took a little longer, dreamer that I was.

As far back as I can remember I've always talked to people in my head, or composed endless monologues. Pathologically shy at times I hardly ever dared speak out. And moving from place to place didn't help much either. Later, as I grew older, I penned and pinned the endless rambles down on paper. Some of them condensed and crystallized into poems and short stories, later into novels. Writing became my solace, my friend in need. Still is – right now.

O

I look up, take a break, stretch, sit back, peer around, shake my arm, my wrist, let my hand flop about, and twiddle my writing fingers. I get up and walk around, kick my left leg a few times, and spill hundreds of pins and needles over the floor (I shouldn't double up my legs so tightly while writing). I have to laugh it off. As I'm awkwardly hopping about I spot another manuscript, skillfully illustrated, titled: *The Preparation of Medicine from Honey*. What a poetic title. All the little dots and squiggles flying around the script above and below the miniature painting remind me of busy bees. I lose myself in the drawing of the pharmacist stirring the preparation and my eyes drink from this visual drug. The elixir refreshes and I sit down in the wicker chair and continue.

O

Words, words – paltry purveyors of meaning, though they're often all we have. As writers we're always trying to hit the sweet spot with our words, where meaning and medium meld to convey the essential thoughts. So we stir, like the ancient pharmacist, tasting them for their medicinal properties.

32

I love words, especially when I am distressed. They come flying, or well up like fish from the depths. I'm obsessed by them. When I'm feeling down, I go for the dictionary instead of the bottle. I frantically look up words that I've circled in the books I read. I collect words to liberate them through use – or so it seems, each time I've made a word my own, or gotten to know it more intimately, by mining it for subtleties of meaning. Some words have been reduced to ugly frogs, but are really princes. Some words elude me and I need to go in search of them, again and again. Others flee if I neglect them for too long. Words don't like to be neglected. They need to be nurtured like any other living being. They need to be fed, taken out, talked to, put to work, enjoyed, and most importantly – loved. Otherwise we have a multitude of words at risk, who'll wreak havoc in the careless minds of the unsuspecting. There's anger in the word world. The media isn't fair. Favoritism causes irreconcilable conflict. Buzzwords have the same effect as drive by shootings. Wards in the word infirmary are filled with ailing, wounded words. Many caring teachers, poets and writers are frantically trying to save the lives of words, but daily patients die like trees in the Amazon forest. They fall – a discarded, wasted and rotting pile. Double plus ungood.

My fourteen year old daughter, Alicia, surprised me the other day. Over brunch, Sunday morning, just before driving her back to her mother's up in Duchess County, she suddenly riled, "I hate our incestuous past. It's to blame for all my weirdness, my random thoughts, my inability to socialize without making a complete fool of myself, yeah, even my unibrow – I hate plucking it by the way – and also my stuttering… everything really – down to my pathological compulsion to say words backwards – *sdrawkcab*."

"Hey, that's funny," I chuckled, amused at her eruption. How I missed these spirited outbursts, now that I only saw her on weekends.

"I constantly have to say words backwards. I can't help it. It just happens – *sneppah*."

I burst out laughing. "What do you mean – backwards?"

"Exactly what I'm saying – backwards. Go on, test me. Throw out any word you want and I'll say it backwards. I don't even have to think anymore – *eromyna*. It just pops right up in my mind. Come on, dad, shoot – *toohs*."

"Okay," I said, still snickering, "how about… butter?"

"*Rettub*." Come on, that's a baby word. Something bigger, more challenging."

"Fine… let's see… how about Metropolitan?"

"*Natiloportem*," she answered without the slightest pause. I whooped out loud. It was too hilarious. Each word was perfectly enunciated. It was uncannily satisfying and uniquely thrilling.

"Technical."

"*Lacinhcet*."

"Rudimentary."

"*Yratnemidur*."

I tossed out word after word and she hurled the inverted versions back at me with stunning immediacy. By now I was doubled up with laughter, tears running down my cheeks. But I hadn't heard anything yet: not only could she say whole sentences backwards, but she could have a conversation in 'backwards talk.' The clincher came when she recited a Shakespearean sonnet in reverse. "Most of the poems we learned in school I can say backwards – no big deal." It was an almost frightening revelation. How could I not have known?

"How come you never told me about this?" I asked, almost accusingly.

"Oh, come on, Dad. You never noticed; that's all. I often talked in backwards talk. You were just too busy doing your own thing, I guess."

"I guess." I poured myself another cup of coffee. "Did Mom know?"

"Of course she did. She knows everything."

"You're right there," I answered, almost bitterly. I was never as involved in every detail of Alicia's life as I should have been.

"I've been doing it since I was six," she explained. "It all began with street signs: *Stop* was the first word I transformed into its mirror image – *pots*. You know, I'd get so bored when we'd walk around, sit on busses, or on the subway. It gave me something to do. Billboards came next, and before long it became an irreversible habit: I read everything twice – once forwards and once backwards. I can read a whole book in 'backwards read' and understand everything. In fact, I've developed specific pronunciation and grammar rules."

And I thought my counting craze was weird.

O

I take one more look at the *Koran Text*. I find out that the border text reads: *It is written: Baghdad, may God protect her in the months of the lunar year 707* (1307/8 A.D.) The auspicious nature of the words rings on as I walk slowly back down to the Great Hall. How long before America will attack Baghdad? All the rhetoric in the media is intimating the worst.

Surrealism

Guggenheim Museum

The Guggenheim. I spiral slowly up the rotunda, the continuity of the slight incline steadily disagreeing with my system, making me resent the twelve dollar entrance fee. On entering the 'inverted ziggurat,' landmark of the museum mile, I felt fine enough – but now I'm nauseous. A full two rotations up the ramp I stop to scold myself: *Hey, dim-wit, you're supposed to take the elevator to the top of the building and then walk down at a leisurely pace – otherwise you're viewing the exhibit in reverse.* Maybe that's why I'm feeling out of sorts – didn't follow the instructions. Hoping to fix the situation I let the elevator whisk me to the top, where I found out that I still had to walk up two thirds of a spiral. Enervated, I look down from the topmost railing and succumb to the added sensation of vertigo. Frank Lloyd Wright is an innovative architect, but my body is rebelling against the double feature of the big hole and the expanding circular ramp. It had the same effect on me when I came to see the *Surrealism* exhibition back in '99.

Be that as it may, I start my downward spiral focusing on the visual Americana of the Norman Rockwell exhibit, which seems at odds with the organic, geometric and sculptured shapes of the building. The humorous captions of typical American life (not without its slight undertone of tragedy) remain dead on the wall. Though I pay them due attention, nothing's happening. I'm not even entertained, as I have been in the past while visiting the Norman Rockwell Museum in Stockbridge. Truth is: I cannot stomach any art today, though I hold his work dear.

Eventually, I hide out in one of the seventy-four niches, hoping to recover in this slightly removed but level enclave, resting comfortably on one of the plush seats. I close my eyes. My spinning head begins to settle and I'm remembering the Surrealists: The *Two Private Eyes* exhibit; the collections of Nesuhi Ertegun and Daniel Filipachi. Back when I was still in college the Surrealists were my favorites next to the Dadaists and the Impressionists. I was intoxicated with the possibilities of Surrealism, as much as the art itself. The idea of liberating the workings of the subconscious excited me because of the option of experiencing life beyond the limitations of day consciousness – another inroad to the possibilities of spiritual dimensions. The Surrealists stimulated me to think differently about reality, the rational and the irrational, inner and outer existence, day and dream consciousness, objective and subjective soul states. The pursuit of surrealistic aesthetics became a path of knowledge that included the inexplicable – the world of the unconscious that is just screaming for us to tap into, to study and reveal. I emulated and idolized the main representatives with an almost cult like zeal. Studying the works of Salvador Dali, Yves Tanguy, Max Ernst, Joan Miró, Marcel Duchamp, Picasso and others went hand in hand with reading the writings of people exploring expanded consciousnesses such as the Beat poets, Aldous Huxley, C.G. Jung, Carlos Castaneda, Guillaume Apollinaire – who coined the term *surrealism* – and, of course, Andre Breton, the undisputed leader of the surrealist movement. He was the momentum behind the literary movement before the visual artists latched on to the same ideas. But ultimately I was disappointed with the results of the movement. They were twentieth century *men* trying to break through 19th century stuffiness – a hangover of the Victorian age. Taboos and social conventions needed to be challenged, all part of the necessary breakaway from dense materialism; a further manifestation of the ongoing desire to break through to realms more profound (the 'other side'), even if that meant entering another, finer form of materialism, a kind of spiritual *physicalism*.

But mostly I was disappointed at what many of the surrealists actually found in their 'subconscious.' Too many of them couldn't get beyond depicting their repressed desires, prowling (almost indulgently) just below the surface of their consciousness. Now, the flaunting of suppressed lust, dreams, wishes and wants is no longer my idea of reaching into the depths of the vast unconscious. It was a starting point, but now, something else is needed. Nevertheless, I fully recognize its place in history: the surrealists tried to dip into inscrutable and invisible realms, realizing that the dead intellect is pitifully inadequate in humanity's overall makeup, relegating us to a spiritual indigence. And for that I revere them still. The point is that I needed to break through the solid ranks of my personal taboos and conventions, which have besieged my emaciated psyche – and still do. "Fetch me my rapier…"

There is something that wants to be said, but my mind cannot muster the right format. But what exactly? I need to find it; I need to stop circling the airport. Cogency demands clarity of mind, but doesn't necessarily guarantee useful insights. Maybe that's what led André Breton to write his poetry in the manner he did. Why not follow suit and let my subconscious dictate my thoughts? I'll give myself over to automatism in true surrealistic style – a foray into uncharted territory. Let reason take a break, I'll not control my writing. Maybe that'll help me find the right relationship to my hang-ups, open up to the closed sectors of myself; and help me home in on the essentials – the true motives behind my writing project. I've got to try different things to see what works. A window to crawl through is all I need.

I slip into another one of those bay niches, sit down on the carpet, lean against the wall, leave reality and reason behind, and dive right in… a current charged with life…

O

Breaking the spell that flew from willow wands, fate found us hugging and kissing on the Imagine Mosaic in birch and elm embalmed, homage-rich, Strawberry Fields. No Tivoli, but cheap dollar store surrogates, symbol circles, pushed onto finger fortune's hearts. We go, quite sane, walking steadily in single crowd, down to the altar. We squeal with unborn daughter's delight, smelling the perfume rendered waste by the priest's barking confession. Is down the same as up when entering time's spatial clock-word clementine? She must come now. If she does not, I'll never know if the night is brighter than the day's offshore body touch. Red rivers flow through the ache, pounding unraveled rope of hair across my chest – luscious, velvet blood strands that tickle as foliage pools widen to welcome the throbbing diver. And the crooked man in his infant forties wishes in vain. Baboons pummel the thirsty camel with sharp rocks as it walks the extra mile through the humpy desert into the soft snail's wet little house. Beat the jealous blame and balance the throbbing strength of knobbed intruders. Violence is a scourge that nobody can sequentially escape. Seed it anyway. All future is linked to the past and the present proves it.

○

I come up for air, resisting the temptation to review what I've written. But something is pushing through, that's clear – about Arietta and the moment I proposed, the pregnancy and wedding; the sensuous, seminal moments of our ring-sealed love… the arrant sense of my loss. Is there more? I jump back under:

○

The crippled wayfarer is the broken antenna of a yellow taxi cab. Or a dog's tail tucked between the leash-fastened ankles of a seen-it-go-round Cuban grandma. Witness the warm watered serenity of Winston's blasphemous white hanky on the battlefield? My church is ill. I'm a world at war, waged because I plucked the dart that cupid planted, unwittingly. Shot a bullet into the temple and saw Pallas Athena melt from the wound with a wilted olive branch. You wished to be more than soap rivulets on a hot afternoon's pavement, draining into the gutter after the frothy sponge squeezed and stroked the length of my insatiable desires. There's someone here talking and it's more than me, so I swim the backstroke in order to reach you sooner, but flail around in frantic, tormenting circles. Still, I embrace you from afar, for your arms are love-limbs, and every motion is caught in the bubbles' reflections before they burst. Keep it secret till the future birth may clomp two stones together, creating sparks, igniting old moss, protecting the new, midst the insistent relentless rolling. Fire me from the circus cannon through the supernova to you.

○

Like candy on a soft sucking tongue, the sweet chaos of kaleidoscopic images calmly dissolves. I'm relishing the aftertaste – like fragments of dreams that call for interpreting. Was it Freud who said that dreams not interpreted are like letters not opened? Anyway, the literary bonbon took care of my nausea and I feel invigorated. A window was opened and I caught a glimpse of myself mourning the loss of love.

Surrealism is a loosening device, if nothing else. I'm ready to spiral down and out, feeling more myself than when I came in. I'll go to Café Sabarsky, a few blocks down, for some good Viennese coffee and torte. There, I'll review my notes – to see what modest insights they might yield. There's always a lot going on underneath it all.

Melting Pot Me

Mother and Child, Mali, Barmana people, Wood

For a while I watch the film on Mali dancers in the African section of the Michael C. Rockefeller Wing. Usually I'm against films in museums unless they're in a closed off room or auditorium – it disturbs the contemplative silence I cherish in any museum – but in this case it merges well, the small screen discreetly placed, the volume low. The ritual dances and music are captivating, giving me ideas for the African play, *Cheating Death* I'm currently working on with the drama club. Stimulated, I sit down on the soft grey carpet, leaning gently against the *Africa – Kingdom of Benin* partition, right next to the *Carved Altar Tusk*. There's a primal pain that seeps through my flesh, and I give way to it. I suspect the source of my incomprehensible and yearning love for Africa lies in the homeopathic dose of my distant ancestry.

O

I didn't know about it till the day when someone shouted, "Get out of the way, you nigger," almost hitting me with his car as I was riding home from school on my bicycle. I was nine at the time and had never thought of myself in terms of race. My mother and her partner (at the time) were both white, and the question had never come up. That afternoon, after I told her about the incident, my mom revealed the truth about my real father. "Sit down, Clarence; it's time I told you something about your Dad." We were in the kitchen. She poured me a glass of milk and I added a spoonful of cocoa. Up till then I knew next to nothing about him, except that he'd died just before I was born. That evening, after her admission, I looked in the mirror and for the first time recognized the faint trace of my distant African heritage: the texture of my light brown complexion, the shape of my nose, and the woolly (though not curly) hair – bleached straw blonde in the hot summer sun.

Mom had kept the explanations brief and simple. Only later did I fully comprehend what had happened and what my mother must have gone through.

I was conceived in a small *dorpie* called Genadendal, about an hour's drive north of Cape Town, South Africa. While on a six months college exchange program my mother had fallen in love with Jan Leipoldt, a tall, blonde, and blue eyed Jazz musician. He held down a day job as a printer, and played trumpet in a Jazz club on the weekends near Clifton Beach, where they'd met. By all appearances he was white, but in fact, he was a 'colored.'

Jan only revealed this fact to her once they found out she was pregnant. His straight, blonde hair and white complexion was a hand-me-down from his great, great, great grandfather who'd emigrated from Germany and fathered numerous children with his black female slaves. As sometimes happens, Jan was born with not a touch of blackness – a genetic aberration – and he could easily pass off as white and enjoy many of the 'European' privileges in apartheid ridden South Africa, which, however, reaped heavy resentment from some of his fellow 'coloreds.'

But now, in her new circumstance, he vehemently urged her to return to America before giving birth, to elude the grave racial problems that would inevitably ensue should she stay: a family split apart; the stigmatized and labeled child, unable to partake of the legal rights relegated solely to the whites. At first she defiantly refused, only relenting when he promised to follow her out to California as soon as possible. She left when I was barely a bump in her belly. Permission to leave the country was repeatedly denied my father, until, at last, through my mother's untiring effort, he was granted a three months visa. But fate chose otherwise: two weeks before flying out to the States he was murdered in poverty plagued District Six (a couple of years before it was bulldozed down to make way for a designated white area – the coloreds, Malaysians and Indians relocated to the Cape Flats, the present day ghetto), beaten up and stabbed to death by a gang of *skollies* who thought he was a whitey encroaching on their territory. She only found out the devastating news after days of frantically trying to contact him. By then he was already buried.

Hearing about my father made me curious about the bloodline on my mother's side, which, in turn, spread all over Europe. Mom, who grew up in the Bronx, until her parents moved out west, to San Diego, California, was the result of an Italian/Irish union, which caused inevitable friction in both camps. The Irish stream, I learned, could be traced back to include English, Dutch, Swedish and Ukrainian roots. In contrast, the Italian side of my mother's family was all too pure of blood. The family hailed from a small village in the mountains, a few miles inland from Palermo, Sicily. Apparently the entire clan was rife with incestuous mergers even before my grandfather, at the age of forty-one, courted and married his fifteen year old niece. This is what my daughter Alicia was referring to when she railed against her incestuous past. Only in my late teens was I struck by the enlightening fact that my multi ethnicity also included many religious streams: Catholic, Protestant, Calvinist, Huguenot, Russian Orthodox and Jewish (my Jewish great grandmother having fled to Scandinavia to escape the pogroms in the Ukraine), and, of course, animism.

Such my lineage.

O

I get up; shake myself back to the present. As usual, my left foot has fallen asleep and I leave the Rockefeller Wing behind me and limp up to the many galleried European section, stopping by El Greco's *The Miracle of Christ Healing the Blind*. I pause in front of this painting, and then let my eyes roll over *View of Toledo* and *Vision of Saint John*. They have a distinctly modern touch to them and I have to remind myself that they were painted at the end of the 16th, beginning of the 17th century. Is it the color, or the bold use of form? Without waiting or thinking of an answer I walk on till I'm seated in the company of the early Netherlanders' paintings, my eyes intrigued by Jan Van Eyck's *The Crucifixion* and *The Last Judgment* – mesmerized by the rill of blood from the heart of Christ as the centurion Longinus pierces his side… was it an act of compassion, duty, vindictiveness – divine necessity? He jabbed Him and was converted. How many times do we take a stab at God before we attain higher knowledge? I'm intrigued by the paintings as much as the themes. In between my contemplative perusals I write – in standing.

○

There's more than I can fathom flowing through my blood. Melting pot me. A challenge and a relief. I have no ties except for the human tie. I'm color blind, though I see them and celebrate them. I'm a cosmopolitan down to the last pore of my physical make up. Foremostly, I define myself as an individual and I love the ancestral blood in my veins. It's molten, like future's gold. It's who I am. *Blood is a very special juice* – Mephisto, the god of lies, tells it truthfully in Goethe's miraculous and monumental *Faust*. The 'pure' blood as well as the mixed blood carouses through my veins – the old and the new, the red and the blue, the thick and the thin, the healthy and the sick, the blood of my sundry ancestors and that of my unique self. On the one hand, it's robbed me of my sense of identity, sense of belonging; it's made me homeless, thus vulnerable and lonely; it's contributed to my feelings of insecurity, caused me to feel like an outsider, a stranger. But it's also given me strength, the ability to rely on my own resources, to see myself as a distinctive individuality – a 'creative outsider,' as a friend once remarked. My blood has become my destiny, and now it's up to me to cleanse it of my own mistakes, moral missteps – unequivocally through my own forces. All the atrocities practiced in the name of ethnic cleansing, epitomized by Nazi Germany's Holocaust, but shamefully continued in Kosovo, Rwanda, Indonesia, and other endemic pockets of the world, are just a tragic inversion of a 'cleansing' that should take place within oneself – solely and utterly, a purgation of one's own impurities of soul, and never those of others, for freedom's sake.

It must have been *divine necessity* – the piercing of the human brother on the cross; a revolutionary moment… distilled drops, marking the site, watering the seed of individuation. And as I'm staring up at Jan van Eyck's monumental works, mulling over my heritage, I admit that as much as I'm pondering the bigger picture of race, religion and art, as it intersects with my own life, I'm aching for love lost, for Arietta. Was our relationship too good to be true, too ideal? Now that we're apart it's almost as if the failed marriage nullifies the source of our love, or even worse: makes a mockery of it. Maybe I haven't suffered enough to forgive? Maybe I need to remember before I can forget?

Curved Altar Tusk, Wood

Break-up

Benches in Central Park

Packed. The Christmas crush. It's almost impossible to focus. I'd specifically come to see the exhibit of Pieter Bruegel the Elder's drawings and prints, but my mind won't let me. I persist, but it's no use. Arietta's phone message keeps on ringing in my ears – slightly nasal, but silky soft as ever: "Alicia won't be down this weekend. Her basketball team has a make-up game on Saturday. Of course, she'd love it if you came. But we know how very busy you are. Bye." She always calls when I'm out. First she dashes my expectations, then she makes me feel guilty. All with an edge.

I keep walking. In between I sit down to write, but fail. The crowd is anathema to me today. The plebeian platitudes of the gawking throng are found fodder for my acrid cynicism as I involuntarily suffer through the abundance of cultural baseness. Today the inane babbling infuriates me. They shouldn't be talking in museums anyway. "Lumpenpack," I mutter, latching on to mad Nietzsche's view of the masses. It's so easy to slip into a negative mind set, though it's nothing more than a quick fix to cover up an undetected fault line within the substrata of my mental constitution. It's in moments like these that I go slashing around deliriously at other people's failings. My antisocial tendencies are running amok. My antipathy gauge has entered the red zone. Everybody's a threat. I'm smothered by their proximity. Maybe my grim discontent stems from the agreement I finally signed yesterday afternoon. Yes, it's over. I'm officially divorced!

A tall, grey haired man laughs, turns and steps on my toes. I can smell his Eau de Cologne. He pats me patronizingly on the shoulder. I shrink away, brushing up against a withered look-alike of Queen Elizabeth, who grumbles something under her powdery breath, before shuffling off, nose upturned.

That's it! I rush off, dodging people. "Just gotta get out of here," I hiss, jumping down two, three, four, five steps at a time. I run right out of the museum till I drop down on a vacant green bench in Central Park – finally free of the claustrophobic crush. Dazed and detached, I sit and watch the children play… the meek shall inherit the earth.

Though it is a cold Saturday morning I lean back and relish the sun gradually emerging from behind the thinning clouds, warming my face, until digital strands from Mozart's 40th symphony from a nearby cell phone annoy me out of my vacancy. It sets off the playback of Arietta's nettling message: "Alicia won't be down this weekend… Alicia won't be down this weekend… Alicia won't be down this weekend… but we know how very busy you are… but we know how very busy you are…." It's the caustic undertone of her sweet voice that fuels my anger, triggering a slew of disturbing memories that take me right back to the haphazard replay of the breakup. I take my pen, determined – once and for all – to rein in those random and painful images. I'm compelled to bring order to those unattended memories that run wild, that always leave me emotionally drained. I've denied confronting them for too long. Trembling, I reach for my notebook and thumb it open. Let the writing begin.

O

Initially, I'd braved the shocking news relatively well. It was a Friday evening; Alicia had just left for the movies and I was about to pop *Dinner with André* into the VCR, when Arietta said, "Clarence, I need to talk to you." The tone of her voice was ominously mild and I sensed my cherished TGIF mood was in jeopardy.

"Sure, what's up?" Something was up, for sure. "Hey, I also rented *Sleepless in Seattle*; you want to see that instead?" I said, smiling.

"Clarence – no! Just listen to me, will you," she answered with unexpected force, glowering at me fiercely. Clearing her throat she continued in a softer tone. "We have to talk. I can't put it off any longer." She sat down on the coffee table, almost knocking over the flower pot.

50

The hibiscus needed water and her thick copper hair was tied back too tightly. Funny, the things we notice and remember.

"Okay," I said slowly, gesturing for her to go ahead.

"I've been meaning to tell you for a while…" She hesitated, then looked straight at me. "As you know, things haven't been going too well between us lately… in fact; we've been living past each other for too long."

I was in no mood for this. "What do you mean, 'Things haven't been going too well between us lately'? Sure, some ups and downs – whatever, as far as I'm concerned things are fine. And yes, I do love you."

"Will you just shut up for once and let me talk." She rolled her eyes.

"Fine, go ahead, I'm all ears." I threw my feet up on the coffee table, rubbed my toes teasingly against her thighs, leaned back and said, "Shoot."

"Your flippant response is exactly what I'm talking about. So, no – things are not fine, and the downs far outweigh the ups. Let's face it, we've grown apart, and the sad thing is, you don't even realize how far. You've been doing your thing for so long that you've forgotten what it means to be in a mutual, healthy relationship. You're oblivious to my needs, let alone the kind of things I might be going through. You've lost all sense for our relationship."

"Oh, come on, I can always tell what's up with you. Hey, it's Friday night; cut me some slack, here. I've had a long week." I began to feel annoyed. "I really don't feel like handling your PMS crap right now."

"Screw you," she said, pushing my feet off the coffee table with surprising power. You just don't get it, do you?"

"Get what?"

"That I'm serious – dead serious about the simple fact that it's not working out between us anymore… that–"

"Slow down!" I raised both my arms in a silencing gesture, fingers slightly splayed. After a moment's silence I let them drop again (typical teacher kind of thing to do). "Okay, now what the hell are you driving at?"

"What do you think?"

That seemingly innocuous question hit me. I froze. For the first time I realized the situation really was serious. Beads of sweat formed on my forehead – intuition is immediate. "There's someone else, isn't there?" I asked. My voice sounded disembodied.

She didn't answer. With a pencil she poked the dry earth around the hibiscus.

"You haven't answered my question." My voice trembled involuntarily. "Are you seeing someone else?"

"I tried talking to you... many times. But you never listened."

"Who is it?"

"It's not like you think it is," she mumbled, still poking away at the dry earth, some of the dirt spilling over onto the polished wood – maple.

"But there *is* someone else?"

"Yes," she whispered.

"I knew it. I fucking *knew it*. Who is he? How long have you been seeing him?" I shouted, jumping up in sudden anger, walking over to the kitchen counter, simultaneously sapped of all my forces. I saw my life – the way I'd known it – shatter around me. But I felt nothing, no pain, though I knew I'd just been critically wounded. There was something phantasmal about the unfurling moment, even welcoming in a weird way. I became conscious of a sudden and distinct disconnect between my mind and my emotions, while my body momentarily turned to styrofoam. I could see myself thinking: *I've been through this before, so have millions – I'm just another jilted lover.*

"So, who is this lover boy of yours?" I asked sarcastically, reeling back from the initial blow. "Do I know the shit?" My words were like acid, meant to brand her. "And for how long has this whole affair been going on, anyway?" She just poked away at the roots of the hibiscus in silence with the HB 2 pencil. On impulse I grabbed my favorite coffee cup from the rack and banged it against the marble kitchen counter, shouting, "Say something, damn it!" She winced and turned her back on me. "Not good enough for you, am I?" I had the urge to kick the trash can across the living room, but I caught myself.

I flopped down onto the couch, trembling. I entered a vacuum. I felt nothing. The beating of my heart was amplified, but the pounding came from the periphery.

"I'm sorry," Arietta said at last, turning toward me. Her sincere and submissive apology was unexpected, and it sucked me out of the cozy vacuum. To make it worse, she looked utterly beautiful as she said it, like a pieta. I didn't want to be hooked by her beauty. Not now. And why did the word 'pieta' have to come to mind? Her flushed face, the sheen of her clear skin in the ambient light, enhanced by the luster of her teary eyes were excruciatingly enticing. I wanted to devour her. Ravish her. Hurt her. I registered guilt and shock at my reaction, but they were bullied from my conscience.

"Did you?"

"Did I what?"

"You know… sleep with him?"

"I told you, it's not how you think it is."

"But you had sex with him?"

"No – I mean yes."

"What do you mean? It's either the one or the other."

"No, because it's not a man. It's Sylvia from the theater. There, I've said it!"

"Sylvia? You mean *the* Sylvia? Wait a minute, you're telling me that there's no man involved and you're in a lesbian relationship – with Sylvia?"

"If you want to call it that."

"And it's the real thing, sex and all – the whole shebang?"

"You have all the right in the world to be angry," she said in a way of an answer.

"Unbelievable! Who would have thought? My wife a lesbian. And with Sylvia. What fucking irony." I snatched up the half empty mug from the coffee table and impulsively smashed it on the tiles of the kitchen floor – the mermaid mug I'd given her just before we got married, on which was written in red: Lucky Catch. Arietta ducked instinctively. "All these years, and I had no fucking idea…" I wanted to hurt her with my words.

"Okay, I'm really sorry, Clarence. I should have told you sooner. Go ahead, say whatever you want. I'm glad you're angry. I deserve it." Her quasi apology and acquiescence only deepened the wound; left me impotent.

I knew, of course, that things had not gone well between us, but I'd ignored the tell tale signs. Faced with the possibility of losing her I was finally willing to look at my own shortcomings. Extended confessional talks followed over the next few days which I hoped would lead to reconciliation. I played the mature and understanding victim as I started analyzing our relationship's demise. Enthusiastically I admitted my failings, took blame and offered good advice about her conflicted state. I was almost proud of the way I was handling myself, how understanding I was of her situation. I was convinced that she'd see reason and things would get back to normal. But soon I realized that I was doing most of the talking and that she appeared preoccupied and distracted. For all my heroic efforts she wasn't really interested. Incrementally, the hopeless reality set in – she'd dumped me for someone else and her mind was made up: she was leaving me for Sylvia. Nothing I could do or say would change her mind. Our relationship was kaput.

O

I cannot continue. I'm cold, spent, but calmer. I'll get a bite to eat, and then proceed. Finally I'm doing what I was meant to do all along at the Met – face up to things. It took me a while to acknowledge it, to get to that point. It wasn't easy.

Suicidal

The Harvesters, Pieter Bruegel the Elder

Back with Bruegel. My head is cleared, my psyche stabilized, helped along by an olive and mushroom pizza and some coffee at Serafina's on Madison. The crowd – even bigger – does not bother me anymore. My mood had righted, my appetite to absorb, whetted. Bruegel's paintings have been part of my life long before I even knew his name. As a kid I remember gazing at Bruegel's *The Harvester* on an album cover of Beethoven's Pastorale, whenever my mother brought out her favorite 6th symphony, and losing myself in the rustic peasant scene. And during the times we visited my grandparents in San Diego, I was drawn to a framed and faded copy of *The Peasant Dance*, fascinated by the weird characters unabashedly frolicking around, unencumbered by their follies. During my year abroad I relished the encounters of his paintings in the museums around Europe. But more than all that, the paintings epitomized the love Arietta and I once shared; for on that sunny morning when I ceremoniously proposed to her (at the Strawberry Fields memorial in Central Park, just a few weeks after it was opened in October 1985), I gave her a beautiful print of *Peasant Wedding* (purchased at the Kunsthistorisches Museum in Vienna) moments after we symbolically slipped our surrogate dollar store rings on each other's fingers. I still carry it around with me in my wallet. Those were the insouciant days when we both still imagined we'd be living our lives together in peace… to the end.

And now I feel driven to chronicle the unfortunate and painful episode of our split up. But I'm procrastinating. My urge is challenged by resistance. I'll give myself another fifteen minutes.

The work displayed here is new to me and again I'm fascinated, easing my way intuitively into the brown ink drawings and engravings. I'm most taken by *The Seven Deadly Sins*. Bruegel's attention to detail and artistic perfection is astounding; the grotesque, almost otherworldly element of the figures caught up in their foibles reminds me slightly of Hieronymous Bosch. I can't help but smile, seeing aspects of my own failings displayed so accurately, naturally and humorously in these medieval scenes. Sauntering over to the *Seven Virtues* I realize it takes as much effort to uphold the virtues as to overcome the sins. They both address aspects of evil. I ponder the word *evil*. It has resurfaced. Not too long ago it was considered outdated, an anachronism, politically incorrect. But that's all changed since the 9/11 turning point, when the world got jolted with implosive rapidity. Its very taboo nature has added to the power of the word, now used deliberately to charge up hatred against the enemy – the bad guys *out* there. Over the last few months it's reigned supreme on top of the buzzword charts. But what if it's not just the word, but a living force, proudly incarnated and dressed to kill? What if Evil *is* both the playwright and the director of a play performed right now on the stage of world events? I'm wondering, because I've often felt an uncanny, even diabolical presence welling up in my own inner life. And when ignored it gets the better of me. It makes me think: how many of my thoughts, feelings and deeds are truly my own? How many are really expressions of me?

The gravitational pull of *The Seven Deadly Sins* is strong; its modern incarnation is far more fascinating, subtle, enticing, and luxuriously insidious. The hardest part is to recognize the full range of evil, to discern and acknowledge the multifaceted face of evil, to see through the layers of disguise. I love my personal evils in a skewed sort of way. The trick is to transform them into *good* through love. To ease out of the belly of the beast, no matter how comfy it might appear. To ease out is to stretch one's strength over time, so that the bad is metamorphosed into something virtuous. Moral mutation.

That'll do. I'm ready now. This mental discourse has given me strength to crawl back into my own story, self debasing as it is.

O

A week after she told me about Sylvia I was suicidal. The pain had finally set in. I roamed the streets at night provoking a mugging; went for long, lonely walks along the Hudson River; climbed up buildings and bridges, intent on taking the ultimate leap (something always stopped me – the image of Alicia, my late mother, or Arietta herself). Started smoking again. On days when nobody was at home I'd take out my old vinyl albums and play Hendrix, Led Zeppelin, Black Sabbath, Metallica, Judas Priest, or any of the other veteran heavies at full blast.

I desperately wanted to talk to someone, to unload, to get some perspective, some sympathy – to get it all off my chest. But I was too proud. I couldn't open up. On top of all that I had to accept that I didn't have any close friends anymore. Arietta had become my last confidant, and I hadn't even opened up to her for quite some time. Acquaintances galore, but no close friends! The ones I used to have are scattered all over the planet. Call me Iron Hans.

On one desperate day I drove out to Long Island, chose a beach at random, and lay flat in the wet sand, face down at low tide, determined to let nature do me in. Nothing mattered anymore and all I wanted was to be released from the relentless pain, enhanced by my own sense of utter worthlessness. Sounds of seagulls and surf, the distant drone of a private plane, the intermittent gusts of wind over the dunes, and the thumping of the blood against my temples, all compounded into a foreign presence. I felt bugs crawl over me, and before long the encroaching tide began tugging at my toes. I was ready to die. But as the waves got bigger and stronger, creeping up my legs, buttocks and torso, the agonizing pain in my chest began to subside. Each new wave was like a massage by the hand of Mother Nature, a soothing sensation from behind. Then, from above, came the rain, a steady, soft drizzle. I could feel the sand beneath me give way, shifting my body slightly this way and that. Nature was enveloping me from every side, kneading me. I opened my eyes and watched creepy-crawlies scurrying around over the sand, feeling them move under my shirt, across my neck. Nearby, some birds were pecking at a dead fish. I could smell the stench and breathed deep. A wave chased them away for a few seconds. Another wave momentarily washed over my head. I tasted the salt between my lips. Almost instantaneously another, stronger wave broke over me. I let myself be pushed and pulled by the swash and backwash, like a log, this way and that. More waves assailed me, increasing in force. One particularly powerful breaker rolled me over three or four times, leaving me lying parallel to the water. In that limp state I felt all my senses heightened – becoming preternaturally aware of every sound, smell, touch, taste, and sight. I felt more alive than ever before. Another wave hit me and the undercurrent pulled me out a few yards. Now my tossed head faced the ocean. After a respite of nine smaller waves (I was still counting), a whopper attacked me with a savage roar, and my body was battered by the full impact of the water's tumbling punch. Euphorically I choked and spluttered, and as I was violently flung around, I got a sense of self like never before – a primal current charged through my limp body. It restored me to my senses – my senses restoring my will to live. The wave's ruthless impact beat me back into myself. Dazed I got up, stumbled to the car, tore up the suicide note and flung it into a ditch. The words I wrote suddenly seemed silly – all about how I still loved Arietta and Alicia, and that it was my own free choice to put an end to it all, and that they should, on no account, feel guilty. I knew, of course, that if I really loved them I would never, ever have considered killing myself. I drove back home, drenched but revitalized

Though no longer suicidal, the pain persisted and came in spurts. During unbearable spells I wished I could just break down and cry; I tried to force it, but I couldn't cross that threshold. Tears and the resultant feeling of relief simply wouldn't come – the result of false pride, coupled with years of trying to tough things out, be a man.

The only person who could have helped me was Arietta herself, but she just looked at me with her sad, dark eyes, shining out from underneath the canopy of red, suave hair. To make matters worse I wanted so badly to make love to her – an inexorable urge. Rejection and pain is often like an aphrodisiac. But I was relegated to sleep in the study – the first step in our separation. Her bed was off limits to me, and in that she was firm. Still, I wanted to be with her, more than ever. I loved her desperately, though much of that love was born out of self pity, and often it turned to hate.

One night I awoke, aching for Arietta, the touch of her soft skin, the sensuous feel of her voluptuous body, the way we used to wrap our legs together, her warmth. She'd loved me so much, so how could she just turn away from me? (The *dumpee* always asks that question, instead of just figuring it out.) In a relationship there are a thousand little things that we tend to take for granted. My passion for her hurled me into the lower levels of extrasensory perception. Wild, exotic landscapes spread themselves out in front of me, populated with fantastical animals and naked people – waking visions that inevitably turned violent. Even with eyes wide open the grotesque shapes, figures and colors persisted. They were delirious manifestations of my lust for Arietta.

Plagued by these unsavory visions I got up and quietly tiptoed to her bedroom, heart pulsing down to my flaming loins. She was sleeping. I slipped under the covers and felt the familiar touch of her body – an excruciating recognition. I pressed myself against her, scenting her, gently caressing her. I was trespassing, but the familiarity of the moment dispelled my guilt. She was part of me – *how could I be kept away from myself?* I rationalized. How I craved this intimacy – the alchemy of charged bodies connecting. Her body responded and I took it as an invitation. But it was a reflex reaction and moments later, realizing what was happening, she urged me to stop. I couldn't.

"Please, Arietta, one last time... for the sake of closure."

"Don't be ridiculous. There was closure."

"For you maybe, but not for me. Please don't send me away... for our lost love's sake... please, just this one last time."

"I'm tired. I just want to sleep. Go away."

"Come on, Arietta. I've been through enough pain. I love you, and I must still be there, somewhere deep inside of you. Please, Arietta... yes?" In a small recess of my mind I knew how miserably pathetic my behavior was.

She didn't respond, which I interpreted as acquiescence. So I took her, first gently, rediscovering her body, then violently, giving vent to a lascivious drive that was uncannily satisfying. If I'd hoped that I'd fulfilled her in any way I was sorely mistaken. After I had my carnal satisfaction she whispered, "Now, get out of my bed," sobbing into her pillow. Like a thief in the night I slunk back to my study, more alone than ever. For hours I lay awake mulling over my vile action. I felt polluted. Yes, it was a form of rape – that's how low I was capable of stooping.

The very next day she left. I found her waiting for me as I returned home. "I'm moving in with Sylvia," she said definitively, as she noisily pulled her little black suitcase with the worn casters along the parquet hallway. "Alicia will be spending the night with us as well. She's already there." She paused at the mirror, adjusted her hair and slipped into her coat. "I wanted to tell you in person."

"Why even bother." I said, regretting my snide remark immediately.

"Because I have some civility left in me, or would you have preferred a note saying," – and she bobbed her head from side to side – "'Hi, I'm moving out and I want a divorce'?"

"Divorce?" I was dumbfounded. "We've never ever talked about divorce. Has it really come down to that?"

"For me it has… it was clear from the moment we split up. And after last night?" She bit her lips and her chin was quivering.

It was 6:12 pm (according to the digital clock above the shoe rack) when she lifted her suitcase over the doorstep, shrugged and walked out. I wanted to say something significant, but choked up. Once the door banged shut behind her, I mumbled, "I love you." Moments later I opened the door and shouted down the stairwell, "I'm sorry for last night, and I love you, I swear," just as the front door slammed shut. I doubt she heard me. Quickly I ran over to the window overlooking the street. I saw her hurrying away, dragging the black suitcase behind her. I desperately hoped she'd look up. She didn't.

O

Finally I've tackled one of the buboes of my biography. At least I've got it down on paper, even if I haven't quite come to terms with the whole ordeal. I feel lighter and freer for it. I've gained some perspective. All along I was afraid of facing my weaknesses, but simultaneously they also served to highlight my strengths. After all, I didn't commit suicide. I saw things through and kept on going. It's worth shifting the focus on the inscrutable power of overcoming, rather than wallowing in self pity, dragged under by regrets and failures – difficult as it is.

It's a start, but I'm done for the day. I've discovered it's more powerful to write something down than to just think and replay the images at random in one's mind. It's an ordering activity. It's taking a stand.

I pass slowly through the crowd. In contrast to this morning I can love them again. Leaving the Met I catch a cab down to 48th street, slowly walking west past Manny's music store, taking a left down 7th, heading for Broadway. I have no plan, stopping here and there, swayed by fancy. A troupe of breakdancers show their incredible skills… further on, a single bucket drummer, ferociously ensures that the beat goes on… around a corner an old, white haired woman with a pink purse dangling from her shriveled arms plays a trumpet in an alcove, alone and ignored... at Times Square a rubber man in sleek silver spandex moves like mercury to the sound of Tangerine Dream and Techno... I leave a trail of dollars.

The Lover

Autumn Rhythm, Jackson Pollock

I'm sitting in front of Jackson Pollock's *Autumn Rhythm*. A precocious girl of about eleven sits down on the corner of the plush bench, scratches her knee, and says to her mother standing behind her, "These modern painters have lost their minds. I don't know what comes over them. It's like a three year old."

"The artist is expressing his anger. While pouring the paints over the canvas he was pouring out his emotions," answers the mother, wanting to move on.

"Couldn't he control himself? What was he so angry about anyway?" Now she's scratching the other knee.

"Life, I guess. He had problems. Women problems, alcohol problems, and he was criticized by many people for the new art he was creating. He died in a car crash when he was only forty-four, you know. Total destruction. Fits his lifestyle, just like this painting."

"Was he drunk when he crashed?"

"Yes."

"No wonder. Stupid man." She jumps up dismissively and squeals, "Oh, look at that crouching, naked woman hanging upside down from the wall. What's that supposed to mean, mommy?" referring to Kiki Smith's intriguing *Lilith*. Off she goes; pink boots, bare legs, white dress, stomping down the stairs, followed by her heavy set mother, shouting, "Wait," while thumbing through the Met's guide book.

It's as if the girl's reactions to Pollock were personally addressed to me – curtly summed up with the words: *stupid man*.

○

No doubt, it was stupid that I hadn't recognized how far we'd drifted apart; stupid that I'd pursued my personal goals at the cost of our relationship; stupid that I'd ignored her numerous requests and invitations to do things together; stupid that I'd let the demands of my job as a teacher eat me up and wear me down; and really stupid that I'd taken my life with Arietta and Alicia for granted.

People had always commented on how we were the perfect couple. True, in many ways we were. We hardly ever argued, never raised our voices, settled differences quickly, agreed on most things, gave each other space, shared interests, had good conversations – it was, in short, a relationship based on mutual respect and freedom. With that in mind the break-up made no sense; but then again, I'd let it happen by not noticing the gradual erosion of our bond. Relationships need to be nurtured, and in this respect I'd fundamentally failed.

Still, it was hard to accept. We had so much going for us. When we were first married we did everything together. We were cofounders of a struggling Off-Off Broadway theater company, and acted, produced, and directed many plays together. Alicia basically grew up in the theater, falling asleep backstage, in the lighting booth, or in the dressing room. Off and on we gigged with a rock band; Arietta was the singer in the band and I played the drums (my dismembered kit is still in the basement). Practices were sporadic because the theater always took priority; still, our résumé included a stint at the infamous, graffiti filled CBGB's – birth place of America's punk scene. We were always doing something: going to concerts, art galleries, museums, sundry shows, and poetry readings – or just hanging out in one of the parks, having coffee, visiting friends. We got by on very little. Our theater company rarely made any money. We considered striking even a success. We wouldn't have survived without our day jobs. Arietta was the proverbial waitress, and I tutored children in English and made my rounds as a substitute teacher. It proved impossible to keep that bohemian lifestyle going. With Alicia's needs growing it became increasingly clear that changes had to be made. The confluence of different opportunities, wants, wishes and events gradually changed our lives.

For one, getting offered the lucrative position as drama director and English teacher at a lower Manhattan high school was too good to pass over. A few months later the lease on our cheap, but squalid apartment in Queens ran out which forced us to move. Luckily, through a school contact we got an apartment on the lower west side in "Little Italy," – a whiff away from Chinatown. It was expensive but close to the school. Arietta took over the management of the theater company – a part time, salaried position – which meant more administrative duties at the cost of working the boards; but it boosted our income. Though we were busier than ever, we'd regulated our lifestyle, felt more comfortable and settled, but spent less time together.

I was gone most of the day, either teaching English classes or directing plays and musicals, while Arietta took Alicia to school, waited tables, and spent most evenings at the theater. On top of that I began spending much of my free time – weekends and vacation – immersed in my new passion: writing novels – the best seller that would end all our financial woes. Over the years we slowly grew apart. It got to the point when sharing a common meal – just the three of us – became a rare event. Unintentionally, I'd made myself progressively more unavailable to both Arietta and Alicia. That's when Arietta began to spend time with Sylvia – not without some irony due to an incident that had happened many years ago between Sylvia and me.

I'd known Sylvia from the drama department at NYU. We didn't have anything to do with one another, but immediately after graduating, I acted opposite her in Tennessee Williams' *Cat on a Hot Tin Roof* – my first professional gig. She was cast as Margaret and I, against all expectations, had landed the part of the alcoholic Brick. Sylvia was experienced, having acted professionally even as a kid. Initially, I felt intimidated by her ease, confidence, and her sexy Marilyn Monroe looks. And I froze up whenever we arrived at the play's finale where Maggie coerces Brick to sleep with her. The director had her straddled on top of me, seductively remove her negligee, revealing all, and kiss me as the lights slowly faded. I was loosely bound up in another relationship at the time, and I felt uncomfortable every time we kissed. My guilt only grew when I noticed myself falling for Sylvia. The director was getting exasperated, shouting, "Come on, man, there's zero chemistry between you two... heat it up, damn it." As we got closer to the performances the kisses got more passionate. We'd joke about it and say things like, "Yeah, next time I'll stick my tongue right down your throat." Kidding around helped us to loosen up and get into character. She had a slight build, but her breasts were voluptuous, well rounded and firm like an Indian goddess; her skin, however was marble white which contrasted beautifully with my maple wood complexion. The last scene became increasingly steamy – enough to get each other dangerously aroused, but at the dress rehearsal I froze up again. During the blackout she whispered, "Let's rehearse this scene again later on, when everybody's gone." Inconspicuously we waited until everybody had left the house, and then proceeded to reenact the last dialogue between Maggie and Brick, starting from when she says, "Brick, I used to think that you were stronger than me…" right to his last line, "Wouldn't it be funny if that was true?" which is when she pushed herself tightly on top of me. Tacitly, we gave in to each other's unrestrained passion and had sex on the little squeaky bed, right on the edge of the stage in front of the dark and empty, cavernous auditorium.

We never alluded to the incident again, but from then on the performances were infused with excitement and wild intimacy. Nothing further developed between us. After the run we parted ways. She went on to Broadway and I left for Europe, where I met Arietta.

How strange, then, after so many years to be reintroduced to Sylvia by none other than my wife at the opening night of Anton Chekhov's *The Sea Gull* in which they were both acting. I could see that Sylvia was as surprised as I was, but all she said was, "Oh, I remember you from the drama department at NYU." She'd changed. Though still beautiful, the soft luxurious roundness of her face had given way to a hardened, almost gaunt look. And her figure wasn't quite as sensuous as I'd remembered it. She'd gained weight.

It had never crossed my mind that Arietta might be attracted to women; but, as she assured me, "Only this woman." Yet, in retrospect, I recall her telling me that as teenagers she often slept in the same bed with her best friends, and that they occasionally explored each other's budding bodies. "It's what girls do," she said, and I left it at that. After all, I see girls hugging, kissing, and holding hands in our high school every day.

But from the moment Arietta moved in with Sylvia, gay and lesbian relationships took on a whole new meaning. I was forced to examine my own relationship to the matter, and come to terms with it. I'd always seen myself as a professed liberal. Intellectually, I was an avid proponent of gay rights, and I felt strongly about the issue, because it had to do with individual rights and freedom. So why was I so disturbed by it all? Or was my sudden inexplicable prejudice just fuelled by my anger and jealousy? I hoped so, but I was at a loss. Nevertheless, I wondered whether I would have been less upset had Arietta left me for another man. I doubted it – possibly even more. And then there was the added dimension that I'd known Sylvia intimately (or had we just acted out Maggie and Brick's relationship to the last consequence?). In the end, the only thing that really mattered was that Arietta had left me for someone else – and that's what hurt.

It's hard to fathom that it's been two years since the initial break-up and almost a year since they'd moved up to Red Hook in Duchess County, where they founded *Dionysus Reborn*, an independent theater project, devoted to bringing new and little known plays to the stage.

Now I keep thinking: was it masochism, weakness, guilt, or just plain emotional exhaustion that made me submit to all of Arietta's demands during the divorce proceedings? Or was it a form of love, shielding a hidden purpose? All along I just wanted to get it behind me as quickly as possible, so that I could get on with my own life. Even so, it took way longer than I ever imagined – especially in the state of New York, where it is particularly hard.

O

A man with squeaky sneakers walks by and says to his friend, "What's the name of this one – Chaos?" chuckling superciliously. They're wearing denim jackets, blue jeans; the one sporting a perm, the other a mullet. I want to give them the finger, but check myself. *Autumn Rhythm* does have a wind tossed quality about it, expressing the 'fall' of man; but it's also a canvas splattered with seeds, promising new growth – the 'rise' of the revivified human. Of course, Pollock didn't think in those terms, but the conflicted nature and anxious state of mind is abundantly, even beautifully, expressed. What he was conveying abstractly from within is nevertheless an objective rendering of our age. He wanted his paintings to 'confront you,' and they do, like a force of nature, as does the violent history of the century we've just overcome – survived. Maybe it's apt that he's sometimes referred to as "Jack the Dripper."

An invasion of about twenty little kids stops me from any further rumination. Their two instructors get them to quiet down and they sit patiently on the carpet peering innocently up at Pollock's work. They can't be older than six or seven. Sweet little things.

"So how does this painting make you feel?" asks the lady who seems to be the one in charge. I squirm at the question, as much as at the absurdity of exposing the children to a pseudo intellectual 'confrontation' with a painting of this ilk. My common sense and pedagogical instincts immediately rebel against it. Talk about age appropriate education. Yet, I'm intrigued, because children are so refreshingly honest with their answers.

"Messy," one boy shouts out and shivers in mock disgust, which is immediately followed by some of the others, accompanied by lively laughter. Another auburn haired girl with bangs puts up her hand.

"Yes Rachel?"

"He was a silly guy because he didn't paint real pictures."

"What do you mean by real pictures?"

"You know… pictures like of stuff you see… like a house, a cat, trees, cars –"

Immediately other children chime in, offering all sorts possibilities.

"Well, you're right," interrupted the male instructor, "but let me tell you what Jackson Pollock, the artist, said. He said, 'My paintings are like drama; they tell a story, but without any characters.' So you see, kids, you have to make up the story yourselves. You have to *supply* the characters. And you can only do that by going inside the painting. Do you like to make up stories?" The instructor looks expectantly around at the remarkably attentive children. One child who has been sitting very quietly on the edge of the circle puts up her hand, waiting patiently until she gets called on.

"Yes, Judy, what story can you tell us?"

"No story. But will *you* tell us a story? Please tell us what you see in this painting?" All the children get excited at the idea, shouting together, "Yes, please, tell us your story."

"Maybe another time. We still have a lot to see today." They all voice their disappointment. One boy says, "I want to go inside the painting, but I don't see a door…"

The instructor missed a pedagogical moment. She would have redeemed herself – certainly in my eyes – had she told them an imaginative story of what she sees in the painting.

I've heard enough, and move on to the north side of the mezzanine gallery, stopping briefly in front of Georg Baselitz's *Man of Faith*— thinking: yes, you're the upside down modern man. You nailed it. I'm reminded of the precocious little girl who was puzzled by naked *Lilith*, hanging upside down from the wall. Maybe we can only have a semblance of faith if we turn ourselves upside down and inside out. Modern life does that to us. The trick is to remain conscious.

Lilith, Kiki Smith

The Nightmare

Equestrian Court

There's muck beneath the surface. I always forget that. I thought I was over the worst of it. I thought I'd gained enough composure to face the black holes of my past. My up-front writing efforts over the last few months are proof of it – so I thought. Then comes this nightmare out of nowhere and shreds my valiant attempts at self-possession and forgiveness – jolting me awake with such visceral force that all the old wounds are ripped open again.

It was a dream about Arietta; that much I know, and we were at a party. Once I lay awake in those surrealistic wee hours of the sweaty, dark night, vengeful coulda-shoulda-woulda suppositions plagued me. I tried to empty my mind in Zen fashion, but the stubborn little harpies relentlessly pecked away at my raw feelings, until they finally left at sunrise. The searing discomfort has been with me all morning, and it was an effort to get through my lessons.

Throughout my life reminders of my undigested emotions have assaulted me during the night, mostly due to some relationship gone awry. I've been hurt many times, but I've also hurt others. At least, by now, I've learned that to forgive and forget is never a onetime thing, but an ongoing exercise. Any kind of peace of mind I might have attained has always rested on fragile ground. Like last night, when another nightmare shattered my placidity. What sets them off, those landmines buried in our sleep? I can hardly remember the harrowing dream, just the painful aftereffects; though it is right there, teasing me on the tip of my tongue. How irksome that they dissipate so rapidly, that they're so hard to hold on to. But in their wake I'm a wreck; in this case a jealous and wretched one.

O

It is lunch break and I'm at the Met, calming myself down through writing. I'm in the spacious and almost empty Equestrian Court, leaning against the wall, intermittently looking up at horses and knights decked out in resplendent armor. As I'm gazing around a thought comes and repeats itself again and again, until I write it down, to shut it up. *It's not a matter of indulging, but of divulging.* Writing often feels like an indulgence, especially if my personal problems are the main focus (egoism or self awareness?). But everything is always part of a bigger picture, I rationalize. And every life is a research project, from which others can benefit. Arietta would have rolled her eyes at that thought. She would always keep me in check when I took things too far, when I became too clever or 'preachy.' Nevertheless, I always hope I can divulge something of universal value; though I realize it is mostly only a humble attempt. I wish I had someone to bump these thoughts around with.

O

Anger was at the core of the dream, fed by covetousness, born from the raw pain of betrayal. And anger bolted down from the loss I had to bear. It raged against the snuffing of self esteem. Obviously it represented all the unadulterated anger I still harbored against Arietta. There was no need to consult a Freudian psychologist.

O

Again I glance up at the silent knights in their magnificent glory and have to think how the armor must once have served as steel encasements for anger – not so much to protect, but to direct rampant wrath. Warriors throughout the millennia have had to come to terms with their anger, as far back as Achilles, whose epic anger is the driving force behind

72

Homer's *Iliad*. It had its place. Anger is not only a destructive force; it is also a corrective and an agent of growing consciousness. Anger, like love, can be blinding, but it can also wake one up – especially once the passion has cooled. I'm rationalizing my own anger; I know it.

O

Anger was my middle name – proverbial angry young man that I became. But I was a late bloomer in the realm of choler. As a child I was mostly quiet and mellow. My melancholic nature only turned choleric when I stepped into high school, after a few laid back years of home schooling. I rebelled against all the restrictions and the inane education that was pushed down our throats. If there was something to rebel against I was part of it, getting actively involved. Even trivial topics, like fighting the dress code, or lobbying for a smoker's corner, became major issues which I championed, at the risk of expulsion. Later, as a student at NYU, I became socially and politically active, taking to the streets, handing out flyers, speaking at forums and mass meetings. I especially fought for the rights of the underprivileged, the underdogs, the so called dregs of society. Any perceived injustice would ignite my ire. Playing drums was another outlet for my anger. Our punk band *Up Yours* often played at political rallies, or we'd just set up in places like Washington Square Park and scream our views out to the world. Getting busted by the police was like receiving a badge of honor. Youthful idealism and self indulgence went hand in hand, indistinguishable at times. I was awful and full of awe.

Intermittently, I still burn with sentient outbursts, though now the bright-eyed tiger is more easily tamed and shamed. I've witnessed its lethal bite, seen its blunders in the form of consequences, contorted under its deadly serum. I sometimes wonder if my anger's source can be found in the loss of the blood-father I never had – a need unfathomed. There's always stuff broiling away underneath it all. It's always more than we think.

○

Then – all at once – it's back: the dream – in uncanny detail. I can see it clearly. My anger must have commanded it – reeled it in, willed it back. Imponderable, the way the psyche works. It's more than a memory, it's a re-dreaming. I abandon time and focus sharply on the apparitional images, scared they might dissipate as suddenly as they appeared.

○

I'm caught in the throes of a wild party, trying to find Arietta. A big band is playing, but I hear only the shrill laughter of people around me. Everybody's in happy mode... stretched smiles, baring pearly white teeth, or open, red gullets, heads bent back. Every sense tells me something's wrong. Pushing people aside I wade through the gyrating throng. I spot Arietta talking to a bearded man – tall and dark, wearing a black suit. His red, silk shirt is undone and a gold chain, with a heavy cross, dangles over his hairy chest. Raw antipathy shoots up. I shout, "Arietta, where've you been? I've been looking for you all night!"

"Ah, Clarence, there you are. Having fun?" she answers, slipping me a dismissive smile, ignoring my distress. James Bond takes her by the arm and leads her through an arched doorway to the next room, whispering something into her ear. She laughs, tilts her head sideways, flicking loose strands of red hair from her flushed cheeks. He grins, and hugs her tightly. For a moment I think, "She's entitled to her freedom... I mustn't interfere." At that point they kiss passionately, one hairy hand moving down her back, further... squeezing her tush. She's purposefully hitting on him to hurt me.

Pumped with jealous rage I lunge at him, throw him to the floor, pin him down and pound my fists into his face. He throws me off with ease, grinning. Again I attack, out to kill, to shut him up, to injure him. But he's immune to my punches, nothing hurts him, and he is ceaselessly laughing. Exasperated, I take a Chinese vase from the mantelpiece and smash it over his head. The whole room erupts with laughter. On the wall I spot a decorative samurai sword; I snatch it and slash wildly at him. I want to harm and wipe him out. I'm charged with savage fury, and with one sweet blow I lop off his head – a formidably satisfying act. But still *it* laughs as it bumps and rolls across the marble floor like a bowling ball, leaving streaks of red. I run after the autonomous, guffawing head, but slip on the sleek blood, falling hard. I get back up, gripped by an insane rage, intent on crushing the dismembered head beneath my feet.

I'm stopped by a bevy of six scantily clad women, smiling seductively, fondling a large undulating python, its forked tongue jutting back and forth erratically. Aroused I let myself be taken prisoner, bound tightly against a marble pillar with a long, gleaming chain. Sensuously they caress me as they stuff my mouth with marshmallows.

Arietta steps forward dressed in white, diaphanous veils, the black bearded man's bloody head pressed to her bosom. She throws me a look of reproach. I try to scream, to beg for her forgiveness, but my mouth is stuffed. Slowly she turns the decapitated head around, and it takes on the features of Sylvia – smiling and alive. I strain in vain against the chain. The six girls walk toward them, now dressed in black gowns forming a protective ring around Arietta and Sylvia. Slowly they walk off, and I see that Sylvia – fully restored – is walking arm in arm beside Arietta, both in lavish bridal dresses. I try to follow them but cannot. I wake up with dry cotton wool slowly dissolving in my mouth.

O

Again I'm sweating. I'm emerging from the nightmare a second time. But the anger is gone.

I rise from my cramped position and leave the Arms and Armor Gallery, my left leg once again caught up in a buzz of pins and needles. I'm in search of contrasting impressions.

Up in the south mezzanine I stare at Paul Klee's *Angel Applicant*. We're all hybrid angels, diseased with human failings. To suffer through is the cure. Suffering puts us on the outside, so that we can look inside and gain perspective. We're all outsiders some of the time. It's part of retaining or becoming human. I want to put a microphone to Klee's hollow eyed phantom, turn on the power and hear his nightmare. I want to be a purged Angel Applicant.

The Scandal

Ink in Water, Martina Angela Müller

Spring! The fountains outside the Met are on again. It's a beautiful morning. The vendors are setting up their stalls. There is a little boy on the edge of the fountain trying to blow up an orange balloon. Failing, he asks his father to help him. Excitedly he watches his dad, while waving his arms up and down in anticipation. The balloon swells... bigger and bigger, until it suddenly pops with a bang. The boy loses his balance and falls backwards into the fountain. The cold water takes his breath away. Bewildered, he grins half heartedly, then bawls pitifully. His father helps him out. He leads the drenched and crying boy away.

I get up from the green bench on the pavement and go to the Petrie Café for my usual coffee and croissant. I look languorously out through the glass wall onto Central Park and get lost in the people enjoying this warm Saturday morning. I both love and dread spring. Nature, with all its budding, blossoming and flowering is a picture of endless potential, of hope in a glorious and better future. It's a powerful metaphor for our own striving, but I can never keep up with the natural world. On the contrary, I often think I'm losing my mind and my emotional stability gets rigorously tested during springtime, in one form or another. The blooming beauty around me is like a mirror, clearly reflecting all the things I have *not* achieved. So many of the expectations and hopes I've had in life have been thwarted – and spring rubs it in. It's interesting to note that some of the most trying times of my life, such as my mother dying, or Arietta leaving me, have occurred in this season of rebirth. Maybe it's an interior spring cleaning – a form of purging, where the old is burned up to make way for the new? After all, Easter is a time of death as well as resurrection. It means going into the basement of our cluttered past and facing all the junk that needs clearing out – to make room for new and future events. Left untended it rots or gets moldy.

This leads me directly to the nasty scandal that flared up around the Katrina Griffin incident – a former student – which hammered another nail into my coffin. The upsetting episode is just another example of a biographical node I've left unexamined until now. Again, it was pride that got in the way of self reflection. It's highly unpleasant to look at these things.

The Petrie Café has filled up. It's too noisy to concentrate. I make for the Robert Lehman Wing, enjoying, as always, the spacious and quiet ambience, perfect for collecting one's thoughts and writing. But first I take a quick walkabout. I say hi to the *Princess de Broglie* by Ingres (not that I particularly like the painting, but we've become good friends over time), wave wistfully to *Diana and Actaeon* and the other godly maidens, smile at Renoir's *Two Young Girls* at the piano, wondering once again what piece of music the blond girl is playing, and pause pensively in front of *The Martyrdom of Saint Paul* by Taddeo Zuccaro – ah, the indomitable spirit of humanity. That done, I hurry to a vacant bench to unburden my soul *on these spindrift pages*, as Dylan Thomas would say. It's as good a time as any to take a closer look at the unfortunate developments regarding Katrina that led up to my disgrace.

O

The pretty new girl was an enigma when she first arrived. Nobody knew anything about her. She appeared in late October. Quietly, she'd sit down near the front of the class and try to look attentive; but I could see her thoughts meandering within the first few minutes. She'd make an effort to catch herself, but it never lasted long. It was clear she was

Above: *Two Young Girls at the Piano*, Pierre Auguste Renoir

tired, confused and overwhelmed. She never talked to anybody and kept to herself. Though quiet she appeared windswept, as if she'd just escaped a hurricane. Her long, wavy, dark brown hair was always ruffled and unkempt, and she was continuously chewing on wayward strands. It gave her a wild, feral look, though her features were rounded and soft; her vanilla complexion almost transparent. Her eyelids were heavy, as if weighed down by her long, but natural eyelashes – in sensuous accord with her pouting, glossy lips. She seemed oblivious to the attention she was arousing among the boys. She was either unaware or ignored their comments and inane histrionics, which made her even more desirable. They were out to break through the real or imagined façade. The girls were unsure about her. I was assigned to be Katrina's advisor.

That's when I found out some of the details of her past. She'd come from Redwood City, California, where she'd lived with her father. After he was busted for drugs and locked up, she returned to New Jersey to live with her mother. However, they fought constantly and after only a few weeks the mother kicked her out and she moved in with her aunt who had an apartment near Battery Park. Katrina had been diagnosed with severe ADD and was put on medication. That explained, in part, her distant, confused look in class. Together with the school nurse I fought and succeeded to have the dosage reduced. I met with Katrina on a weekly basis to ensure that she was getting all her work completed, and to facilitate her integration into the school. I'd never felt as concerned for any student before and I was pleased to note that positive differences could be observed in Katrina's behavior after only a few weeks. She was increasingly interested in the lessons, could focus for longer periods of time and made friends with some of the girls. Yet, I remained concerned, justifiably so.

On one occasion I'd asked the junior literature class to write a fictional or true account of a tragic event in their lives, as a lead-in to our study of the great Shakespearean tragedies. Most students wrote either outrageously fantastical stories or drab and trivial tales about the death of a pet or a minor accident. Not so with Katrina. She handed in eight handwritten pages describing in vivid detail how she got beat up and raped in the girls' bathroom at her old school in San Francisco, as payback for her ex-boyfriend's actions in a gang related incident. She'd scrawled it all down with a red ballpoint pen – her handwriting as wild as her hair. She'd called it *Victim*. And in parentheses she wrote: true story (underlined three times). I was as shocked by the revelation, as I was awed by her literary skill.

Only two days after I'd read her outstanding, albeit disturbing composition, I observed her sitting uncommonly apathetic and red eyed in class. Something was amiss. Later, when I met with her, she confided that her aunt's boyfriend tried to force himself onto her while she was doing her homework. Luckily her aunt had returned home earlier than usual, which saved her from another instance of severe sexual abuse. It also put an end to the aunt's boyfriend.

It was a setback, and the incident played itself out in various ways. She flung herself at the boys who were chomping at the bit to be with her, entering into these flings with a vengeance. None of the relationships lasted long, and she never seemed fazed after a break-up, though she left a trail of gloomy guys in her wake. She had trouble focusing again, and she upped her dosage; said she needed to. I persuaded her to see the school counselor, but after only two sessions she refused to return to him.

But she did get involved in the drama club, where she quickly proved to be a born actress. After a successful production of Neil Simon's *Fools*, where Katrina surprised everybody, including herself, with a striking performance, I cast her as Vilma in Vaclav Havel's relatively unknown play *The Temptation* (giving the Faust legend yet another provocative twist). She slid into the character with ease, intuitively knowing what was required. For the first time I saw her wild hair as a true reflection of her spontaneity, her artistry. While on stage, I saw her grow and embody long neglected parts of herself. After rehearsals she was more upbeat than I'd ever seen her during normal school hours. The drama work was dismantling the protective wall around her, brick for brick. Her face, naturally attractive, looked less dolled up, more relaxed and beautiful. And she began to smile. The anger was dissipating, the random flirting with the guys eased off, and all her energies went into acting. It was during this time, however, that I unwittingly overstepped the professional boundary between teacher and student; advisor and advisee, which consequently landed me in deep disgrace.

It began innocently enough. During the rehearsal breaks I'd go to the Java Jive, a funky place where they made lattes to my liking – hot, strong and dry. It was a bit of a walk from school, but the upside was that you hardly ever bumped into colleagues or students. A good place to take five. As I entered the café one afternoon, Katrina and two of her friends were sitting by the window drinking mocha frappuccinos. "Oh, Mr. Somerset, what are you doing here?" asked one of the girls.

"What do you mean? I come here all the time. The question is: what are you doing here?"

"Oh, we're just hanging. Wanna join us?" Katrina asked, scooting over to make room for me.

"Why not?"

From then on I often met with some of my acting students at JJ's, as we called it, discussing all aspects of the play – what scenes needed more attention, which ones worked well, blocking possibilities, props, costumes, lighting, set design, staging, et al. I hardly noticed that I was often sitting alone with Katrina.

However, after all the performances were over it dawned on me that Katrina was intentionally seeking me out at the café. That's when I should have put a stop to it all, but we kept on seeing each other. The play was no longer a topic of discussion; instead she began opening up about her home situation and her past. She'd tell me about her father, how he used to send her around to distribute drugs to his various clients when she was still a young kid in grade school – always in a plastic shopping bag. "I thought I was delivering spices." She'd tell stories of wild parties to which she was dragged; of drug induced orgies, witnessed throughout her childhood; of rolling and smoking joints when she was nine, and of dropping acid and snorting cocaine at age thirteen. Then her parents split up. For a while she lived with her mother in San Francisco (where the rape occurred), but when her Mom moved back east to New Jersey, Katrina returned to Redwood City to stay with her Dad, up until his arrest.

Then, one afternoon, just as we were leaving the café, she handed me a poem she'd written. "Let me know what you think, okay, *teacher?*" That's when – in an instant – I realized she'd fallen in love with me. But I wasn't at all prepared for the intensity of her affection. Reading and rereading the poem I was taken aback by the passion of her words, and though flattered on some ignominious level, I saw all too clearly the mess I now found myself in, and felt sickened at the probable and inevitable consequences I'd have to face. Why didn't I notice it before? How stupid and careless of me! How could I have let our conversations become so intimate? How could I have let myself spend so much time with her – alone? The truth was – I'd enjoyed her company, the raw, youthful femininity; her promise and potential. Maybe she made up for something that was lost, or no longer alive, in my relationship with Arietta. Regardless, I'd stepped into a minefield and I knew I had to retreat immediately.

Consciously, I distanced myself from her, making up excuses of having to attend meetings, prepare lessons, write reports, grade papers, or run errands. I told her I liked the poem, but didn't let on that I knew it was a love poem intended for me.

But distancing myself from her and acting as if I was unaware of her infatuation didn't stop Katrina. She requested an advisee meeting and came to see me in my office the same day. For the first ten minutes I managed to keep the conversation objective and away from us. I inquired about her school work, if she was keeping up with all her assignments, how she was getting along with her aunt and if she'd heard from her respective parents. She answered dutifully, till she broke down crying in the middle of a sentence. Repeatedly she tried to control herself, but the tears kept on coming. In between the sobs she stammered apologies. I went over and put my arm around her, consolingly. It only made her cry all the more, and she buried her head in my chest. Kindly I stroked and patted her wild hair until she calmed down. I was surprised how soft her hair felt, in contrast to the tousled appearance. She smelled good (was it the perfume or the shampoo?). At last she looked up, and whispered, "I knew you cared for me… the way you touch me… it's so…" And then she kissed me. Her passion took me off guard, and a few seconds elapsed before I had the presence of mind to pull myself gently away from her, saying, "We can't do this, Katrina. It's wrong."

"Not if we love each other," she answered softly, throwing her arms tightly around my neck again, kissing me even more fervently, groaning slightly.

"No, please, Katrina. Someone could walk in through that door at any moment," I said, panting, knowing that I should have pulled away sooner. "I care for you, but it can't live itself out on this level. You have to understand."

"All I understand is that I love you, and I know that you love me too."

"Katrina, I'm a teacher, remember. It's an impossible situation."

"No, it's not. Hey, this is as weird for me as it is for you. But remember, we've been seeing each other for months now. Nothing has changed except we've finally confessed our love for each other," and she wanted to kiss me again, but I gently put my arm on her shoulder.

"On the contrary – everything's changed. Those kisses just changed it all. Beforehand, when we met in the café, we just talked – that was it. Let's keep it that way. We can't let romance come between us."

"Whatcha mean, 'come between us?' It's been there for weeks. You know it as well as I do."

"Katrina, seriously, it cannot continue. I am married. I love my wife." I was getting frantic. I couldn't just give in to her, nor did I want to say or do anything that would upset and hurt her even more. I noticed she hardly heard anything I was saying; she just looked at me with her dilated blue-green eyes, caressing my arm that was still resting on her shoulder, and drawing me towards her again for another kiss. "No, really, I could lose my job over this." I said at last, firmly separating myself from her embrace and putting on my jacket. "I have another class coming up, and so do you… here, take a tissue. Your mascara is all messed up."

"Wait, you can't just lead me on, and then dump me like this," she said, taking the tissue and dabbing her eyes, her fingers trembling.

"Nobody's dumping anybody, and I haven't led you on," I said, my hand already on the doorknob.

"Of course, you have," she said accusingly, her voice rising, quivering. "All the times you paid for my coffee… the endless talks we had alone at JJ's… all the encouragements you gave me… the extra attention… the way you kept me after rehearsals to go over a scene, even back when we were doing *Fools*… admit it, you gave me the lead in *The Temptation* because you had an eye on me!" She stopped, as she tried to control her stuttering inhalations, choking back tears. In frustration she fiercely pulled another two tissues from the box and blew her nose. I watched her, perplexed. I couldn't believe the situation I suddenly found myself in. I felt stuck, helpless and threatened.

"Just listen to me for a moment," I said, trying to console her and calm her down.

"No, I'm not done yet," she retorted. "I want to know from you how you feel about me. I want you to admit that you love me. You can't tell me I was wrong… the way you touched me when you showed or demonstrated a gesture… the look in your eyes. Or the hopeful and cryptic notes you wrote at the bottom of my papers. Come on, you can't tell me you don't have feelings for me. Or were you just playing me?"

"Of course I wasn't." Silence ensued. She just stood there, looking at me, her hair more ruffled than ever, her face flushed with emotion, the eyes puffed and watery. I met her gaze guiltily, and saw the tragedy of her life – a girl abandoned, abused, rejected, exposed to the dangers of the world since infancy – sucked into its destructive vortex, unprotected and vulnerable. I repeated softly, consolingly, "Of course I wasn't."

"Thank you. That's all I wanted to hear." Katrina picked up her backpack, slung it across her shoulders, brushed passed me and left, whispering, "See you tomorrow." I closed the door quietly behind her, and fell heavily against it, completely dazed. I breathed deeply and sighed – her perfume still lingered in the air, on my face and in my hair.

Survival instincts took over. I had to act radically. The next day I called her into my office again and told her straight off and in no uncertain terms that she'd entirely misunderstood the attention I'd paid her, and that from now on there would be no more meetings between us. Further, I told her it would be in the best interest of both of us if I ceased to be her advisor; but that I would do everything in my power to ensure her academic success. I suggested she should make a concerted effort to let herself be helped by the school counselor, who was more equipped than me to help with her problems.

She just stood there on the other side of the desk, taken aback, contorting her mouth into various shapes, biting her lower lip. Her hair was braided back into dozens of little sleek snakes that highlighted her beautifully formed facial features. I'd never seen her hair so neat and orderly before. "What a fool I've been," she said at last. "And I thought you'd be different... but you're just like the rest of them. In fact, you're no better than those three guys who jumped me in the bathrooms back in Cisco... same old – used and bruised." She shifted the weight of her body to the other leg – striking a cocky pose. "You were just flattering yourself all along, weren't you? What did you think? That you were my savior, prince charming in shining armor? Well, excuse my French, *sir*, but you're just one fucking phony. Up yours! I'm outta here... thanks for nothing – oh, and see you in class, *teacher*." She turned around, walked out and slammed the door in my face. Talk about being 'shafted.'

From that moment on things spun out of control. I saw her hanging out with her band of girls again, whispering conspiringly and snickering behind my back in the hallways and in class. Flirting with the boys resumed. Students with whom I'd always had good relations began to

84

evade and ignore me, even refusing to greet me. Boys mocked me behind my back, and I heard words like, "cradle snatcher" and "sugar daddy," murmured in passing. It tore at my guts and I wondered how I could right this untenable situation. One morning I found a note stuck on my desk with chewing gum. It read, "Get out, you fucking pedophile."

Rumors spread. Slander takes on a life of its own, and it was almost unbearable to teach any classes anymore. More poison notes followed: "Check out the boys' bathrooms, if you dare." I did, and the graffiti was disgusting – crude, sick cartoons and scribbles that referred to me in the most depraved and offensive manner. The next day's note read: "If you think that was bad, you should check out the girls' bathroom. You ain't seen nothin' yet!"

That's when I went to report the whole incident to the principal. And it's a good thing I did, because that same afternoon he got his first telephone call from a concerned parent, demanding an explanation and an inquiry into the whole situation. I put into plain words what had led up to these cruel accusations, the rumors and awful calumny. I did, however, omit a few details: the full account of what had happened in my office, and the number of times Katrina and I had met alone at the coffee shop.

On hearing me out, he said, without hesitation, "There will have to be an investigation, Mr. Somerset, and I recommend that you resign immediately, or I will have to suspend you. I'm sorry, but there's zero tolerance for this sort of behavior nowadays." His tone of voice was dismissive and I sensed he'd already written me off.

I resigned. The story did flare up, and the school community was divided between those for and against me. People were advising Katrina to press charges, to sue me for sexual harassment, or at the very least to insist on a public apology for my inappropriate actions. A task force was set up and the proceedings began: I was called in for numerous meetings, repeatedly answering the same questions to different people in various committees; going over every detail of my dealings with Katrina, in and out of school – ad nauseum. The situation did not look promising. I was under fire, and judging by the questions and the harshness with which they were posed, I was culpable, in their eyes, of blatant sexual misconduct. I could already see the headlines in the newspapers: *Educator arrested on rape charges*; *Girl's harassment by teacher sparks protests*; *Police investigate sexual abuse of teen.* Hardly a week goes by without some such heading, somewhere. Am I next?

In the midst of these onerous proceedings Katrina was caught dealing drugs on school property, which resulted in her immediate expulsion. This changed the situation. Public opinion was swayed. She wasn't regarded as an innocent victim anymore, but as a hussy trying to bring down an esteemed and popular teacher. My name, however, remained tarnished, and although marginally redeemed in the eyes of some, I was not reinstated (nor did I want to be). Shortly after, she ran away from her aunt, back to Crescent City, to be with her father who was recently released from prison. With her absence the whole business ceased to be a hot topic of discussion and people focused on other issues.

Fortunately, Alicia went to school on the Upper East Side, and we were able to spare her the details behind my resignation. Furthermore, I would never have ended up teaching at Stone Ridge – a prestigious private high school up on 79th – had I not been forced to quit. Not only was it a better school, which emphasized the arts as well as the sciences and humanities, but it was located only a few blocks north of the middle school Alicia attended.

The ordeal hadn't been easy for Arietta; yet, in the face of the public, she'd stood by me all the way. Even so, I'm convinced the shameful episode had been the catalyst for her leaving me in favor of Sylvia just a few weeks later. On a number of occasions she'd probed me about my relationship to Katrina. I'd always made light of it, never telling her about the poem, the kiss, or the number of times we'd met alone at the Java Jive. I know she doubted me, but all along, I was trying to delude myself as much as her. The scandal and Arietta's subsequent exodus both happened in the spring and summer of '99. What a year to end the millennium with? What a lead-in to the year 2000?

O

My hand and fingers are cramped, but I got it out of my system. I finally faced that ill-fated affair – my awful public and personal disgrace. But, in the spirit of owning up to the truth, I have to admit that Katrina had, in fact, been right on some level: I had developed feelings for her. I'd enjoyed talking to her, consoling her, and offering good advice. And now, as I'm writing all this down, I realize full well how indulgent and selfish that was. Furthermore, it's true: I'd unwittingly led her on; I'd made her feel dependent on me. And in the end it wasn't so much my moral compass that had made me reject her so vehemently, but my drive for self preservation. I sensed my acute vulnerability, saw myself teeter on the brink of an abyss. I'd failed her, this girl-woman caught up in the sacred journey of her formative years. I'd failed her as a teacher, an adult, and as a friend. But more than all that – I'd failed my wife, and I'd failed my daughter.

Still, I've often wondered what's become of Katrina.

Over four hours have passed. I've never written so much in one sitting. I've filled three of my pocketsize notebooks. *Princess de Broglie* is staring at me. She looks pale.

The Princess de Broglie, J.A.D. Ingres

Riding with Alicia

Portrait of a Young Woman, Johannes Vermeer

Whenever I walk through the galleries of the museum's collection of European paintings dedicated to the Old Masters, I feel a little lost. I must admit, I do not have an immediate and natural connection to many of the old works coming out of the diverse European schools. Of course I have my favorite artists and paintings, but I always tire easily while dawdling through these relatively small galleries on the second floor, populated mostly with religious themes. The creaking floorboards, the muffled mood and the tang of age also add to my feelings of displacement. Yet, I go back again and again, reacquainting myself with the themes, the art and the artists. They represent a soul space that is slow in opening within me, with notable exceptions of works by such artists as Rembrandt, El Greco, Bruegel and Vermeer.

So it comes as no surprise that I gravitate to Vermeer's *Portrait of a Young Woman*. I lose myself in her. I can hear the tone and timbre of her voice by the way the lips rest on the delicate smile, breathing in unison with the clear, dark eyes that are both trusting and giving. Here is a spirit, clothed in an unblemished soul, lucid with inner strength. It is as if she's listening to seeds of wisdom that the world is always ready to impart to those who are receptive. I see a girl whose innate dignity has been shaped by her intimation that all human interactions need tending. For a long time I stand in front of this girl, this young woman, who has been compared to Leonardo's Mona Lisa. Though the smile is just as rare and ineffable, it is lighter, more tenuous and untainted. The words "mirthful Madonna" come to mind. Mona Lisa, on the other hand, is grand and all woman, and her spellbinding smile reaches down to her womb as much as out into a knowing world, while remaining aloof, sensuous and archetypically mysterious. Together they portray the faces of innocence and experience. And the more I look at Vermeer's girl, the more my mind gives way to a mood as chaste as the light from her pale cheeks, enhanced by the blue-white fabric shrouding her shoulders.

I cease to think and stand transfixed, as if looking into a mirror – seeing my soul's potential reflected back to me. Moments later it is Alicia, my daughter, who is staring at me with inquiring eyes. I see the child she used to be. I see the woman she's turning into. I am overcome with an inexplicable emotion that thickens into a deep longing for her. It is painful, and I walk out onto the balcony overlooking the American Wing atrium to recover.

I miss my daughter, the little girl who has grown up so fast; the fun-loving child, who used to be my constant companion during the first few years, before I became too preoccupied with school and personal ambitions. I think of all the times I took her to the zoo, ice skating, boating or swimming; I think of the long walks we used to take along the Hudson River and through Central Park, eating hot dogs or ice cream. And I ask myself why the precious dad-daughter times had to end, and why I chose to pursue my own activities over her needs. I see sadness in her eyes.

I feel momentarily crushed. I've been at the Met for almost an hour. I had the firm intention of hanging out with the expressionists and impressionists today, but my little detour to the Old Masters led me to the questioning eyes of Vermeer's 'young woman' who is still whispering in my ear, urging me to write about my Cape Cod weekend with Alicia. Why, I wonder.

O

Shortly after my resignation as the high school drama director, due to the Katrina incident, I suggested to Arietta that we take a family trip somewhere – just for the fun of it, something we hadn't done in a long time. Arietta, who had just started rehearsals on *Arcadia* by Tom Stoppard, couldn't afford to take time off, but encouraged me to go with

Alicia, if she was game. Alicia hesitated initially, but agreed as soon as I took her up on the idea of going to Cape Cod. The two of us hadn't done anything together for years.

Early Saturday morning we hopped into the car and headed north. I'd brought along a bag of provisions making sure I included all the goodies she used to like as a little girl. Once we were out on the highway I hauled it out from under my front seat. She laughed when she saw my purchases. "Dad, you're sweet, but I don't eat these things anymore.

"You don't?"

"Haven't for a while. I'm already thirteen, in case you've forgotten. I hardly ever eat junk food anymore. Mom and I have been super conscious of our diet for a couple of years already."

"Hmm, you're right. Now that you mention it: muesli in the morning, organic vegetables, no more meat, hardly any dairy… I always thought Mom was behind it all."

"She is, but I'm with her one hundred percent. Not that I won't make a few exceptions, like now" – and she tore open the box of Cheezits that I bought – "for old time's sake, you know," and she laughed, stuffing a handful into her mouth.

In fact, there was very little of the little girl left in Alicia. By the time we pulled into the motel near Provincetown I realized I was sitting next to a very different person from the one I thought I'd started the journey with – a confident, outgoing personality at the beginning of her adolescence. I was impressed with the kind of books she now devoured, her social and political awareness, her insights on the environment, and world events as such. Not only was I talking to her as an equal, but her insightful opinions were buoyed with the healthy idealism of youth.

That evening, as we drove along on our way to dinner, Alicia suddenly blurted out, "Oh, look," and she pointed to a large sign on which was written White Sands Stables. "That's where I went to horseback riding camp a few summers ago, remember?"

"Yeah, I remember; you went with your friend Greta, didn't you? … So this is where it is?"

"Right. Oh, it was so much fun," and she began to tell stories of what had happened, the trails she had ridden, the manner of instructions, and how she cared for the horses.

I didn't say a word, but the next day I got up before breakfast and drove over to the stables and made reservations to have a guided tour along the beach, scheduled for later that morning. During breakfast I casually suggested we go down to the beach behind White Sands Stables. "That'll bring back memories," she said, excited at the idea.

It was close to 11:00. Alicia was just getting out of the water, when a group of riders approached. Alicia noticed them too. She stopped and looked at them wistfully, as they trotted along. I walked down to her and said, "Bring back some memories?

"Sure does."

"Would be nice to go for a ride along the beach right now, wouldn't it?"

"Ah, I'd love it... we used to do it all the time when I was at camp, just like those guys."

"Okay, then, let's do it," and I waved my hand at the group of riders and shouted, "Hey, we're over here!"

"Dad, what do you think you're doing?"

"We're going for a ride – just as you wished. I organized it this morning while you were still in bed. I made arrangements for them to meet us... and here they are to pick us up." I had to laugh seeing her face frozen in astonishment. "See, they've got two horses ready for us... so, kiddo, are you ready to rock and ride?"

"Oh my God, and how! ...Dad, you're the best!" she squealed, running off to slip into her jeans.

I will never forget that hour we spent together, riding along the beach on those docile, friendly horses. On the way back the tour guide, who remembered her from camp, allowed her and one other rider to gallop the last stretch. When she finally dismounted, her face was flushed and I saw the little girl in her again.

O

We haven't spent time like that together since.

Voodoo Woman

Madagascar Couple, Africa, Wood, Sakalava Peoples

I'm sitting in the museum café, right up front, hugged against the wall, left of the sign that reads: Maximum Capacity 544. I feel slightly surreptitious about coming here, sipping coffee and writing during school hours. But only slightly. I'm still doing my duty; sort of. I schlepped my elective creative writing class along with me; gave them a quarter each to get in, and an assignment – *create a story centered on a painting of your choice, and imagine you are telling it from a child's perspective* – and then let them loose in the museum. That gives me just under ninety minutes to get on with my own writing. They know where to find me if they need me.

O

A few days after Arietta moved out, Alicia followed; not that she had much choice in the matter. Arietta made sure of that. Alicia was conflicted and I saw how the separation pained her. While Arietta was waiting for her downstairs, I told Alicia how sorry I was that it had come to this. Alicia's eyes welled up immediately, and I quickly hugged her. She held me tight for a few seconds before pulling away abruptly, whispering, "Bye, Dad," and hurried down the stairs.

It made sense, however: I was in no shape to take care of her – even her most basic needs. Only Arietta could now offer Alicia the desired stability. Fair enough, but why did Arietta have to see her lawyer and initiate the divorce procedure that same afternoon? I laughed it off – the coincidence was just too absurd. "You got to ride this one out alone, sucker," I said to myself, pacing around my empty apartment, which had ceased to be home. Their absence was overwhelmingly present. Memories crammed my cracked mind like pushy apparitions, vying for attention. More and more appeared until I screamed. The phantoms scattered, but I could hear them hoot and howl like vindictive coyotes. I slunk to the ground in the dark hallway next to the almost empty shoe rack and mumbled, "Wife gone… daughter gone… reputation gone… job gone. How much worse can it get?"

I went out and rented a bunch of videos, bought a carton of cigarettes, two bottles of Jack Daniels, three six-packs of beer, a couple of large pizzas, and enough milk and cereals to last me a week. Well stocked I returned home, closed all the windows and blinds, disconnected the phone and plunked myself on the couch, watching one movie after another, smoking and drinking, till I passed out. As soon as I awoke I continued from where I'd left off. On the third day of this pathetic, self-indulgent debauchery I came to my senses and decided to clean up, shower, and go out for a decent bite to eat. Getting up, I stumbled stupidly over some ill-placed beer bottles and fell heavily on the floor, knocking over the rickety foldout table cram-stacked with stuff. For a few seconds I lay there, cursing. Then I saw myself from above – a pitiful figure looking like a homicide victim lying amongst old pizza boxes, dirty mugs, bowls, videos, magazines, beer bottles, and umpteen cigarette butts catapulted from the toppled ashtray. I snorted sardonically at my own wretched state. "Okay, enough of this… get your ass off the ground and act your friggin' age." But the moment I was on my feet again, a searing pain shot straight up my spine, and down I went with a slipped a disc. *And I thought it couldn't get any worse!*

I'd often thrown my back out, but nothing like this. The slightest movement put me into excruciating agony. The smallest task became an ordeal, and the pain only got worse – it crept steadily up my spine, forcing me to turn my whole body whenever I wanted to look to the right or left.

Nothing helped. The chiropractor offered temporary relief at best. My stumped doctor referred me to a specialist who gave me the most painful injections I have ever had – directly into my spine. It made no difference. Eventually he suggested surgery as the only alternative. I was dead set against it, but what else could I do? The day I decided to go ahead with the operation, Jake, the doorman of our building, stopped me at the elevator as I was returning home with two bags of groceries, and said, "Let me help you with those, Mr. Somerset. I been noticin' that you been walkin' funny these last few weeks," taking the bags from me.

"Yup, threw my back out, bad. Now it looks like I've got to have surgery."

"Nah, you don't want to be doin' that." We stepped into the elevator, and once the doors shut he continued. "Are you're willin' to try something different... you know, unconventional?

"Anything, Jake, to get rid of this stupid pain."

"I kinda suspected that. That's why I'm suggestin' you visit Voodoo Woman."

"Who?"

"Voodoo Woman, that's what everybody calls her. She's a faith healer from Ghana. She's somethin' else, man. I been to see her myself when I had sarcoidosis. She took care of it. Don't ask me how. And I know many others who've gone to see her and she's helped them all in one way or another."

"For real?"

"Sure. She lives up in Harlem. Next time you come down, I'll have the address and phone number ready for you."

"Well, I might just take you up on that."

A week later I took the subway up to 125th Street, walked up 8th Avenue for a few blocks, crossed over and found the apartment just a little off 129th and Seventh Avenue. I realized I hadn't been in this part of town since I was a kid when I'd gone to the Apollo Theater with my mother to see James Brown (while visiting my mom's cousins in the Bronx). Now I stood in front of the old brownstone apartment complex, not knowing which button to press.

"You're looking for someone?" asked a boy with hair braided neatly into cornrows, sitting on a beat up bicycle, wearing a faded and tattered red basketball t-shirt, # 23.

"Yes," I said, suddenly embarrassed because I didn't even know her real name. "She's a healer."

"You mean Voodoo Woman."

"Right."

"Thought so. Do you have an appointment?"

"Yeah, for 2:30."

"Follow me," and he popped a wheelie and zoomed off.

"Hey, not so fast," I shouted, hobbling after him, down the street and into an alley, where he waited, chewing gum, sitting on his bike, one foot resting on a fire hydrant, smiling. Once I'd reached him he got off his bike and led me down five steps, opened up a metal door and motioned for me to enter.

"Walk right to the end of the passage. There you'll find another door. Knock and wait."

I had some reservations about where exactly he was leading me, but I just said, "Okay," and entered.

"Oh... and do you have a dollar I can borrow."

"Sure. Here, take two," I said

"Thanks." And he clanged the door shut after me, leaving me in total darkness. I felt my way forward until my hands met a door. I knocked three times, the sound echoing around. While I waited my eyes accustomed themselves to the darkness. Dim light seeped through underneath the doors behind and in front of me. The passageway smelled of urine. I lit a match and noticed the walls were covered with layers of graffiti, spanning decades. I knocked twice more before I heard footsteps approaching and the light in the passage was switched on. My imagination had not prepared me for the visual impact of Voodoo Woman.

When the door opened I was met by a colossal woman – she must have weighed about 300 pounds. The word *fat* pushed itself to mind, though I'd struck the word from my vocabulary. A red sequined cotton cloth was draped around her massive waist, but her large, drooping breasts were exposed, except for innumerable necklaces of various lengths that dangled around her corpulent, multilayered upper body – with pouches, tiny bottles and vials attached. Her nappy hair was interlaced with extensions – long strands of colorful plastic and glass beads that fell down past her shoulders. But the most striking feature was a big, milky-grey, blown up, natural balloon woven into her hair – presumably an inflated intestine, stomach, or kidney, almost matching the size of her head. She was blind in her right eye, and its filmy opaque gaze was in mobile partnership with the bobbing distention fixed on her head. She had numerous bracelets, trinkets and charms around her ankles, upper and lower arms; and decorative rings around her toes, fingers, and through her ears. I stood transfixed, intimidated and perplexed. She took her time looking me over, her good eye slowly perusing the periphery of my body, until, in the end, it met my confounded stare, while the blind, foamy eye and the inflated equivalent peered right through me. I wondered whether I should say anything, but instinctively I knew to shut up.

"You got the food?" were her first words (I was required to bring any three of my favorite foods).

"Yes, here they are," I said, handing her the plastic bag containing a peach, some gorgonzola cheese and a box of Lübecker marzipan. I wondered why she wanted the food.

"The spirits help us if we give them food," she answered, as if she'd read my mind. "Now, take off your clothes."

"You mean… everything?"

"Yes." I detected a slight dismissive irritation in her voice. I felt like a fool for coming here. What was I letting myself in for?

But I complied, and once I was disrobed she pointed to an old gurney and grunted, which clearly meant – "get on." I obeyed, though it hurt like hell to climb onto that old, cold steel structure. She wheeled me slowly down the passage into a large, dimly lit hall where the air wasn't quite as stale. Leaving me lying on the gurney she walked towards what appeared to be an altar – two picnic tables pushed together against the wall, covered with a white sheet – her bracelets and other accoutrements tinkling with every step. After careful placement of my 'offerings' she lit seven candles. Now I could clearly distinguish fetish statues of various sizes, and other ornaments, circumspectly placed on the table, amidst bouquets of flowers, roots, more food, bunches of leafy branches and other greenery. Another white sheet was stapled onto the wall which was festooned with colorful scarves and more greenery. Lined up behind the candles was a row of liquor bottles.

Picking up a small rattle she began pacing around the large hall, which I now recognized to be an old, derelict theater, stopping intermittently and shaking it. After every shake she listened intently. Sometimes she just snapped her fingers or clucked softly with her tongue. Once she'd circumnavigated the entire space in this fashion, she appeared to have found what she was looking for; and from a small bottle that hung around her neck she sprinkled a few drops in a circular motion, after which she pushed the gurney into the circle. Taking two wooden statues of seated women from the altar, she placed the bigger one by my head and the little one by my feet. From the same bottle around her neck she sprinkled a few more drops of the malodorous water over my naked chest and legs. Every one of her movements I followed closely, trying to determine what would happen next. I felt vulnerable and powerless, enhanced by my nakedness. "Close your eyes," she said as if to increase my defenselessness. I did so reluctantly, keeping my curiosity at bay. I wanted to see all her actions. After all, it was somewhat bizarre, and not in the least what I'd anticipated. I'd told her briefly about my chronic back problem over the phone, and I expected her to ask me a whole slew of questions, and then give me some remedies – herbs, tincture, drops, or something. Whatever my expectations, it wasn't this.

She began chanting, softly. I felt her placing objects on various parts of my body. They felt cold against my skin, and I presumed they were stones of different sizes – or was it metal? I didn't dare look, and she removed them after only a few seconds. I presumed she got them from one of the numerous pouches she carried on her body. The repetitive nature of her chant put me into a comfortable daze. I felt her big hands massage my body, up from my toes to my neck. Intermittently she tarried in one area or another, adding oily tinctures that gave off pungent or sweet smells, mixing with her sweat. Sometimes, her chanting would erupt, as if she were bursting forth in cacophonous laughter or unearthly wailing; then she'd quiet down again, almost to a whisper. At one point she said, "Now turn around," which I did, ever so slowly, to avoid the piercing pain. Once I was in a prone position, she repeated the whole procedure, again placing the cool objects on various parts of my body while chanting; only this time she massaged me from the head downwards.

All at once she stopped. "Aau! Got it," she shrieked and cackled in delight, as she pushed into my lower back with her thumb. I screamed in pain. "No, no, you relax, it's okay. No good to fight the pain. Accept the pain," she said, her voice now sounding like a calming ululation. "The pain is your friend. The pain is in your body because there's poison in your heart. The pain you feel saves you from the invisible poison." She pressed again – hard, and this time I did not scream, though the pain shot up like a boiling geyser. Thinking of the pain in terms of a friend, helped. "But the poison is also in your thoughts," she continued. "Let the body absorb the pain. The poison in the heart and head is the venom that makes people go crazy. Crazy people are more difficult to cure. Yours has entered the body. It's become visible. That's good. Are you ready to give up the pain?" These words were spoken slowly and softly.

"Yes," I mumbled, groggy with the relentless waves of pain.

"Good. Now, relax, and let me push the pain out of you."

The chant started up again. It was more rhythmic, and she began to stamp her bare feet as she sang and massaged, the bracelets, bangles, and necklaces forming a polyrhythmic tapestry of sound. The percussive cadence of her voice put me at ease. For the first time I could relax. Every muscle began to loosen up under the massaging of her strong and prodding fingers, though the pain was ever present. In my mind the pain took on form – a dark greenish-yellow amorphous blob. It began to soften under the kneading of her hands, and the pain turned into a throb, as it swiftly swelled. Her voice grew louder and louder, increasingly ecstatic, until I was drawn into its trancelike state. I became the chant, I became the pain, I became the embodied poison, and I ceased to fight it, until I'd released the monster from my body – that giant amorphous snot-colored blob of pounding pain – and broke out in uncontrollable sobs. Immediately her chant transformed into a plaintive melody, as she placed her large, fleshy hand on my forehead. Incredible calm accompanied the release and I drifted off into a deep sleep.

When I awoke I was still lying on the gurney, except that a white sheet now covered my nakedness. I looked around. I was alone. The altar was gone. Light from a single bulb hanging from the ceiling gave the old theater a forlorn look. Cautiously I got up, expecting pain, but felt nothing. Warily I moved around, turning my head to the left and right, and then bending down. Nothing. No pain. It was utterly gone. Each movement felt smooth like melting butter.

"She healed you, didn't she?" I shot around, startled, and there was the little boy with the perfect corn rows, and faded Bulls t-shirt. He was sitting on the left hand side of the old stage, legs dangling, chewing gum. Where'd *he* suddenly come from?

"Hey, you frightened me," I said, strangely relieved to see the boy. "Say, where's Voodoo Woman? I want to thank and pay her. I feel like a newly oiled machine."

"Oh, she's long gone. You been sleeping for about five hours, man," and he laughed out loud, his high pitched voice echoing around the empty hall like little silver bouncy balls. "I thought you'd never wake up."

He stared at me, blowing a large pink bubble. After it popped he said, "If you want to make a contribution, you can give me the money." Noticing my hesitation, he added, "She's my aunt, you know... kind of. Anyways, I live with her. Don't worry, I won't run off with the money."

"How much do I owe her?"

"Nothin'... but fifty will do."

I got up, went over to my pile of clothes, got dressed, and took out a hundred in fives, tens and twenties and gave it to him. He fanned quickly through the bills and smiled. "Which reminds me" – shaking the wad in my direction – "she says you gotta understand women better... especially the women in your own life. If you don't, the poison will build up again." He blew and popped another bubble.

"What does she mean by – understand women better?"

"I dunno, but that's what she told me to tell you." And he jumped off the stage. "And I only told you because you paid more than fifty. It's my prerogative," and he enunciated the word *prerogative* like a connoisseur tasting vintage wine. "Come, I'll show you out."

A period of gestation had begun. I was freed of the pain in my back and that alone felt like a transformation. It gave me the strength to tackle some of the outer aspects of my life, such as looking for a new apartment and a job. A couple of weeks later I was hired as the new English and drama teacher at Stone Ridge High School. Though it redirected my focus I was still a long way off from getting my inner house in order.

Compassion

Shoes, Vincent van Gogh

There are many passions, but the most sublime is compassion. Now, for instance, I stand in front of Vincent van Gogh's *Shoes*, and I want to weep, just thinking about the world's cumulative pain, the ongoing suffering. It's inexplicable why the painting triggered this mnemonic moment, or why I should suddenly be overcome with such unbridled compassion for all of humanity. But I am, powerfully so. Was it something in Vincent van Gogh's wild brush strokes, his deep love for the world as it mysteriously imparts itself through his work? Was it the sacrifice and insurmountable hurt that went into all of his paintings? I'd like to think so. Then again, I've stood or walked past this painting many times without being so emotionally moved. Undeniably, the times when art chooses to speak are unpredictable. If there's lawfulness, it's beyond my grasp. Today I'm moved by *Shoes*.

O

Shoes are ever subservient, and it's their humble job to cover, protect, adorn, and facilitate travel, every step of the way. Shoes' soles hug the ground. They fulfill destiny, submerged in the deep sleep of our will – the will to walk the miles, or to stand, to wait patiently, as encounters change life, as greetings and farewells take place, as work calls, as hearts follow their yearnings. Shoes become well trodden homes for the feet. There are shoes for every occasion. They uplift or degrade, sometimes fitting the fashions more than the feet. Shoes lure and tease, invoke fear and scorn, but also laughter, respect and reverence. Often they simply perform a basic utilitarian purpose: to move from here to there, depending on the need.

As I stare at the painting of those rustic working man's shoes, a procession of my own trusty past pairs marches through my mind, those I've worn since infancy – dumb couples, now long lost, buried, forgotten, discarded, misplaced, outgrown, stored, given away, even sold. But there was one pair, like the hallowed van Gogh exemplar – that I treasured above all others; shoes that had accompanied me through my studies at university, the subsequent trip across Europe, and right up to the birth of Alicia, when I finally accepted their passing. I gave them a sovereign and honorable farewell. The gaping and toothless twosome were put on a meticulously constructed funeral pyre and cremated to the scintillating sound of John Coltrane's bebop sax while I narrated highlights of their biography in my sermon (held alone in the community garden one grey, cold Thursday afternoon).

And today, for me, van Gogh's rustic old shoes become the embodiment of the world's deeds, as enacted or experienced by each individual on earth – receptacles of fate inherited from the past, as much as forgers of a freeing destiny leading into the future. I picture myself in the shoes of others, and it engenders an understanding of their daily struggles. Compassion is a deep-felt understanding of the other person's underlying tragedy; and to suffer with them is to get to know them better – they come closer. Does it help to alleviate some of their pain? I like to think so.

O

A little girl of about eight, wearing lacquered red shoes and a white, frilly dress that contrasts beautifully with her deep brown skin is crying. A female guard walks over to the weeping child and puts her hand gently on the girl's shoulder.

"What's the matter, sweetie?" she asks

"I lost my mommy," she sobs quietly.

"Oh, don't you worry, we'll find her."

Closing my green notebook I get up and walk over. "I saw your mother walking into the next gallery just a minute ago," I say, smiling down at the girl and meeting the eyes of the guard, whose name I notice from the tag is Carrie. And I also note that she's exceptionally attractive. The guard takes the little girl's hand and quickly reunites her with her mother. On her return the guard says "Thanks," and smiles.

"Pleasure."

I buy a print of van Gogh's *Shoes* at the gift shop to hang up above my shoe rack – a reminder to practice compassion.

Sitting on the subway back to my apartment I feel free and unencumbered. I close my eyes and a beautiful face appears – Carrie's.

PART TWO

Flowers in Great Hall – (a continuing gift of Lila Acheson Wallace)

Invisible Worlds

Finials from Slit Gongs, Oceania

I want to see her again, but I keep my desire well hidden behind my firm intention to take in and contemplate art. Today I'm more alert and receptive than usual. My mind is ready to be stimulated.

O

I savor the spacious quietude of the Michael C. Rockefeller Wing. The hushed air lures me in. Hardly ever is it crowded, most people just passing through en route to the twentieth century exhibits or back to the Museum Restaurant. Though displaced, the art from Africa, Oceania, and the Americas speaks secrets of the invisible worlds: the common world of *all* of our forebears, the heritage every one of us shares – the preternatural spheres, alive with spirits, gods and goddesses, nature sprites, benevolent and demonic beings, and our ancestors. A world infinitely more spiritual than the mainstream of our modern and 'enlightened' era; reminders of a time when all of humanity was connected to a spiritual counterpart. Nothing was *not* spirit instilled. Every moment had its season, presided over by living entities of an invisible source. All matter was only a manifestation of the spirit, an echo and embodiment of something greater, more ethereal and divine – part of a being-imbued cosmology.

I've just returned from an almost three hour tour through the museum. I leisurely made the rounds of the different eras and cultures – China, India, Persia, Mesopotamia, Egypt, Greece, Rome, Middle Ages, the Renaissance, right through to the romantics, until at last, after passing through the Lila Acheson wing of modern art, I reentered this wondrous wing of mystifying works – my point of departure. I followed the gradual spiritual separation, as it is reflected through the ages, ending with the crisis laden moderns, epitome of spiritual doubt – that 'wasteland' that made T. S. Eliot famous, the 'howl' that got Allen Ginsberg going ... yet, driven by a relentless search for meaning – the lost chord; something to take the place of paradise lost. And all along my elusive nether mind was looking out for Carrie, though, on the surface I didn't let it interfere with my lofty thoughts – on the contrary, I was mentally buoyed by the possibility of seeing her. I let my mind breathe the rarefied thoughts streaming toward me from the artworks.

The bulk of the Met's contents are a testimony of "Man's" belief, search and struggle with the unseen world. In this respect the Met is a microcosm of the world's ever-evolving consciousness; the works of art as analogous to larger life and our special place in it. Modernity has basically denied spirituality, but it would appear we've not put anything that satisfies in its place – though we have, in fact, an insatiable craving for it, embodied in our constant struggle for *freedom*. In our scramble to understand freedom, and what it means for the individual and society, we'll discover the new spirituality needed for our age, of that I'm convinced.

My thoughts are back with Carrie. It's silly that a meeting of mere seconds can get me obsessing about a girl who's hardly anything more than a figment of my fervent craving for feminine intimacy. While fulfilling my intention to follow the development of human consciousness from one epoch to another – as expressed through art of the respective ages – my eyes checked off, one by one, every guard I saw in every gallery. But I didn't see her. Not a glimpse. I'm almost amused that I can't let go of her. Again and again I relive the moment of our brief meeting; when I saw an immediate recognition of compatibility emanating from her eyes. And I wasn't just registering my own raw, self-projected longing. Thinking back, it was almost obscenely obvious – a naked expression of a shared sixth sense moment. Call it carnal clairvoyance, or sacred second sight.

O

Now I'm sitting on the long bench by the slanted and massive window-wall facing Central Park, slightly despondent. The possibility of meeting her was an added draw to my visit to the Met today – the raison d'etre. I'm no longer denying it. I've removed the mask, and wonder: Am I in her proximity? Is she somewhere in the building? Does she work here full time? How old is she? Married? Would that sweetly sensual moment repeat itself if our eyes met again?

Now that I've exposed myself and listened to my other mind, I can go back to my first – unburdened. Carrie, who presently personifies my hope and desire to love and be loved has – strangely enough – become the catalyst to ennobling thoughts. And there's something freeing and satisfying about meditating on deeper and more idealistic themes. I continue to give way to those reflections that might satisfy on a deeper level.

O

If I could only muster my cognitive forces and follow them through to their logical conclusion; and if I could only be an engineer of the mind through enhanced mindfulness, then there'd be no telling what I could accomplish in the creative and social realm. Clear thinking leads straight to the gates, beyond which lies the metaphysical world. But how to open those gates consciously? Some do it through a guru and meditation, others with drugs. I want to make the new territory my own – on my own. All too often the beyond jumps its walls and infiltrates me unconsciously. I've had my share of unstoppable voices, delusions, hallucinations, irreconcilable urges, neuroses, pathologies. I've kept them at bay for the most part. I wonder, however, if my mild obsessions, like having to count steps or collect pennies, are a direct expression of needing something spiritually more meaningful in my life. I feel the walled frontiers all around me, constantly. Even the visible and the obvious easily elude me. I have to work hard to perceive telling details of everyday occurrences, like the shape and shifting of clouds, or hearing the difference between an ash, elm or poplar, as the wind hushes through. And maybe I'm trying to resuscitate my ailing spirit through my penchant for rituals and ceremonies.

O

I gave way to higher notions, and clearly, I've exhausted the breath of this feeling.

O

I've just realized that I haven't thought of Arietta and the attendant problems for a while. My mind is constructing a protective myth, pieced together out of fragments of imagination – a mosaic of how I imagine Carrie to be. That confirms an overcoming of sorts, similar in feeling to the time after my weird visit to Voodoo Woman. But what is it founded on? Does it have any reality? Over the last few days I've caught myself talking to Carrie, confiding in her. If nothing else, it makes for a welcome change because it gets lonely when you can't share your innermost thoughts with anybody except yourself. Even lonelier when you have the unequivocal experience that everything around us must have an esoteric counterpart – in a world where people either don't believe in the spirit, or have a sentimental, solely faith based view of it.

It wasn't alone the lively, scintillating eyes that attracted me, but the pathos of her full lips in relation to her delicately formed nose. Her hair was neatly and tightly bundled up, like a second cupola on top of her head. I'm a sucker for hair, and I wonder how long and lush it looks when loose. It was lustrously black.

Dreaming about someone is rather pleasant. I'm making a goddess out of her, though she's merely an evanescent dream. But her image fuels my musings, gives me fresh wind.

Lifting my head from my green notepad I look around. I see art born entirely out of ancient traditions. And tradition means ceremony, means active ritualistic worship, means intimate relationship with the lofty beings of the supernatural world. Means many rites of many passages. Means survival. Means total integration and unity. Sacredness.

Everything was sacred – from the enormous split drum next to me to the terrifying and splendid masks, to the statuettes, to every power figure… to the shields, boats, poles, stools, vessels, bottles, weapons, instruments – sacred potency in every detail. And all that's sacred demands sacrifice. And the prerequisite? Pain. Pain, joyously suffered for the greater good. For the community. Communion with the gods for a salubrious social life. Down to the most private practices. To sex, a most sacred right, only allowed after sacrificial rites have been performed – the community's blessing.

As much as I revere them, I am glad that I'm not confined by all these traditions anymore, though I'm just a few generations removed from these kinds of strict customs. At times I can almost feel the subterranean tributary of my African ancestors, hear them whispering, like now – strange as it may sound. Yet, how can I regain the richness of such ancient, all inclusive cultures, where every action was aligned with the gods, the spirits, and the entire hierarchy of the invisible worlds, without giving up my present state of mind? It would mean relinquishing individual freedom. And who wants that? I'd forego a chance to live in paradise if it meant giving up the freedom I now have – pathetic as it may be.

A tour guide with his predominantly tired looking troupe starts lecturing about the rather gruesome facts behind the *Mbis Pole* from New Guinea and my thoughts slowly disintegrate.

☾

I turn around and face Central Park. It's a clear blue day out. A few diehard joggers and bicyclists are about. Hours have passed since I sat down to write. I'm loath to leave. My mind is dazed, but my soul is warmed through. Walking out via the Greek Sculpture Court I stop and stand on the front steps of the Met, seven from the bottom to the right.

It's past five. The Met's closed for the day and the last of the visitors are leaving. I pace back and forth on the steps. Eventually I sit down and wait. Just when I'm ready to leave I spot her – or, at least, I think it's her – Carrie standing in line about to step onto a bus. With only a moment's hesitation I get up to get a closer look. I want to call her, shout out her name, but of course I don't. I start running towards her, but she's already stepped onto the bus. I take some more futile steps, then stop and stare as it drives away. I see her moving to the back of the bus, the M4. For a moment I fancy she's looking at me through the window? I wave. It feels like a declaration of love. She's gone. I doubt she saw me.

The Meeting

Burghers of Calais, Rodin

I'd forgotten how crowded it gets around Christmas time. Manhattan throng. The Met's no different. And foreign languages abound, though predominantly German and Japanese. 2002, the year of the palindrome is coming to an end. There is little of the new millennium fever left. It cooled down fast after 9/11. All in all, the prognosis is that it's been a terrible year, socio-politically speaking: wars, AIDS, poverty, hunger, sex trafficking, torture, drugs, epidemics, global warming, et al. Nothing new, really. I guess it's just my present torpor that's calling forth these depressing thoughts. And though my listlessness is clouding my thoughts, augmented by the tiresome stream of visitors, I still uphold my positivity like a prayer.

I can't get going this morning. The weather might have something to do with it – wet and overcast with the sky looking like oxidized copper. Or maybe it's because Alicia couldn't make it down this weekend – again.

Anyhow, I park myself in my favorite corner of the Petrie Café in the proximity of Rodin's *Burghers of Calais*. As always it's quiet here at this time of the morning. The crowds are rushing off to the special exhibits. For my petit déjeuner I have the usual coffee-croissant combo. Let's hope it'll help me rid my mind of the morning cobwebs.

Because I want to find a quiet place to write, I walk up to the Asian Art section, on the second floor. In my desultory wandering I come across the beguiling copper sculpture of Yashoda and Krishna – a kind of sensuous Madonna and child. I ponder the exquisite pair, realizing how rare this motif is in Indian art. It's movingly tender and I'm struck with this exemplar of motherhood (albeit foster mother) in its exhilarating, almost enraptured state – the voluptuous breasts suggesting ample fertility. The almost erotic intimacy makes me wonder whether it led Krishna to seduce Radha and the other countless milkmaids later on. Its similarity to any of the European virgin and child statues is as striking as it is different. In the Virgin Mary of medieval times, all the emphasis is centered on the inner terrain of the soul, to evoke a devotional and sacred mood in the viewer. Depictions of Mary are oftentimes ethereally beautiful, though rarely as sultrily sensual as Yashoda.

Krishna and Christ are both gods inaugurating a new age, sharing similar names; but more than that, they're both sons in need of a mother's nurturing. Without the motherly love they might not have been able to fulfill their mission. I lose myself in Yashoda's naked splendor, the innocence with which baby Krishna nuzzles up to those curvaceous breasts. There's soul warmth in physical touch. I thirst for it.

I climb up the narrow wooden stairs (three, then turn and seven more) that lead to the marvelously carved ceiling of the Jain Meeting Hall. There's nobody there and I lean heavily on the railing looking down at the *Loving Couple* from Orissa in India, sculpted from ferruginous stone. The naked couple is locked in the act, the girl's leg lifted and wrapped around his. Sighing, I sit down cross-legged on the floor. It is dimly lit, and it takes me a while to adjust my eyes.

My listlessness, though not dispelled, lifts gradually. I'm determined to break my lethargy. The trouble is I don't want to face myself today; I can't stomach this in-depth search-pilgrimage that I've come to pursue for more than a year already. Today it feels stifling rather than freeing.

Above: *Yashoda and Krishna*, Early 12th Century

114

I hear footsteps on the stairs and out of the corner of my eye I notice a guard. I sense he's going to tell me to get up. I bend over my notebook, determined to ignore him.

O

Twenty minutes later.

I heard footsteps on the stairs and out of the corner of my eye I noticed a guard. I sensed he was going to tell me to get up. I bent over my notebook – scribbled away – determined to ignore him. But when I furtively glanced up at him I saw, to my surprise, that it was none other than Carrie. Instantly, my weariness vanished. Here was my opportunity. I couldn't let it slip by.

"Excuse me, is it okay to just sit here and take some notes?" I asked, feeling embarrassed as I looked up at the woman whose gossamer image I'd unwaveringly carried around with me over the last couple of weeks.

"It's fine by me," she answered, already turning her back on me. There was no recognition on her part.

"Hey, wait a minute, I remember you."

"You do? ...Do I know you?" she asked guardedly, stopping at the stairs.

"Not really, but remember the lost little girl in one of the galleries by the impressionists? I helped you find her mother," I said, getting up and facing her.

"Can't recall... I see thousands of people every day." I was disappointed she didn't immediately remember me or the incident, and there was nothing emanating from her eyes.

"It must have been about two weeks ago. She had a white dress and red lacquered shoes."

"Oh yes, now that you mention it, I do remember. She was a cute little girl," she said, smiling briefly.

Even in that sexless uniform she was drop-dead gorgeous. "You know," I hastened on, feeling slightly emboldened, "I come here all the time. In fact, I'm writing a book that revolves around this place" – and I waved my notebook in the air – "I'd love to interview someone from the inside... someone like you, who actually works here."

"An interview?"

"Yes, you know, questions like, um… how long have you worked here at the museum?" She hesitated. Feeling tense I quickly added, "I'm sorry; it's none of my business." I didn't want to appear too intrusive. "It's just that I've always wondered what it must be like to be a guard. I mean, it must get quite boring at times, or not?" That was silly. I need training in tact and I always talk too much when I get nervous.

"Well, it all depends on the day and the kind of questions people ask," she answered nonchalantly, smiling ambivalently, adding, "and Wednesdays and Thursdays tend to be a bit slow."

"Right," I said, momentarily lost for words, having picked up on her subtle put down. "Hey, I'm sorry for assuming that your job might be boring. Actually, you must meet all sorts of interesting types."

"There's no shortage of those, though we usually don't have much interaction with the public," she responded, turning her back and taking two steps down the stairs.

"How about the art? Do you have to know a lot about art to get the job?" I had to stop her before she got away.

"It helps, but no, not really." She paused. "The tour guides take care of that. In fact, some guards don't even know the full layout of the place, even though we change our stations every two hours. Anyway… gotta go now."

"Okay… so, how about that interview over a cup of coffee? Would you be up for it?" I asked, stepping forward and putting both my hands on the railing.

She stopped in mid step, turned round and stared straight back at me. For a moment I thought she was going to kick me right out of the Met.

"I understand if you can't. It's okay."

"Well," she said, hesitating, "maybe I'll answer a few questions over a cup of tea." At that very moment, and only for a split second, I saw the same mysterious sensuality emanate from her dark, lucid eyes – the look I'd caught at our first meeting.

"You will?" I asked, in disbelief. "Great. So when are you off duty?" I asked, feeling encouraged, but feigning cool insouciance.

"My lunch break is at twelve-thirty. Let's see… we could meet in the employee cafeteria, if you know where it is?"

"Nope."

"You take the stairs down to the rest rooms, the ones next to the auditorium, on the way to the Egyptian Art section; and it's right there on your left. You can't miss it… well, maybe you can," she said, smiling furtively, as she hurried down the last three stairs, brushing past a panting elderly gentleman in a white suit who glanced around for two seconds before heading up the next fourteen steps to the *Ragamala Paintings*, still panting.

○

And I'm still up here. More than an hour has elapsed since we spoke. I recorded our meeting, but mostly I've just been sitting here, looking up at the masterfully carved ceiling of the Jain Meeting Hall, feeling stunned and excited.

Jain Meeting Hall

Draupati

Shiva, as Lord of the Dance, India

It's Saturday evening and I'm sitting near the pianist in the museum restaurant with more than an hour to spare before Carrie gets off work. People are hustling and bustling in and out, and the piano man is playing a Schubert impromptu. The music always adds a festive mood to the place. Fine time to write.

O

It's been over six weeks since the 12:30 rendezvous in the employee cafeteria. I did most of the talking – just superficial chitchat, little anecdotes and vignettes from my life. By the end of our time I realized that I still didn't know much about her (so much for my 'interview'), except that she had worked as a guard for almost seven months and that, on the whole, she liked the job, especially the people she was working with. I asked her out for dinner and she accepted on the condition that she could choose the venue. "Let's meet outside the Rizzoli Bookstore on 57th around about seven," she said, smiling furtively. "I know a good restaurant nearby."

I felt like I was passing straight through a turnstile into another installment of my life.

O

The pianist is now playing a nocturne by Chopin, the fluency of the melody resonating with my undeniably romantic mood, conjuring forth images of moonbeams reflecting off pristine lakes surrounded by shadowy hills and woods. I'm infatuated, I admit.

O

When I saw Carrie the next evening I barely recognized her, dressed as she was in something other than the dark Met uniform. Her long, smooth, melanic hair fell loosely halfway down her back, and she wore an elegant, close fitting, cream colored coat and red silk scarf. The stern look on her honey hued face was absent and with a slight smile she took me by the arm and said, "Let's go," leading me to a classy Indian restaurant.

The moment we entered we were warmly welcomed and immediately led to a secluded table next to a tiny pond with goldfish, flanked by two palm trees. She greeted the servers as if she knew them. Two water lilies were blooming.

"How do you like this place?" she asked.

"Love it... kind of elegantly exotic." All around there were bowls of patterned petals next to sculptures of Hindu Gods and Goddesses in various poses, well placed amongst beautiful tropical plants and in little alcoves and niches – like little shrines. On the walls were framed paintings depicting scenes from the Mahabharata and the Ramayana. "It sure gives people a taste of the orient."

"And wait till you actually taste the food," she said, laughing. "How much do you know about Indian food, anyway?"

"A little... I like curry vegetables, samosa, spinach dishes... well, uh, to tell you the truth, I don't know too much."

"Okay, then; how about I give you some suggestions." She began to go through the menu, amused at my ignorance and urging me to be adventurous, especially in regard to the spices.

"You're like an expert on this stuff. Are you an aficionado of Indian food or something? How come you know so much?"

"Because I work here in the kitchen four times a week."

"You what! Seriously, you work here?"

"Yes."

"No wonder all the waiters here seem to know you so well. But how did you learn to cook all this Indian stuff?"

"I grew up with it. I'm Indian."

"You are?"

"Yeah, I thought it was obvious."

"Well, I was wondering about that. But you don't have the slightest accent. You know, when I first saw you I thought you might be part Latino or something, but I didn't give it much thought. Anyhow – Indian, huh? Tell me more? When did you come to the States?"

"Let's order first and then we'll talk, okay?"

O

Now the pianist is playing the first of the *Trois Gymnopédies* by Eric Satie. Its slow, plaintive melody, so simple, but so effectively pleasing in its almost stark beauty, is like a tonal meditation. Arietta, dilettante pianist that she is, used to play this piece whenever she was upset and wanted to calm down. It's followed by a contrasting Scott Joplin rag.

O

"I was a baby when we came to America, not even two years old. My first memories are of running around the fabric and clothes store my father opened with my uncle, in Cambridge, Mass. We lived in a small apartment above the store. As soon as I went to school I wanted to be just like any other American kid. In fact, that's when I changed my name to Carrie."

"So what's your real name?"

"See, I'm still embarrassed to say it, even now."

"Oh, come on, that's just silly."

"I know. Whatever. It's Draupati Sarabhai – not an easy name for Americans to twist their tongues around."

"Drewpaty Sareebay – how did I do?"

"Not bad," she said, laughing, "though the pronunciation is a little off. Listen – Draupati Sarabhai."

"Draupati Sarabhai."

"Excellent. You got it... well, almost."

"Draupati. It sounds like the name of an Indian princess or something."

"Correct," she responded, leaning back, slowly brushing her glossy black hair over her shoulders, exposing her smooth neck. "According to the Mahabharata she was the princess in the court of Pancalas... but what was I just saying?"

"How you wanted to be like all the other American kids."

"Oh yeah. You know, I felt so self-conscious about being Indian, and never invited any of my friends over to our place. My mother could barely speak English and my father forbade us to hang out with anybody except for the people from our Indian community."

"That's pretty restrictive. So where in India are you from?"

"A small village north of Madras. All along my father intended to go back to India once he'd earned enough money, to live as a respected man among his relatives. I dreaded the idea of returning to India and was glad that, year after year, the move back was postponed."

"Do you have any siblings?"

"Two brothers – an older and a younger. They had to work in the store every afternoon after school. I was spared that, but when my father opened up an Indian takeout joint, I had to help my mother cook everyday. Later, when I was already in high school, we expanded and my father opened up an Indian restaurant, leaving the fabric store to my uncle and his children."

"That explains your expertise in Indian cuisine," I said, taking a bite of chapati.

"Yes, I led a kind of double life. At home I was the dutiful daughter, doing all the chores, working in the restaurant and sticking to all the traditions, and at school with my friends, I became the stereotypical American schoolgirl. I followed the prevailing fads, put on makeup, listened to all the cool music – you know, whatever was a hit and on MTV – smoked cigarettes and weed, went to parties, drank and hung out with the guys."

"How did you get away with it? I mean, didn't your parents find out? Didn't it conflict with all the work you were forced to do?"

"Sure, it was hard. I often snuck out at night after work without my parents knowing. They were so busy that they couldn't always check up on us – you know, my brothers were doing it even more; especially my older brother. I got away with a lot of stuff, because I was getting good grades. I was always on the honor's list. So, when my parents thought I was studying or participating in a school function. I was often out with my friends.

"But I also rebelled – big time. I hated that my mother and I had to cater to the whims and wishes of the men – you know, cooking, housework, washing and cleaning up after them every day. It pissed me off that we had to eat separately and that my father's word was law. I hated that my mother never stood up for herself, that she even let him beat her. My girlfriends and their moms weren't treated that way. In fact, I was shocked to see how much freedom they had, compared to us. Once, when I confronted my father on some of these issues he slapped me across the face, told me never to talk to him like that again and ordered me to my room. I was just as angry with my brothers, because they never stood up for me or my mother. Just accept it, they'd say. Easy to say for them." Carrie got flushed when she talked about the inequalities she'd endured. "One thing became clear to me: I would never live the way my mother lived. I was determined to break away from home as soon as possible."

"And it looks like you did."

"Yes... well, sort of. After I graduated I wanted to get a degree in social work, and I enrolled at Northeastern."

"And do your parents still live in Boston?"

"No, they eventually returned to India – back to the same little village, surrounded by all of my father's relatives. But my older brother is still in Cambridge, and my younger brother is in the computer business on the West Coast in Silicon Valley."

"So do you go back to India often to see your parents?" I asked, surprised when she hesitated, turned pale, and bit her lip. Abruptly she changed the subject, asked me about my life, and took a sip of red wine. As she lifted her glass a tremor crossed her chin.

○

Now it's Beethoven's 8th sonata, the famous *Pathetique* that's sounding through the halls. Arietta, I remember, was always frustrated that she could never play it properly, though she tried, again and again. Now I'm virtually moved to tears by the ten slow and grave opening measures; but as the pianist bends into the pulsating, will dominated rush of the second motif, my heart jubilates… carried along by the current of the faster tempo – *allegro di molto e con brio* – into a state of sublime exaltation.

○

I don't even know Carrie's address; just that she's living somewhere in Carroll Gardens, Brooklyn. Nor has she come over to my apartment. We haven't spent a night together. She's often evasive. I respect her space, and never try to push her to say or do anything. She's protecting some vulnerability that's hard to place.

But we spend as much time together as possible, given our busy schedules – going for long walks through Central Park, window shopping through the city, having coffee and tea and talking. Sometimes we dine out or go to movies. Mostly she's vivacious, even unpredictable – kissing me at the most random moments, making spontaneous plans, or changing a day's program just to sit quietly on a park bench, watching people go by.

But I worry when she retreats into herself, barely responding to what I'm saying, looking lost and staring vacantly into the distance; or, even more disconcerting, looking straight at me, almost accusingly, sizing me up. When I ask, "What's up?" she smiles, apologizes and changes the subject immediately, feigning effervescence. I can't place it. But over the weeks I've seen her smile more readily. I've seen the girl in her emerge – which, I suspect, wasn't allowed to flourish enough when she was young. Underneath her approachable and warm demeanor I intuit a painful past, some anguish she's not willing to disclose.

○

There she is, I see her coming, just as the pianist is playing the opening bars to Gershwin's *Summertime*. The Met has taken on a whole new meaning for me.

Carrie's Secret

Terrifying Terrain, Elizabeth Murray

Last night it all came out, like a festering boil that has finally popped. I'm dazed by her disclosure. It made me aware again how blind I am to what's really going on in the world right now. Well, in a sense I do know, but it mostly remains abstract – intellectually registered knowledge that you can discard like the news at the end of the day. It often takes a personal connection to really wake up to something. In my case it was Carrie.

All stirred up I walk through Janice Levin's "A Very Private Collection" of impressionistic paintings, a rare exhibit. I've not seen any of them before though they're all so familiar – like good friends revealing new and different sides to themselves. Looking at them relaxes me. I need to feel self-collected before I can record what Carrie let out. Art has that power.

The impressionist painters give me joy. Always have! Their love and courage for color, their looseness with lines and playfulness in regard to form, their ability to transcend time by slipping through the eye of the transitory moment, their capturing of universal human traits through telling details, their exploration of the psyche and their undeniable authenticity, have all helped to school my sensibilities, while forming the foundation for the ultimately liberating elements of abstract art, which I've come to appreciate so much. Before I understood modern art with all its intangibles, I connected to the impressionists. I didn't need to understand them intellectually. They spoke to me directly. They were my base in any of the major art museums I visited throughout my life. And now, to see a whole new collection of paintings never before exhibited publicly – what a treat. Already I feel less agitated.

There's comfort in viewing these paintings, both through their familiarity and their innate content. I amble slowly from painting to painting. I become privy to a very private moment in Renoir's *Seated Female Nude*, the girl, in all her soft-fleshed innocence, sitting naked in a meadow after a bath in a brook. Surely it's one of the *filles* I've come to know so well, seated by the piano or in the meadow (maybe the same meadow) wearing pink and white. Or then there's Monet's view of his garden at Argenteuil – I can almost smell the fleeting scents of the flowers. And the familiar rural landscapes of Bonnard, Camille Pissaro, Alfred Sisley and Eugene Boudin gently open up inner landscapes, funneling the outer reaches of nature, right down into the dark, rich ground of my soul, where the spiritual depths weave their inscrutable wisdom. At length I sit in one of the comfortable chairs with armrests. My body feels weak, and my hand limp, but I'm compelled to write. I'm ready to record Carrie's affliction, which has become my own..

O

Yesterday afternoon, while correcting English papers at Le Gamin Café, around the corner from my small apartment in the East Village (to which I'd relocated shortly after Arietta left me), Carrie called me on my cell. By the quiver in her voice I could tell something was wrong. "I need to talk to you... can I come over?"

"Sure. Where are you?" I answered, anxious and surprised because she'd always put off coming to see me at my place.

"I'm at home," she said, and started to sob. "I'm sorry, but something bad has happened."

"You're not hurt, are you?" I asked, worried. I'd never heard her sound so put out. "What happened?"

"No, I'm fine... I'll tell you everything when I see you."

"Okay. I'll meet you at Astor Place Station in say... thirty minutes?"

"Thanks... please wait for me if I'm late... will you?"

"Of course. See you soon."

I packed up my papers and left, wondering what this was all about.

As soon as she saw me she ran up and hugged me tightly. Her eyes were red from crying. We walked down St. Marks and past Thompson Square Park to my apartment in silence, a frigid wind cutting into our faces, and the sky was dark with clouds. I guessed it would rain soon. As soon as we got home I made some herb tea, and for a while we just sat there, looking at one another, sipping hot Lemon Zinger, holding hands. Intermittently, she braved a smile, before becoming teary-eyed again. Whatever she wanted to tell me; it wasn't going to be easy.

"Okay, so this is what happened," she finally said, breathing deeply. "When I got home from work today I found my roommate in hysterics. Someone had broken into our place and torn it to shreds. I tell you, it was a complete mess – you wouldn't believe it." She pushed her hair out of her face, pulled a tissue from a box, and carefully wiped away some tears. "And the thing is, it's all my fault."

"What do you mean – 'It's all my fault?'"

"Just that," she said, and sniffed, pulling out another tissue to blow her nose. "I feel terrible because my friend was drawn into the whole thing. And now maybe you too."

"Okay, out with it! What's all this about?"

"I'm sorry Clarence, I was waiting for an appropriate time to tell you, but it never came. I guess I was scared... and I wanted to get to know you better, first."

"I don't know what's wrong, Carrie, but whatever it is, you can trust me."

"I know that, Clarence." She got up, dropped the tissue into the trash can and looked out the window. The wind could be heard howling through the open steel gratings of the fire escape. "Anyway, you'll understand why I've kept it all to myself. It's a long story – even the brief version."

○

I pause, the anguish returning as I relive the conversation. I glance over to Monet's *Cliffs at Pouville*. From nowhere George Harrison's *Isn't It A Pity* goes through my mind. I let the wistful melody unwind for a while before I shake it off.

○

She sat down again, sipped some tea and began. "As I've already told you, my parents returned to Madras the year I graduated from high school. They'd wanted me to go back with them, but I persuaded them to let me finish college before considering such a move. I had, of course, no intention of ever living in India again. I'd become an American citizen and felt more American than Indian. Except for one short trip to visit relatives I'd spent my whole life in Boston. I couldn't imagine going back to India for good. However, four years later, with a degree in social work in my pocket, I did go over to see my parents during the summer break. I'd already enrolled at Hunter College for my grad studies.

"As soon as I arrived I sensed something was wrong. My mother seemed ill at ease, whereas my father was uncommonly friendly. But I didn't think much of it, and initially my stay was great; you know, reconnecting with my parents and relatives and enjoying the vibrant life of India. The smells, sounds and sights are just so intense – especially coming from America, where everything is kind of watered down, bland and disinfected. Just breathing the air is kind of an excarnating experience – it really is… smells of manure, dung and sewage mingling with the aroma of incense, jasmine, spicy cooking and tasty bread." She smiled sadly and took another sip of tea. "Anyway, I was treated like a guest of honor, everybody coming by or inviting me over, asking about my life in America. But already after two weeks I wanted to get out of there. The lifestyle was just too different from the one I'd gotten used to. I wanted my space. And sticking to all the customs and traditions, especially the Hindi religious rites, from which I'd totally freed myself, was difficult. I felt stifled and like a stranger." She paused, shook her head, and cried, "Why, why, why didn't I see what was about to happen," punching the puffy pillow next to her. "I guess I'll never fully understand what happened to me and why. Some things are just stronger than we are. We like to think we're in control of our lives, but mostly we aren't."

Carrie looked straight up at me, her beautiful dark eyes, glistening sharply in the warm light of the bedside lamp, and said, "You see, the sole reason why my parents were so insistent on my returning to India was because they'd arranged a marriage for me."

"Marriage!"

"Yes," she said softly.

"So how did you get out of it?"

Thoughtfully she sipped at her tea, before continuing. "I didn't – and that's the problem. It was presented as a done deal." Carrie sniffed, swallowed and fought back tears. "I remember it like it happened yesterday. One afternoon, three days before my scheduled departure, my father casually told me about this successful computer programmer from Madras who was well off, and who they'd met several times over the past year. My brother knew him from Silicon Valley and had recommended him. After sifting through and interviewing many applicants they were convinced that he'd be the best partner. It was like a business transaction, and my father pointed out all the indisputable positive attributes – as he saw it: he was above us on the economic scale, educated in America at RPI, had a large house, and he was a landlord, which gave him political clout. They showed me photos of the man and his relatives. Everything was already arranged with his family." Carrie put down her cup, took a tissue and dabbed her eyes. "Obviously, I was shocked and I protested angrily. I pleaded with my mother to speak up for me, but she remained silent, and when I continued to argue she left the room, but not before saying, 'It's meant to be. Don't talk to me about your unhappiness – I'm not interested.'

'But I don't love him.'

'Love? That's silly.' she scoffed. 'You'll learn to love him,' she said as an afterthought, and was gone.

"There was no way out. It was tradition, and she'd accepted it just like most Indian women. She saw no reason why I should be an exception. I didn't give up, and I challenged my father, but no matter what I said, he remained obstinate. They'd already cancelled my flight back to the States without my knowing. The nightmare had begun, and I watched the preparations for the wedding take place. I called both my brothers in America, but they refused to help me. The one in Boston was sympathetic, but wasn't willing to stand up against my father. The one in California told me I was lucky to get such a rich husband who would take care of me. In fact, they already had their tickets to fly over for the wedding."

"So you actually got married to this guy?"

"I did. I wish I could tell you otherwise, but no, there was no way out! It was like being caught up in a maelstrom. I don't even remember much of the wedding. I went through the whole ordeal in a bewildered, somnambulant state."

"So basically they forced you, against your will?"

"There was nothing I could do. The irony is that it was a dream wedding in so many ways. It was held in a large grassy area in one of the semi-luxury hotels on the outskirts of Madras. I was dressed in the most lavish way – beautiful red and golden sari and headdress, sashes, garlands with expensive and extravagant jewelry. A Hindu wedding is a festival of color and sound, and so was mine. But, believe me, I was the most miserable wretch amongst all the splendor. You know, weddings belong to one of the most celebrated and important traditions in India, and my father saw to it that this would be no exception. He had, after all, been in America and made his fortune – by Indian standards, anyway. He had his honor to uphold. And I was being married off to an educated man who'd also spent many years in America and gone to a prestigious university. Make no mistake, this was a big deal. I looked like a bride taken right out of a Bollywood movie. It was a nightmare I never thought I would find myself in. 'This can't be happening to me,' I kept on saying to myself, over and over again, as the women fussed over me, weaving marigolds into my hair, fixing the large hoop earring into my nose, putting tiny jewels into my eyebrows and painting elaborate designs with henna all over my feet, arms and hands. It was like I'd been displaced into another time and place – reliving some former incarnation. Of course, in India it's the norm, but I'd grown up in America." As Carrie was relating all this she stared into the cup, held tightly between her hands, as if she was seeing it replayed in the tiny round circular screen of steaming tea.

"Finally, some hours later, Jitendra, my fiancé, arrived, riding on an elephant, and the ceremony began. It was an unbearably hot day and I was weighed down with my wedding dress. We sat literally for hours on plush thrones under a canopy of marigolds, listening to the priest chant Sanskrit prayers. At last we circled the ritual fire, were sprinkled

132

with holy water, and were married. At that point I broke down crying. I thought I'd never be able to stop."

"You don't have to continue if it's too distressing for you," I said, seeing involuntary tears slip down her cheeks.

"No, I want to… I need to tell you; really." She tried to laugh. "Now where was I? Oh yes. Okay… so straight after the wedding I moved in with my husband and in-laws, and my new life in a household of strangers began. We lived in a large two-story house in a town, south of Madras; about three hours drive from my parents. I was expected to learn from my mother-in-law exactly how to care, look after, and cook for her boy. I was basically reduced to a slave – in the service of the man who had become my husband, who I hardly knew, who I disliked intensely, and who'd robbed me of my freedom, not to speak of my dignity as a human being. What irony that I'd studied to become a social worker. I was living the very life of some of the women I'd learned about. I had known of the dire and unfair situation of women in India, but I never thought I'd share the same fate – not after having grown up in America.

"Before the wedding, on the two occasions I'd met him – or rather, was shown him – he had been friendly enough, promising me I'd be able to pursue my studies and intimating that I would be able to continue my emancipated way of life. Nothing of the sort. I was never allowed to be alone. When I refused to sleep with him he forced himself on me, consoling me that I'd come to appreciate and love him. At the earliest opportunity, I ran away, but was caught only a few hours later. That's when he beat me for the first time. 'You have shamed me,' he screamed. 'You're no longer living in America, and you're mine, and you'll do as I say. If you comply, you'll be happy, and I'll treat you well… but if not, you'll be sorry,' adding, after a pause, in which he gripped me by the throat, that if I ever tried to escape again he'd hunt me down and kill me. From then on I was not allowed to leave the house anymore."

"What do you mean, like house arrest?"

"Yes, essentially. Do you know what purdah is?"

"No, I don't think so."

"When a woman in India is kept in purdah, it means that she can no longer leave the house, or only rarely, like going to visit her parents twice a year. Living in such seclusion is only reserved for the higher castes, or for the economically better off. It's a matter of prestige. Anyway, my husband decided to keep me in purdah. Can you imagine how I felt, confronted with the idea of spending the rest of my life cooped up in a house, working for my husband and in-laws? I thought of committing suicide, but I was under their watchful eye at all times."

"So, how the hell did you get out of there? This is all so damned crazy. God, how long did you live under those horrendous conditions?" I asked, incredulously.

"Too long. After a while I made as if I'd seen reason, and complied with everything that was asked of me. But all the time I was plotting and scheming my escape. I knew where my husband hid my passport, and I still had my own stash of money which I'd kept in a secret and safe place. Every so often I'd snitch some money from my husband's wallet to add to my savings. I was biding my time, but it took a while. In fact, only once my daughter was born did I see an opportunity to get out of there."

"What! You got pregnant? You actually had a baby?" I cried out, almost accusingly. I felt upset at this latest revelation and I fought back feelings of revulsion mixed with pity. Of course, it all made sense, but my picture of her as an Indian goddess was shattered. The very thought of her having suffered through such abuse was sickening. A spurt of jealous anger made me want to beat up this lousy Jitendra guy.

"Well, of course. It would have been strange had I *not* gotten pregnant. In fact, my mother-in-law was already getting suspicious when I wasn't pregnant after just a few months." Seeing my stunned reaction she added, "I know this is all coming as a shock to you, but I had to tell you."

"I'm okay," I said, trying to regain my composure and looking at her with new respect in spite of my initial reaction. "Go on…"

"Things didn't get any better after the birth of my little daughter Indra, though she was the only ray of light in my ongoing nightmare. Of course he'd hoped for a boy and I knew that I had to get out of there before I got pregnant again. I was waiting for my chance to escape.

"I'd planned it for months, down to the last detail. Once a week my husband would get together with his business associates and drink late into the night. It was after one of these evenings, when he was too drunk to move, that I slipped out with his car keys, rolled the Mercedes silently down the hill, and drove off to the Madras airport, with just one bag. I left the car there and took a taxi to the central bus terminal, where I hailed another taxi to the train station, buying a ticket to Mumbai. I did this to get him off track, because there was no way I would have gotten a plane out of Madras before he'd have found me out and picked me up again. From Mumbai I took the first available flight to New York, and from there I took the bus to Boston."

"You actually pulled it off," I asked, awed by her story.

"Though grueling, it was easier than I thought. It would have been a different story had I not had any money and a passport."

"What about your baby?" The question struck a nerve. She covered her face with both her hands, and it was quite a while before she could answer me.

"I knew that my daughter would be safe with my sister-in-law, who'd always been kind to me, and doted on little Indra... but leaving her behind was the hardest thing I've ever had to do." Again she choked up. "I miss her so badly, and I pray for her daily. It's the greatest pain of my life, not having her around."

"I'm so sorry, Carrie. Really sorry."

"I'm going to get her back. Even if it kills me." She said it with such certainty that I had no doubt that she would, somehow.

Outside it had begun raining and the wind was lashing it against the windows. I poured her another cup of tea and asked, "So, what's all this got to do with the break-in?"

"I'm getting to it," she said, taking the purple pillow to her chest, hugging it. "Once back in Boston I went straight to my brother and insisted he help me get things straightened out. Initially he was helpful, letting me stay at his place and communicating with my parents and my husband and referring me to a lawyer. I wanted a divorce, and I wanted my baby. But it wasn't that simple. I'd shamed both families and their relatives. You see, a marriage in India is always a community affair. My father was upset about the big dowry he'd paid, and my husband, who was hurt in his pride, ordered me to return to India immediately, or he would come and get me personally. He told my brother never to help me again, if he valued his life. My brother told me in no uncertain terms that my parents would disown me and my husband would stop at nothing to get me back home. Besides, my brother had already heard that my uncle and his friends were planning to have me locked up and beaten and sent back to India. I didn't stick around to find out whether it was true or not. That's when I left Boston and came to New York. I've been here ever since, living in continuous fear." She took my right hand in both of hers, looked me straight in the eye and said, "Do you have any idea what it's like to live like a fugitive?" Unconsciously she began kneading my fingers with her cold, moist hands. "And I'm constantly afraid that my husband or one of his goons is going to find me."

I embraced her. Slowly we rocked each other back and forth. She was crying silently. "I'm so sorry, Carrie, really sorry," is all I could say. For a long time we just sat there, holding and caressing each other. At length I whispered into her ear, "You know, I can fully understand why you didn't tell me earlier."

"Thanks." She stroked my cheek. "After my house got ransacked today, you were the only person I could turn to. I'm grateful for that."

"So what exactly happened?"

"Well, this morning, while I was already at work, my roommate opened the door to a person inquiring after me, claiming to be a good friend of mine. He wanted to know where I was and when I would return home. Luckily, she remembered that I'd warned her about an old boyfriend – as I put it – who was looking for me and who might show up at any time. She told him that I was no longer living at the address and shut the door on him. As she left for work she saw him waiting in the car. She tried to call and warn me, but couldn't get through. I'd switched my cell off and didn't get her message. By the time she came back home the damage was done. The door was forced open and the apartment had been combed through thoroughly. She immediately called the police. They'd just left when I returned."

"So you think it was your husband?"

"No, it was my uncle. My brother told me. I called him before I called you and he confirmed that my uncle had come to see him wanting information about my whereabouts. My brother is convinced that Jitendra is paying him to find me. I wouldn't be surprised if my father has a hand in it as well."

"Is that how he got your address?"

"Yes, Unfortunately. I'd called him once from my apartment, and he tracked down my number and address. Initially he denied giving it to my uncle, but I pressed him on it and he finally admitted it. I can't trust anybody from my family anymore. My brother's a good man, but he's weak. Jitendra wants retribution and he's dead set on getting it. I'm on my own now."

"No, you're not. You've got me. We'll see this through together."

"I'm glad I called you… and even more glad that I told you my story. I feel relieved." Carrie sighed, leaned back and closed her eyes. In the silence we listened to the rising sound of the rain drumming on the fire escape, ushered along by a yowling wind.

"It's really coming down, now," I said, looking out the window into the darkness, stroking her hand gently.

"I like it," she whispered, her eyes still closed. We continued to sit in silence, while the rain and wind unrelentingly riled each other up into a frenzied state. "Yeah, I really like it," she repeated, a soft smile hovering over her lips.

"Do you want to spend the night, Carrie?"

"Yes."

Blizzard

Twentieth Century Art

That's what they're calling it – Blizzard 2003, hitting the eastern states on none other than President's Day, February 17. Twenty-some inches of snow in our neck of the brick and concrete woods; the city's come to a virtual standstill. What a blast. Streets empty of traffic, people milling about in jovial groups; a big village of kids. A city transformed: sights, sounds, smells, everything. It's nature's way of making a political statement. Even she's getting fed up with the situation, by contributing trillions of tiny little stars to the burgeoning peace movement. On the Saturday before, a different blizzard descended upon the city: between 200,000 and half a million strong, fervently demonstrating against the impending war with Iraq; they came by the bus loads – whole 'peace trains' trundling in. And on that same Sabbath, all around the world, millions more went marching the streets of cities and towns, urging for peace.

It's late Tuesday morning as I'm writing this. And heaven radiates from people's faces today; they're taking joy in the mild catastrophe, helping each other out, shoveling snow and uncovering cars. And the beauty adds significantly to the amiableness – clean white blanket thickly covering over the grimy filthiness that we've learned to accept and ignore. If we could just leave it for a few days – not do any shoveling or plowing whatsoever. I'm amazed at the mountains of snow piling up with just one run of a snow plough. It's going to cost the city a fat fortune: over twenty million dollars I hear, a million an inch.

The Met is as deprived of people as I've rarely seen it. I'm in my usual spot at the Petrie Café. Coffee, croissant, and newspaper. The walk through Central Park was invigorating. Just seeing people sledding and skiing was a lift. Made me quite forget I was in the middle of Manhattan.

But Carrie and I are weathering our own blizzard! The blissful side is that she's temporarily staying with me, and we're elated, tempered only by the ominous reality underneath it all. Quick decisions were made. She quit both her jobs and gave up her room in the Brooklyn apartment, arranging to have her meager belongings brought to my place at a later date. Her roommate fully understood. Today I came to pick up her last paycheck. It's already in my pocket. We don't know how it will continue from here.

I almost feel guilty about how upbeat I am, given the dire world situation and Carrie's sinister plight – but when it snows there's always a bit of heaven that descends. And I'm assured by Carrie's undaunted demeanor, the inner ease with which she seems to be coping with the situation, as much as by her resilience. For the moment she's perfectly content to sit it out for a few days before tackling the next step. And I'm content to have a woman in my life again – though we're living in a bachelor's pad, hardly big enough to swing a cat in. Even so, there's an additional snag: how am I going to explain all this to Alicia? Once, when I'd asked her how she'd feel about my dating other women she immediately responded with tears. Up to now it was easy to keep these two aspects of my life separate. But there's no protecting her from the knowledge of my new relationship anymore. She'll have to be told; she arrives in two days for the mid-winter break. Alicia must be expecting that it will happen at some point, and maybe enough time has gone by that she won't feel threatened anymore. But for the moment I'll let it go. I don't want a good day's art viewing to go to waste. It might be a snow day in New York City, but it's a Met day for me.

Facing Page: From the Faraway Nearby, Georgia O' Keeffe

I'm on the first floor of the modern art wing, plunking myself down on the various plush, comfortable seats, letting my examining eye wander, letting the art works exert their power over me without my mind interfering too much – which it usually does, all the time. Today I can do it without having to treat it as an exercise, though I fail to shut it off completely. My eyes hang for a while on O'Keeffe's *From the Faraway Nearby*. I dream into it, becoming as still as bones in the dry, hot, sun... disturbed only by a gust of wind from a passing intruder blowing unsolicited life back into my consciousness... and I hear myself think: *The gentle blue speaks of the ever present divinity amidst the death-desert bleached antlers, staging tomorrow's resurrection.* I change my position, ready to let my eyes roam once more, but remain moored in front of Yves Tanguy's *My Life Black and White*, caught up by the domino-clatter-brain-game, triggered by the title rather than the artwork. The words remain in a vacuum and the toppled phantom sentences soon vaporize. My listening eye is now pulled slightly to the right by *The Satin Tuning Fork*. Viewing the two in concert they begin to reverberate sympathetically as the question unfolds: how can we rightfully attune ourselves in such a bleak and empty time? And I hear the immediate answer – keep asking the question! I get up and see myself trying to see. I walk on but don't get far. Pablo Picasso's *Man with a Lollipop* gets in my way. I dodge him. He cackles in my wake and I get stuck in the Blanche and A.L. Levine Court. The clickety-clack of two women's stilettos on the parquet floor and the lack of a bench momentarily annoy me. I feel uncomfortable, almost petulant. I don't want to look at Elizabeth Murray's *Terrifying Terrain* but I do. Why? Is it because that's the very terrain I'm caught up in if only I dared to look beyond the narrow confines of my existence? Is it because I'm not doing anything about the terrifying terrain that's spreading across the world like a disease? I pull myself away and take shelter in the little alcove gallery exhibiting *Cityscapes* by Klee and Feiniger. Carpet and comfortable seating – just how I like it. Absolute quiet for quite a while until a big-bag woman with a raspy cough disturbs my peace. She leaves soon enough, and I lose myself in Paul Klee's *Oriental Pleasure Garden*.

That and Feiniger's *Mid-Manhattan* keep me put. I'm in both places and my reverie conjures forth my lovely Draupati, my girl with the soft skin, the color of tea with a soupçon of milk. She's my oriental pleasure in mid-Manhattan.

And outside, people are still frolicking in the white pleasure, holding off thoughts of war for just another day.

Man with a Lollipop, Pablo Picasso

Wishing Well

Fountain with the Young Pan, American Wing

I'm a picker upper of pennies. Three a day on average. That makes for a lot of pennies over time. I'm always on the lookout for them – you don't deserve the dollar if you don't honor the penny, as they say. I cannot bypass them. I have to pick each one up and I don't care if it's heads or tails.

O

The American Wing is almost deserted. It's nearing closing time and I'm sitting in one of the liberally placed wooden benches with sturdy armrests and backs. I do a lot of sitting, I realize. There's not much light in this beautiful atrium at present – too overcast and late. However, Tiffany's colorful stained glass windows still give off their own inherent glow. This open garden court is a peaceful place to reside in, given all the greenery around and the friendly sound of the water fountain. My left jacket pocket is heavy with a plastic bag filled with pennies. For the moment I'm just sitting, writing.

○

Alicia surprised me. When I called her on the phone and told her about Carrie she responded positively: "I'm looking forward to meeting her, Dad." If there was any awkwardness at all it was on my part, not hers. They hit it off immediately. I'd heard all these terrible stories of children hating the new partners of their divorced parents. I'd braced myself for a hefty confrontation. No need. The effect they had on each other was remarkable. Alicia seemed more mature, like a young woman, in Carrie's presence, and Carrie became more relaxed in hers. They were more like sisters, and the bond was solidly sealed after their first shopping spree. They returned giggling like little girls, trying out the new clothes they'd bought, and preparing an Indian dish.

It was, however, an altogether different matter with Arietta. As soon as she heard about Carrie, she called up, trying to find out everything. How did you meet? How old is she? What are her interests? What attracted you to her? I hadn't expected such a barrage of questions. I'd always assumed she couldn't care less about my current personal life. Though I tried to veer away from the subject in an effort to divulge as little as possible, she always steered the conversation back to 'that new woman in your life.' I hadn't talked to Arietta as much in months; it was almost amusing, except for the sharp edge in her voice, which put me on guard. Had Alicia not liked Carrie as much it might even have been easier. Arietta made it clear she wasn't charmed about Alicia spending time with Carrie, particularly since Alicia had returned home with a couple of sexy thongs, which Arietta attributed to Carrie's questionable influence. Her insinuations were obvious.

○

Getting up, I take the three steps down to the gilded bronze statue of *Diana*, half the size of the original exemplar that once perched on top of Madison Square Garden. She's a virginal ballerina goddess, her lissome body poised to shoot her arrow – a girl huntress depicting the act of hunting in its most refined and symbolic state – the hunt for truth, meaning, and love. Diana, the guardian of springs and streams – the sources of all the secrets, outer and inner, the refreshing and rejuvenating substance at the very origin of the enigma called life, as alluded to in countless fairy tales, myths and legends. Diana, the deity who is gentle and stern, pure and knowing. Diana, protector of hunters and wild animals – the hunter and the hunted.

I'm connecting to her as I slowly pace around the 'golden' girl, my rambling mind triggered by her beauty, as the hunter in me is stirred. I think of the wild animals in the pit of my psyche that need her protection in order to be tamed and transformed – my vices; and I acknowledge that some must be hunted down and slain. Diana, the female hunter in purified form, standing in stark contrast to the image of crass masculinity usually associated with the hunter, as he kills for joy, as he lives for the kill, as he exults in the rush of power in the moment of death by his hand. I see her take careful and confident aim at the ideals that need to be pursued. There's no aggression in her stance, no self interest. Diana, naked without shame, is a picture of beauty without vanity, a personification of innate power unburdened by brute force – daughter of God. An angel. A guardian. I touch her foot.

I walk over to the happy splash of the fountain under the rulership of the goat-god Pan, determined to find the Diana within me (my anima), twin sister of Apollo – the god of light and music. Sitting down on the fountain's edge I take out the fist size sack of coins and finger a few in my palm. I thought it would be easy – the wishing – but it's not. I've come to this wishing well to wish away a year's collection of pennies. Last year I poured my pennies into the upturned hat of an Ehru (Chinese bowed instrument) virtuoso, who was playing near the elevators in Penn Station. And the year before that I placed my mound of pennies between the paws of the lion statue outside the New York Public Library. For years I've practiced some sort of penny ritual. Now I'm hesitating. Making wishes is almost like a prayer. And we all know the admonition: careful for what you wish lest it come true. And I must confess, I've never been good at wishing or prayer – not while cutting my birthday cake nor in church.

I scrutinize the first coin. It's dated 1984. Absent mindedly I flip it into the water, watching it shudder to the bottom, while graceful ripples stretch across the surface. I smile because I forgot to make a wish. Is that bad? I take another one. While tossing the coin I whisper, "Let no

Above: *Diana*, Augustus Saint-Gaudens, American Wing

harm come to Carrie." It lands close to the youthful Pan, playing his double reed pipe. I'm satisfied with the wish that arose naturally. I finger another one. "May Carrie be reunited with her daughter," dropping the coin lightly into the water right in front of me, adding, "Indra," as I watch it twinkle and sink… "And may sweet Draupati be granted swift divorce from her husband," – I fling the coin hard and fast to the far side of the pond.

The wishes now crowd in. I feel a power in them, each one like a little charm. Maybe I'm more superstitious than I dare admit, but, if nothing else, I'm getting poetic joy out of my ritual game. "May our new found love be selfless," – another cent goes diving. "May we free each other through our growing love," – a bright copper coin spins through the air. "Let Alicia not suffer under our divorce," – plop. "May Alicia's deepest wishes be granted." And now with an underhand pitch: "May Arietta and I cease to bicker and argue,"– flump. "May we understand one another again like we used to," – plonk. "May I forgive her and may she forgive me," – plunk. Each time I fling a penny it's as if I'm giving permission for my wish to come true – for something to happen. Am I just sentimental? Maybe.

While wishing and throwing my little charms, my mind is centered on the people closest to me. But there's a ripple effect and I begin to think of friends and acquaintances, wishing for their well being, tapping into their diverse wants and needs. Until in the end my expanding wishes embrace all of humanity: "Protect the weak from the violent… supply the hungry with food… give health to the ailing… may peace prevail over war… care for the innocent children… help us to be good stewards of the earth…"

I start to walk around the fountain, dropping, throwing, casting, flinging, flipping, tossing the coins in fast succession, attaching a wish to each, like many little shielding thought-amulets. Each cast coin sounds slightly different as it breaks the surface of the water, as it breaks some spell, setting something in motion. And with the last coin I wish that my wishes will turn out well. My coins and attendant cares have joined the copper and silver carpet at the bottom of Pan's pond – all the other people's hopes and wishes.

Fountain with the Young Pan, American Wing

War

The Entombment, Medieval Section

I follow the main access route from the Asian Art Wing down to the Library and Teacher Resource Center opposite the coat check. The place is empty and I take a seat with my back to the wall, facing the entrance. I place my writing utensils in front of me and lean forward, take my head between my hands, close my eyes. I try to turn myself into a temporary fossil. At length I open up my notebook and stare at the blank page. After another five minutes I print the date on top of the page, in the center.

March 19, 2003

I take my pen and go over the letters and numbers until the date stares boldly back at me. I'm paralyzed – failed ignition. Frustrated, I rush up to the cafeteria – leaving my stuff on the table – drink a cup of coffee and return. Charged, I take pen to paper.

O

What has happened today takes precedence over almost everything else. I had to do something. I gave my students a homework assignment and released them early from class. I sped over to the Met and went straight for the Islamic wing, seeking out the splendid Mihrab – the most significant part in a Muslim mosque, the niche indicating the direction of Mecca. However, it's not the beauty of the intricately placed glazed ceramics, the brilliance of the color, the floral designs, the decorative inscriptions I want to admire today. No, I was on a mission.

Having caught my breath I reverentially took off my shoes and socks, placing them neatly to the side; took two 'baby wipes' from a plastic bag and cleansed my feet. Slipping out of my jacket I placed it carefully down in front of the Mihrab as a prayer mat. As I dropped down to my knees and bowed my head in front of the Mihrab a guard appeared and said gruffly, "What do you think you're doing, sir?" I looked up and around at the corpulent African American guard, the uniform straining against the push of his immured body; his fleshy jaw agape, with disbelief embossed in his curious eyes.

I hadn't expected a guard to happen upon me so soon; in fact, I thought I'd be done with my little ceremony before anybody would even show up at all. I couldn't help but feel a bit sheepish. But my intent gave me confidence, so I responded almost aggressively, "I'll tell you all right. As you most likely know, America officially declared war on Iraq this morning at 10:15 – so I've come here to pray. It's my way of doing something, paying homage, if you will, of showing my empathy and compassion with the innocent Iraqi people who will have to bear the brunt of this preemptive attack." I said more than I'd wanted to.

"Oh yeah, the war…" he said, the edge leaving his voice for just a moment before continuing hoarsely, "but hell, man, this is no mosque. Why don't you go to a mosque? There are enough around."

"I'm not a Muslim. It would be disrespectful for me to just show up and pray; and besides, the Met's a neutral place, and it's a temple of sorts that represents the religions of the worlds through the arts – all under one roof, without any religious affiliation."

"This is crazy, man. I appreciate your sentiment, but you can't do that here."

"Why not? We come to museums to have an artistic experience, to learn and empathize with different cultures. It's as close as one can get to a religious experience."

"But this is going too far… taking off your shoes, praying… come on!"

"It's not much different than artists setting up their easels and copying masterpieces. I'm paying homage to a people who are going to face months if not years of suffering because of this war based on lies."

The guard looked baffled. He took out a white handkerchief, wiped his perspiring head, and said, "Well, I guess you can go ahead, just be quick; I'll stand guard in case anybody comes."

And so I faced the Mihrab again and began my noontime prayer, softly chanting, "La ilaha illa-llahu, Muhammad, rasul, allahi," which I knew to mean, "There is no God but Allah, and Muhammad is his prophet." In my class on Dante and medieval history (which included an overview of Muhammad's life and Islam and its significant contributions to Europe) I would recite this opening call to prayer with my students. My knowledge of Islam, however, was rudimentary and remained intellectual rather than experiential. Not knowing the Quran or any of the chants of praise and worship I simply prostrated myself in utter submissiveness – face to the ground, rump up. After the fifteenth prostration I got up, put on my shoes and jacket, thanked the now smiling, but head-shaking guard, and left.

In the Arthur M. Sackler Gallery I sat down cross-legged on the stone floor in front of the massive *Head of Bodhisattva*, and began meditating, silently chanting *Aum*, again and again, freeing my mind of superfluous thoughts. In the presence of the formidable replicas of holy people around me in this 'Buddhist Hall' I felt easily transported, and soon the colors, like living and rotating mandalas filled my mind. The peace that came over me was the peace I wished over to Iraq, to all the people who'd be involved in this conflict.

Next I walked down to the Medieval Sculpture Hall, taking in the different statues of the Virgin and Child. After contemplating on the intimate mother and child motif, I made for the Medieval Treasury, gallery number six. I sat down on the pew-like bench in front of the *Pieta with Donors* from the 16th century; behind me *The Entombment* – both potent images of mythical dimensions. I'm reminded of Osiris and Dionysus, two gods from antiquity – dismembered and made whole again. I was moved, once

Pieta with donors, Medieval Section

more, to think deeply on the theme of death and rebirth, as encountered in our daily lives. In the chiseled countenance of Christ and those around him, I saw the suffering and torment that will inevitably befall countless people because of today's dubious declaration of war, in ways that go far beyond what we can fathom. Wars always do that.

And I prayed. I prayed in my simple way; I prayed for the people, that they might find the forces to overcome the awful trials they'll be faced with. I prayed for the soldiers – American, Iraqis and all the others, and I prayed for the innocent people involved, and those who would ineluctably be touched by the horrors.

And in the end, in a natural gesture of reverence, I got up and bowed my head. Thus I stood in front of the Pieta in this darkened thoroughfare, my eyes resting on the skillfully carved group in front of me, bleeding compassion.

O

I close my notebook, and sit staring at the ceiling. There are tears in my eyes; tears of frustration and grief. Though I feel helpless and cannot do much to change the situation, I could at least do this.

Buddhist Stella

Steps

Front Entrance of Museum

Steps can always be taken.

O

I sit on the 21st stone step outside the Met, on the left hand corner, overlooking a congested 5th Avenue, five steps above the 2nd plateau. 9:35 and the Met's still closed to the public. My thoughts are running along independent tracks, sometimes interweaving. I jump from one to the other, depending on where the jam is.

O

Today Carrie starts her new job at the Project Hope Women's Shelter in Brooklyn, ironically not too far from where she used to live. She was thrilled to finally get a job in an institution that provides women a safe haven against violence and abuse, where gender equity is fostered, and programs on global issues for women are offered. I'm hoping it will also have therapeutic effects; yet it might be too much for her. I trust it will be to her liking and that she'll feel fulfilled. But maybe it's all still a bit too close to home. In one way or another, we're always on a battlefield.

The battlefield in Iraq is now in the world's spotlight. The first strikes began around 9:30 last night against strategic targets in Baghdad. An hour ago the student body of our entire high school congregated in the auditorium. We couldn't, in good conscience, just let our country go to war without formally acknowledging it – bringing it to communal consciousness. A school is, after all, a place of education. We, the teachers, are supposed to be their role models, and they need to see that we are actively taking part in world issues, that we are concerned and interested, that we accompany world events, thus encouraging them to do the same. And that our inner – if not outer – engagement will make a difference. War cannot be glossed over. It needs to be questioned, scrutinized, analyzed. History is happening in front of our eyes. We have to take a stand. An educated one.

In our discussion at the impromptu assembly, the students voiced how essential it was to look beneath the surface of world events. They recognized that words like liberty, freedom, and compassion have opposing meanings, depending on who uses them, and for what purposes. I was impressed with the mature and serious attitude of the students. Underneath all the outer shlock they have their hearts in the right spot.

I'd tried to get Carrie to do something: to report her husband and uncle to the police; to get a restraining order; or at least to see a lawyer, to ascertain her rights – anything. Was it even possible to press charges against someone living on the other side of the earth? She refused adamantly with the excuse that she didn't want to risk having to go to court – not for anything, not even to get an order of protection. Nor would it do much good with her husband living in India. Besides, she argued, it would demand too much time and money, exacerbating the whole situation. Unfortunately, she thinks that by lying low and keeping silent the problem will dissolve. It won't! I suspect she's afraid to come forward with her story. She feels her own guilt, especially having left her child behind. Working in the shelter will remind her of that, daily and painfully. I worry about her.

O

The doors to the Met open. Strolling in I stand for a moment in front of the octagonal information desk, admiring as always the generous bouquet of flowers (today it's lilies). That's as far as I get. I breathe deeply, sigh, turn around and walk straight out again. My heart's not in it today. I walk down 82nd and turn in at the first opportune coffee shop for a cappuccino and a danish. Sip, nibble, write.

O

Carrie's decision to return to social work and look for a job at a women's shelter was made shortly after Alicia's visit. Carrie had come down with a severe bout of fever, forcing her to lie in bed for almost a week, which got her thinking. The decision relieved her and filled her with enthusiasm.

However, Indra, her daughter, remained her greatest concern. She could not forgive herself for having left her own child behind, yet she knew she would never have gotten her out of India and into America. She simply did not have the correct paperwork. How to get her to America? How to be reunited with her? That was her greatest problem.

Arietta called yesterday afternoon. I wasn't home. She left a message saying she wanted to come down and see an Off Broadway production of Beckett's *Waiting for Godot,* and wondered whether she could sleep over at my place. Impossible! I'll have to call her back tonight and give some excuse. The very idea of it gives me psychic shudders. Why would she suddenly want to stay over at my tiny apartment, if not to check out Carrie? As far as I'm concerned, it's far too soon for any such meeting. It would put me under too much stress. But that's her point, I guess.

While Carrie was recovering in bed we talked a lot. Now that I know the secret of her past we can talk about almost anything. What struck me most is the way she's able to reflect on her ordeal. "You know, living in India, though under terrible conditions, taught me a lot. It's never all bad. There's always something to be learned."

"Like what," I asked.

"This will surprise you, but I really got to appreciate the all-inclusive nature of Hinduism – not so much in the way it's practiced, but in its potential."

"How do you mean?"

"Well, as I told you, I'd turned my back on everything Indian while growing up in the States. I was embarrassed by it, especially as a teenager. And even while I was in India I initially rejected it – with a vengeance. But, after a while, I began to appreciate certain aspects of Hinduism. You see, nobody's excluded."

"Is that really true?"

"Okay, I admit, there are always the sectarian fanatics; but Hinduism, as such, embraces all religions. Of course, I still reject all the archaic customs and I get really mad when people don't think for themselves – which, I know, is true for people in most religions." She stopped, flicked her hair back, laughed apologetically and continued, "Now, I know this might sound a bit corny, but there is a doorway that leads to a new spiritual future – and for me it's the doorway of beauty."

"Beauty?"

"Yeah, people spend a great deal of time every day praying, making offerings and sacrifices. It's not just a Sunday affair. It includes the details of every day life. Over time I got to value that, especially when I was kept in purdah. That's when I took up the custom of making offerings to the various gods and spirits. It gave me comfort and strength. Just preparing the simple offerings had a calming effect. That was my inroad, so to speak. I got a new appreciation for beauty. I was moved to tears at the effort that goes into keeping things beautiful; small things, like arranging petals in a bowl of water, putting strands of marigolds around a statue of Vishnu, hanging lavishly framed pictures of the goddess Kali on the Banyan tree in our courtyard, or preparing the food in colorful arrangements. The spiritual life is celebrated through beauty, and I really like that; I miss that aspect here in America."

"And I've certainly benefited from it," I said, looking appreciatively around at the many little touches of her hand in my apartment.

"Well, it doesn't take much."

"Maybe not, but it's how you do it," I said, lifting both her hands to my lips and kissing them. "So, do you see yourself as a Hindu now?"

"No," she said and laughed. "I've lived too many rebellious years in America for that. I've been disconnected for too long. I don't even really consider myself an Indian, though I am, of course. Just like you, I feel like I'm a cosmopolitan. However, living in India within a Hindu environment has shown me how much care, effort, and time people spend on their spiritual beliefs. I really liked that – the tending of an inner life. And I want to take some more steps in that direction.

The Poison Note

Cleopatra's Needle, Egyptian Obelisk from Heliopolis

Fatigued, I walk up to the Amity on Madison Ave for a veggie burger and some coffee. I just finished a class on contemporary poetry, which ended in a strident discussion on the relevance of rap lyrics, especially those of the late Tupac Shakur. One of the students hip-hopped to the front of the class and spontaneously launched into a rap – dance moves and all – while two of his buddies thumped out a funky beat on the desks and chairs. The words had punch and fed my fragmented mood. Today they taught me.

I feel ill at ease, though I don't quite know why. I pick up the New York Times to distract myself. The news fuels my cynicism. I scan the headlines, rush through snippets of articles, gobble down the burger and fries, and wash away my anger at the ongoing drama of world events with coffee. All the world's a 'hood,' it seems. I wish I could rap like Tupac, or his deceased nemesis, the Notorious B.I.G. I take out my pen and notebook, hoping to slam a few power words onto the page, or at least to glean what's irking me today. If nothing else, I'll get something out of my system. Word-lust, not word-love. Here goes....

I wrote for a solid fifteen minutes, but tore it up again – all stuff about this ludicrous war with Iraq, the corruption of the oil industry, the lies of the politicians, blah-blah-blah and more yada-yada-yada. Nevertheless, I feel much improved. It's better to barf creatively than to hold it all in, I guess. Now I can continue writing with greater equanimity.

O

The conflicts we're confronted with are the little wars we're forced to fight on a daily basis. How do we cope with them? At least we have the power to wage them the way we see fit.

Last Saturday, Carrie's former roommate, Sally (a petite girl with auburn bangs and a silver nose ring, studying comparative literature at Barnard College), called and wanted to see us. It sounded urgent. We met for lunch at the Orsay on Lexington Ave. While waiting for the pizza she took a folded piece of paper from her purse. "I found this tacked on my door last night," she said, handing the note to Carrie. It was written on old computer paper, the kind with the serrated edges and holes along the sides. Carrie's hands trembled as she opened it. Written with a black marker were the words: *You cannot escape – I'll be back!* "At least he still doesn't know where you are," Sally remarked, breaking the silence.

"What do you mean?" Carrie asked, still staring at the note.

"Well, he's taking it for granted that I'll show you this. If he knew where you were he wouldn't have bothered pinning the note on my door; he would have just gone straight to you. He's terrorizing you psychologically. Thinks he's like some psycho Terminator – asshole!"

"Do you think it's still your uncle who's doing this?" I asked.

"No, it's Jitendra," Carrie said, biting her lip. "I know his handwriting,"

"This guy just doesn't give up, does he?" Sally said, leaning back and wiping her mouth carefully with the edge of the napkin.

"Whatever, I won't let him intimidate me anymore," Carrie responded with abrupt resolve, "because that's exactly what he's hoping for. He got away with treating me badly in India, but that's not going to work any more."

I was happy with Carrie's resolve. Working at the women's shelter – although it's only been a few short weeks – has already given her new perspectives. She's building her strength and self-esteem.

O

The weather is warmer now, up in the low seventies. I'm sitting on the stone wall by the colossal Egyptian obelisk – Cleopatra's Needle. It's nice to write outside for a change. The magnolias are in full bloom, and the new warmth and blue sky accompany their grand flowering. They're at their peak. I stare deeply into the flesh of the purple and pink blossoms. Intermittently I look up at the tall, brown, sand-colored needle, contrasted starkly against the spring blue sky. I wonder how it must have looked when this obelisk stood in front of the Sun Temple at Heliopolis together with the other needle that's now standing on the Thames Embankment, London. That they were both cut from a single piece of stone fills me with awe. It's a pity they're separated. The beauty of my surroundings is a picture of peace and calm.

O

Yesterday, April, 9th, Iraq was 'liberated,' symbolically marked by the toppling of Saddam Hussein's forty foot statue in Fridas Square, Baghdad. The news showed us happy faces: kids riding on the head of the fallen dictator, dragged through the dusty streets. But what don't we see? The overwhelming casualties, the dead, wounded, maimed, and grieving mass of individuals; the burning of the library with priceless ancient documents; the looting of the museum. I picture, for a moment, looters entering the Met, ransacking and destroying this cultural haven, and sicken at the thought. And to think that some American marines are supposedly encouraging the looting. I don't want to believe it.

And on the home front the peace is just as tenuous. The poison note spurred Carrie's ire. Though she waited a few days she overcame her fear and called her brother from a pay phone, telling him what had happened and demanding to know exactly what was going on. To get him to comply she threatened to put the police on him and press charges if he refused to be straight with her. The truth came out, and he confessed that Jitendra had indeed come back to America on one of his business trips, and that he would continue to search for Carrie every time he came. More disconcerting was the news that Jitendra had offered friends and relatives big money for any information leading to Carrie's whereabouts. It was small relief to know that he'd just departed for India again. "Now listen to me," Carrie continued in a no-nonsense voice, "I'm going to give you the telephone number and e-mail address of a women's shelter in Queens; and as soon as Jitendra comes to America again, I want you to call or write immediately. They will forward the message to me. If you don't do this, and should anything happen to me, I'll see to it that you will be prosecuted as an accomplice. Got that?"

O

I lose myself again in the mass of magnolia blossoms. My soul rises with the rarefied air, as my gratified senses become the recipient of the gifts of nature. My equanimity has been completely restored. I dream into the ethereal sensation and a line enters my mind: *as long as we help to lighten the burden of others we are not useless.* I take comfort in that thought and wish it on the world.

Good Friday

Christ Carrying the Cross, El Greco

I'm stopped. The guard paces slowly around the car, peers into the trunk and then lets me pass through into the Met's parking garage with a cheery, "You look nice." The affirmative comment takes me by surprise, because usually, whenever I'm traveling and pass through customs or security, I'm stopped and searched, or my luggage is ruffled through. The friendly remark brings a little light into my morning.

I hardly ever come to the Met by car, but I'll be traveling upstate in the early afternoon, after my Met fix. Arietta asked me to stay with Alicia for a few days while she's away with Sylvia, who's landed a small part in a feature length film called *Beneath the Steeple* – an action-horror flick about a fanatical religious leader who inhabits an old ghost town with his congregation while running a drug and arms ring from the basement of the church. Arietta is accompanying her out to Minnesota to help her get settled before the initial filming gets underway. I wanted to take Carrie along, but Arietta nixed the idea before I even finished verbalizing it. I acquiesced. However, since Carrie has now planned to work at the shelter for the entire Easter weekend, I feel somewhat assured regarding her safety.

Though drained of punch, I'm finding mild satisfaction in counting steps – fourteen and sixteen respectively from the ground floor to the first floor by the restaurant. It's still closed at this time of the morning.

The anticipation of coffee at the Petrie Court Café quickens my pace. I'm relieved that the quiet queue is only seven people long. The first cup is lukewarm, which garners a growl of discontent. The refill is more like it, but I'm wary of the amount of caffeine I'm sending into my system. Furthermore, I am just a little disconcerted by the remodeling efforts of my sacred sitting space: they've made it smaller and changed the sculptures around. I really miss sitting right next to Rodin's *Burghers of Calais*. They've moved it over into the European Sculpture Court out of view from where I usually sit; all very well, but it doesn't make me happy. The weather's not too much of a help either: cool and overcast with projected highs of 45 degrees. The croissant dipped in coffee compensates somewhat, but after the third dunk it falls apart, leaving soggy chunks in my cup. The last few weeks have been hectic on all fronts. I just finished directing the musical *Man of La Mancha* – a terrific success, but it's left me a depleted curmudgeon.

O

I half suspected that my impulsive need to write at the Met would end after getting together with Carrie, but something inexplicable is still stirring, poking and egging me on. I'll ride it out, not quite knowing what's really at the source of it all. Carrie finds my excursions amusing, calling my project a compulsive pathology. I tell her it's my momentary path to self-discovery. Admittedly, recording tidbits of my life and our times smacks of self absorption (navel gazing), but I've noticed over the last few months that it's served to increase my awareness; I live my life with greater intensity. My observation skills have improved and everything that occurs in my surroundings is loaded with potential significance, which in turn schools my powers of positive discrimination. Besides, it has a soothing effect on me. No matter how distraught I am, the almost ceremonial process of coming to the Met, discovering a place to write, facilitates the finding of my composure. The architecture, coupled with the cultural dignity of the place, effects my disposition. I'm embraced by greatness – how can that not be transformative? The Met's my couch; the art is my tacit psychiatrist, a relationship based on trust and absolute freedom. I can come and go as I please. No strings attached.

○

After ten minutes of aimless walking I sit down again on a stone bench in the Patio from the Castle of Velez Blanco (1478 - 1546) from Spain. I realize I've never given this hall much time and appreciation. I do now, for it is quiet and spacious, the cool austerity of it easing my throbbing head. I close my eyes, imagining myself back in time, hearing the soft patter of bygone souls on the stone floor sounding out a lullaby. I must have dozed off, for a sudden sneeze from a little boy sounds like a rifle shot, fired off in a cathedral, hurling me back to my senses in a cold sweat. I move on. The mini-hiatus must have done some good, because I feel refreshed enough to venture up and face the "Manet/Velázquez" exhibit.

As anticipated, this special exhibit is utterly crowded. The paintings show the shift from idealism to realism, but for me the reality of the crowd is far from ideal. It's impossible to stand in front of any painting without someone getting in the way, bumping into you, obscuring the view, or talking too loudly; not to mention the smells – too much perfume, aftershave or bad breath. I am back on edge; a combination of post-play burnout and caffeine. And the sounds from the audio tapes are especially irritating – crinkled phantom whispers crawling uninvited through my ears as I try to focus on the paintings. I need and demand inner and outer quietude to enter into the secrets of any artwork. Normally I can shut out the peripheral white noise, the aural litter (an essential survival faculty for living in New York), but today I don't have the mental wherewithal for that discipline; I cannot treat the barring of unwanted sonic bulk as a mental exercise. I need my ears to see as much as my eyes, for when I internalize an artwork I listen to the thoughts that come on the wings of the meditative viewing; I enter into a conversation with the artwork, and in rare moments of artistic sublimity they become alive, or I apprehend tones, a music as clear and scintillating as sunlight through a prism. Hence, my reluctance to ever use audio sets, though at times I've succumbed, for information's sake,

Above: Patio from the Castle of Vélez Blanco

making sure, however, to pilgrim back to the paintings a second time sans the electro-magnetic device.

So I make my round hastily. Nevertheless, Jusepe de Ribera's *Saint Jerome Listening to the Sound of the Heavenly Trumpet* (1626) from the State Hermitage Museum in St. Petersburg stops me in my hurried perusal, magically eliminating the crowd around me, drawing me into its spell. The realism of the painting moves me little, but the thematic content gives me pause to ponder about the harmony of the spheres lost to our ears.

Before leaving the exhibit I glance over my shoulder and see Edouart Manet's (1832- 1883) *Execution of Emperor Maximillian* (1867) from the Museum of Fine Arts in Boston. The painting strikes me. All the faces are obscured; especially the man facing away from the firing squad, standing rifle-erect: his individuality is expunged in the moment of killing, warmth of soul brushed away; and instead of the music of the human face – a blank BOOM. There's a pit in my stomach and it fills with the dead and dying of the present war. Killing obscures our finer selves, irrespective of context.

I remember that it is Good Friday while passing through the medieval wing. I peer around at the various crucifixions and imagine the pain of thorns piercing deep under the skin of my scalp, the nails pounding through my feet and hands, my frail limbs stretched tightly over the hard and heavy cross. I live into His suffering and marvel at the power of compassion to invite such suffering for the sake of others. The imagination is powerful. Instead of revenge, Christ's suffering conceives compassion. Then why is Christianity, as it manifests itself today in its exoteric form, so devoid of true compassion? Why are some of the greatest atrocities perpetrated in the name of Christianity? Why has Christianity such a history of intolerance? And the only plausible answer is that the bulk of what stands as Christianity today is the very antithesis of it.

Agitated by the passion of my inner soliloquy I walk down to the Robert Lehman Wing. In one of the small galleries I sink into a very comfortable couch and look up at El Greco's *Christ Carrying the Cross* (1580). Because it's Good Friday I look at this painting more consciously. There's no anger, self-pity or feeling of injustice in his countenance. He's accepted his fate. No – fate has fulfilled itself. The love with which he is holding the cross is almost like that of a child gently embracing a teddy bear. There's no weight to the cross, as if the very wood has been redeemed of its awful task. The dark arm of the cross is pointing the way upwards – a directive – followed by his glistening eyes, staring into the heavens with a transported look. There's no bitterness in his eyes and the pain he's bearing is of a transcendent nature. The cross is carried lovingly because he is carrying humanity's salvation. It is worth the weight, and the knowledge makes it light.

At that moment two girls sit down next to me, interrupting my reverie.

"I'm not scared of him anymore," says the younger of the two, who looks to be about seven. I smile, wondering why she would be scared. My interest piqued, I listen in on their conversation.

"You shouldn't have to be," says the older one, who's about twelve. "He's not harming anybody, but people are hurting him."

"Was he scared?"

"No. He wanted it that way. He's about to be crucified, but really he's on his way to be resurrected,"

"What does that mean?"

"It means that he's going to be really, really alive."

"What's the difference between being really, really alive and just alive?"

"When you're really, really alive then you can never die again."

"I want to be really, really alive. But I don't want to die like him."

"You won't have to because he's already done it for you... anyway, that's what Dad said."

"Oh." The two of them lapse into a few moments of silence before the younger one asks, "Is he sweating blood?"

"Maybe. It doesn't look like real blood... too watery."

"Is he crying?"

"No, just teary-eyed." After a short pause she said, "You know, nobody really knew who his dad was... but I say it was God."

"Well," said the little girl pointing to *Saint Jerome as a Scholar*, also by El Greco, "I'm sure that was his grandfather. Look at his white beard. It's about two feet long."

"No, silly, that was someone totally different."

"How do you know?"

"I just know. Let's go and find Mom."

"Okay," and the little girl jumped up and followed her big sister out, pointing up to Rembrandt's *Portrait of Gerard de Lairesse*, chirping, "And that's *pig face*."

I retreat into obscurity under the Grand Staircase in the Mary and Michael Joharis Gallery, surrounded by Byzantine and Egyptian art. It feels almost like a catacomb – a space carved between the great brick arches and the walls that support the museum's massive staircase. I take a chair and place it right by the unfinished undersides of the massive stones that make up the steps of the imposing staircase that leads to the second floor. The light is dim and I decide not to write. I'm assured my peace. I wonder how many people feel as if they're still roaming through catacombs of sorts – underneath the mental mainstream of our era (unable to say what's really on their minds). In between, I think of the two little girls talking. They verbalized my greatest wish: to be really, really alive. But what does it take?

Later, after the 2:00 p.m. showing of the film: *El Greco to Goya, and Edouart Manet:Painter of Modern life*, at the Uris Center Auditorium, I go down to the parking garage, get into my car and head north. Driving along the beautiful Taconic Parkway I realize how long it's been since I've enjoyed the open country. Yet, my mind's constantly on Carrie. I feel uneasy about leaving her alone, even though she's safe in the shelter. Jitendra's bound to catch up with her sometime. And who knows what he'll do when he finds her?

Under the Grand Staircase, Mary and Michael Joharis Gallery

The Message

Greek Sculpture Court

I would not be here had it not been for Carrie's insistent call. I suggested we have a bite to eat at the Met's public cafeteria during my lunch break. Now I'm ensconced in one of the plush velvety couches around the large fluted Greek pillar at the restaurant's entrance, amusing myself watching the guard repeatedly ask people not to sit on the ledge at the foot of the pillar. Even the small metal railing (recently installed) has not stopped some diehards from trying to get away with it. And I get just as much of a kick watching the diverse ways in which people pass their time waiting around. It's the Met's own mini Piccadilly Circus, and – as they say – if you wait long enough you're bound to meet someone you know.

I'm a few minutes early so I take the opportunity to catch up on some writing. This is my busiest time of the year and I hardly have a free moment to steal away to the Met with. Apart from teaching, I'm down to the last three weeks of rehearsals for the upcoming production of Albert Camus's *State of Siege* with the senior class – a dark play that focuses on the evils of dictatorship, and the consequent struggle of the human individual to hold onto his dignity and freedom within such a totalitarian setting. Right up my alley. I know I'll be sorely criticized for choosing such a violent and disturbing play. People always want happy stuff; comedies that make you laugh and feel good. Be that as it may, I'm glad to have a few short minutes to write.

O

After returning from my visit with Alicia in Red Hook, I noticed a distinct change in Carrie. On occasion she'd lapse into prolonged silences, staring into a vacuum, responding monosyllabically when I attempted to break through to her, even withdrawing physically when I came too close. Or she'd suddenly snap out of it, apologize and be all over me, want to make love, ask me endless questions about my day at school, the students, the other teachers; rattle off stories from the shelter, some of which were horrific and hard to believe. Both extremes left me uncomfortable and I was unsure which I preferred. They were the same symptoms I'd noticed before she'd told me her secret, except amplified. I never quite knew in what condition I'd find her on coming home from school, and was always relieved when I saw her happily engrossed in a book, or preparing dinner while listening to Ani de Franco or Nora Jones. My gentle inquiries about what was eating her led nowhere. She assured me she was fine.

There was no ambivalence regarding her work in the shelter. She was dedicated – no question. She worked overtime, volunteered for night shifts and any other duty, depending on the need. She connected strongly with the battered and abused women and children – especially the children, the helpless and innocent victims of domestic violence. I half-suspected that her intimate and intense occupation with the consequences on the young ones was the true cause of her aberrant mood swings. It was certainly a foreign world to me, and I was both appalled and fascinated by the gruesome tales she told. To uphold the peace in the nucleus of the family just isn't easy these days. Well, I knew that.

O

There she is. Even from the far end of the Greek Sculpture Court she stands out, walking leisurely along, wearing a paisley designed, riffle gored skirt, and an off-white, lace-knit top with a deep V-neckline, accentuating both the honey sheen of her skin and her bust. The people around her fade as she approaches. She knows how to dress stylishly while retaining her natural poise. But something's amiss. Her gait and taught expression tell me as much.

Time to stop writing. I'll continue later, after we've had a bite to eat.

O

As soon as we got our lunch and found a place to sit, Carrie clutched my hands tightly with both of hers, and said, "He's back."

"Who?"

"You know who."

"You mean, Jitendra?"

"Yes."

"How do you know? Are you sure? I mean – it's so soon."

"Positive. This morning Sally called me at the shelter. She found another note stuck to the door." Carrie's voiced quivered.

"Shit… what did it say?"

"Nothing much, just, 'You can run but you can't hide!' But that's not all. I immediately called the shelter in Queens, and asked whether they'd received an e-mail or a telephone message for me. The receptionist confirmed that my brother had called three days earlier with a warning that Jitendra was on another business trip and was intent on coming to New York – and we all know what that means."

"Why didn't they let you know earlier?"

"Apparently it was a new receptionist, and she just took down the info, and never followed up on it."

"This sucks. This guy's just not letting loose."

"And he never will – not until he finds me… I'm scared, Clarence. I don't want to be, but I am." She began crying, but checked herself almost immediately.

"I know, but we'll make sure you're safe. You'll be fine," I said, gently stroking her hands, though not entirely convinced of my own words. "Maybe you should spend the next few days in the shelter, like you did over Easter. We shouldn't be taking any risks. You don't know what this guy's capable of."

"Well, actually, I do. He's crazy," she said, hastily taking a sip of green tea, as if to expunge a memory.

"Still, it won't be so easy for him to find my address," I said, reassuringly.

"A scheming mind, fueled by pride and anger can be pretty resourceful. No, he'll find me!"

"I guess you're right," I said, half-heartedly.

"Okay then," she said, putting down the cup and tapping her fingers along the rim. "I suppose I should go straight home and pack."

"I think it's for the best. I'll end play rehearsal early today, and go to the shelter with you – just to make sure."

"This is all so ridiculous," she whispered, shaking her head and dabbing her eyes with the edge of the napkin. "Sorry," she said, trying to smile through her tears. "Come home as quickly as you can, will you?"

"I will."

O

She's gone. Most of her food is left uneaten on the plate. Twenty minutes have passed since she left. The news numbed me. Perfunctorily I recorded the essence of our conversation into my green notebook. It's time for me to go too. I'm already late for the rehearsal and I'm a stickler for punctuality.

In the Garden

Astor Court

It's 9:30 a.m. and I'm one of the first to enter the Met, making my way to the seclusion of the Astor Court. In the fashion of the Ming scholars I retreat to this exquisitely recreated Garden Court, in search of quietude. I have always loved the harmony of this microcosmic natural world and the light and airy feel of the place. I sit cross legged on the patterned tiles surrounded by rocks, plants and water, especially positioned according to a formula replicated over eons. My ears receive the sweet sounds of water over perforated and wrinkled rocks, conjuring forth pictures of exotic birds and animals, or caves and mysterious grottos, inhabited by immortal beings. The interplay between the mobile water and the immovable rocks is a perfect manifestation of the yin and yang in all of its feminine and masculine qualities – the polarities of the world in their most complementary form. As I sit, sinking into this order of domesticated wilderness I feel the rejuvenating qualities of water with all of my senses – the shadowy, wet, cool, soft, gentle, and yielding yin, as opposed to the hard, solid, flashy, sturdy, dense, hot, dry, and unyielding yang. And slowly the balancing properties begin to have their harmonizing effects on me, resolving my own dissonances.

Partly restored, I get up and sit on the stone bench of the "viewing terrace," the area where the scholars would come to write poetry or sample new tea during the full moon. I take out my green notebook, not to write poetry, but to record the painful incident we'd hoped to avoid.

What had initially motivated me to come to the Met, apart from wanting to write, was the general turmoil I found myself in, revolving predominantly around my separation and divorce from Arietta. Crises have their individual life span, but I never thought that mine would stretch out like melted Swiss cheese. Is this what they call mid-life crisis? A depressing thought. I feel too young for that. Forty is the new twenty, as they say. Still, I feel as if I'm locked into some sort of life-phase lawfulness that I can't explain. Are there outside forces at play over which we have little control? Is it connected to events in our childhood and youth? Is it preordained, fated, or simply part and parcel of our natural development, like puberty? I think – yes, for all of the above. But even if we do take the time to connect the dots it will still remain a mystery.

○

I find it physically difficult to write. After my night in the hospital where they patched and stitched me up I spent three days at home just resting. Carrie is also off work this week, and we're taking good care of each other. The burn from the acid on her leg is giving her ongoing pain, but I'm more concerned about the life-long scars on her psyche. This is my first outing, and I'm feeling vulnerable. My injured left hand, arm and shoulder make it painful to hold the notebook, my breathing is hampered by the broken rib, and the bandages are wrapped too tightly, stopping my blood in all but a few positions. I don't know how much I'll be able to get down on paper today.

○

When I came back home after the play rehearsal Carrie was packed and ready to go. We anticipated her staying at the shelter for only a few days, no more. We didn't realize how close to home the danger was. Even Carrie underestimated Jitendra's design to get even.

Avove: Viewing Terrace overlooking Garden Court

172

"I'll meet you down at the car," she said, bag in hand and already half way out the door.

"Okay," I said, putting on my jacket, getting the keys, switching off the lights, grabbing the suitcase, before locking up and following her down. The car was parked up near 1st Avenue, and as I walked toward it I heard a muffled yelp and got a glimpse of a shadow disappearing through the iron gates of the community garden. Puzzled, I strained my eyes through the darkness, but couldn't see a thing, least of all Carrie, who should have been waiting by the car. I hastened my step, weighed down by her heavy suitcase. "Why does she need so much stuff," I grumbled, hobbling along, panting heavily. I heard another stifled scream – Carrie's. I dropped the suitcase at once and ran to the open gate just in time to see a tall figure force Carrie viciously to the ground, while covering her mouth with his hand. I ran to him, but he saw me coming and after a quick and vicious blow to Carrie's temple, which sent her crashing into a tree, he stood facing me, knife in hand, slowly approaching. I retreated, keeping my gaze steadily on him while searching peripherally for some kind of weapon I could use against him. My opponent was dressed in a suit, and except for the wild, irrational look in his eyes, did not pass for the regular mugger type. I knew immediately it was Jitendra. So this is how we meet, I thought. His skin looked almost black in the darkness, offset by the whites of his fanatical eyes, blazing with the driving hate of his personal vendetta.

I had no time to think of the absurdity of the situation. I had a cold-blooded madman in front of me, intent on avenging the terrible shame cast upon him by Carrie's escape, and it was obvious he would stop at nothing to get even. He'd take care of me first, then deal with Carrie, who was lying semiconscious in the shadows. Near the gate I spotted two trash cans. Steadily I retreated in their direction. As soon as I was close enough I made a dash for the trash cans and in one quick movement grabbed both lids. Now I had my shields, and could face him. Though I hadn't had any experience in street fighting, I did have a lot of experience choreographing fights. I'd taken fencing lessons at NYU, performed and directed a lot of fight scenes with foils, swords, poles, and, yes – trash cans, with sequences based on the percussive *Stomp* routine.

Never in my life did I ever think I'd face a real opponent, armed with two trash can lids. But here I was, and I wasn't acting. I was desperate. He was clearly stronger, and it was equally clear that he didn't take me seriously, but he soon realized (much to my own surprise) that I wouldn't be a walk-over either. His initial charge, though quick, was clumsy, and I easily dodged him. Every time he lashed out with his knife I successfully blocked his jabs. In between I clashed the lids together making a hell of a racket, hoping it would deter him and attract people's attention, but with all the disparate city noises, our fight in the secluded garden remained unnoticed. After parrying and playing defense for a while I went on the offensive and rammed into him with all my body weight, shielding my torso with both lids, one above the other. That hurled him to the ground and I fell on top of him crashing the lids into his face with all the force I could muster. But they proved to be clumsy tools for battle, and he rolled swiftly to the side, caught hold of one of the lids and wrenched it away. Now he faced me holding both the lid and the knife. I attacked with renewed vigor, used proven stage fighting moves and took courage at their efficiency. Almost too quickly he lay supine on the ground again. Discarding the lid I pinned down his arms with my knees and pummeled him with my fists. But he wrestled himself free, got in a slew of solid punches, and a powerful head-butt. As I crashed to the ground he slashed my lower arm with his knife. I rolled over and picked myself up at once, but he'd already stabbed me again, the blade boring deep into my shoulder, right to the bone. And again he stabbed, but this time I warded it off with my hand, though it sliced through my left palm. Simultaneously he kicked me in the groin and with a groan I fell back, crumpled up in a bundle of excruciating pain, incapacitated. I heard my ribs crack as he repeatedly kicked me in the side. I don't know what would have happened had not Carrie, who'd regained consciousness, battered him across the head with a brick. With blood dripping down behind his ear, staining his white shirt, he staggered over toward Carrie, removing a bottle from his jacket pocket, unscrewing the top. "Watch out!" I yelled as he viciously splashed her. She leaped to the side shielding her head with her elbows and hands. The liquid, however, hit her bare legs and she let out a piercing scream. Struggling to my feet and ignoring the pain I tackled him before he could hurl the rest of the contents over Carrie. He dropped the bottle and it crashed to the ground, shattering the glass – the acrid smell of sulphuric acid ripped through my nose. In return I received a sucker punch to my cheekbone which had me reeling back, releasing fireworks in my head. I shielded a few more punches, but I had no more fight left in me. I was going down. Carrie, meanwhile, had yanked out her cell phone, dialed 911 and was frantically giving them directions. Hearing her, Jitendra stopped pummeling me, lurched toward her, kicked the phone from her hands, and ran.

In the Park

Bryant Park

T here's no rush to get to the Met. I've got all day, and what a day it is, the epitome of a nascent summer's day – clear blue sky, sunny, warm but not muggy. School's out! No more teaching, no more meetings, no more plays to direct; just a little bit of this and a little bit of that. What a relief after the hectic and dramatic events of the last few weeks. Almost perfect, except that Carrie left for India a week ago.

I'm sitting in Bryant Park on one of the little green chairs. Near me the wardens are cleaning up, emptying the green trash cans. The little round green tables are still wet with puddles from last night's shower. A few pigeons are fluttering around looking for tidbits; the fading flowers are glistening with the last of the morning's dewdrops.

I've come here umpteen times over the years, but have never really looked around much. And it only takes a few moments to do so. For instance, as I walked past the big fountain I noticed that it's called the Josephine Shaw Lowell Memorial Fountain, and it is New York City's first public memorial to a woman – a fact I'd overlooked till now. Further, I discovered Gertrude Stein's bronze statue at the opposite end of the park. *How could. I have. Been so. Unobservant?*

It strikes me as symptomatic of how unobservant I have been in respect to women as such – their issues, difficulties and differences – underscored by the women in my own life, starting with my mother, whose biography only really began to intrigue me once she'd died; I'd taken her too much for granted. She deserved the greatest gratitude and affection from me, but I was too self-absorbed to express my true feelings openly, or even notice them. I missed my chance and some questions will forever remain unanswered. And likewise, I missed out with Arietta, the most compatible person I've ever known; Arietta, like Gertrude Stein, was a lion of a woman, with her "violent devotion to the new" – an attribute I so admired. But I couldn't give her what she most desired: an open, true, and passionate declaration and show of love; I could not let her into the most intimate chamber of my heart out of an innate fear of my own inadequacy, out of a spurious perception of my own manhood. The false ego corrodes everything. And consequently, it impacted my relationship with Alicia, who I loved unconditionally, but who I now only see intermittently, making it impossible to be the father I'd wanted, or needed to be. A humbling and humiliating outcome! And then there's Carrie, whose ill-treatment at the hands of her family and husband has left me feeling angry and helpless – Carrie, who has opened my eyes to the magnitude of the abuse and violence against women around the world. Never before have I grasped the deplorable situation with such visceral and painfully poignant insight.

Nor will I ever forget the demented look in Jitendra's eyes, motivated as he was by his insoluble grudge, on the night of the fight. He was defending his inherited, but antiquated right as a man to treat his wife as a possession, a beast of burden, a nonentity, with fanatical zeal, thereby gravely violating the dignity of the individual that is every person's basic right. I sigh, deeply relieved that part of the ordeal is finally behind us.

The police arrested the crazed Jitendra within the hour, at the corner of East Houston Street and Second Avenue. He was charged with attempted murder, first degree assault, trespassing and criminal mischief, and resisting arrest. After his arraignment in City Court he was sent to a correctional facility without bail. He now faces a minimum of ten years imprisonment. Carrie showed her metal during the proceedings, and for the first time found the courage to come forward with her story, volunteering delicate information beneficial to the prosecution.

Knowing her husband was safely behind bars; Carrie immediately filed for divorce and began focusing on reuniting with her daughter – her foremost priority. Referred to the Madras Counseling and Resource Center for Women by her own shelter, Carrie left for India last Saturday where she's receiving moral and legal support in getting her child back. Though happy that Carrie finally feels empowered as a woman and is making full use of the help available to her, I'm apprehensive about the success of the venture. Not only Jitendra's family, friends and relatives, but her own parents, especially her father, still pose a serious threat to her well being. Her daily e-mails, however, are upbeat; assuring me the people at the shelter are friendly, supportive, experienced and entirely devoted to exerting pressure for the sake of justice. With the help of a lawyer and the police she expects to be reunited with Indra early next week.

On her return we'll have to find a new place to stay. My apartment's small enough, even for one.

O

On the green benches behind the public library overlooking the park I spot a strange group of eleven costumed kids aged between about nine and sixteen, sitting in a frozen state of immobility. Getting up I amble towards them hoping to satisfy my curiosity, and realize with a chuckle that they've all succumbed to the charms of J.K. Rowling's latest: *Harry Potter and the Order of the Phoenix*. Dressed in the weird and bizarre outfits of their favorite characters, they sit transfixed and at one remove from reality. I'd quite forgotten about the midnight release parties held at thousands of bookstores throughout America and the world in honor of her fifth book, a tome of over eight hundred pages.

Magic is in the air. I miss Carrie and wish she were here. I send her my love. That too is a kind of magic.

I'll forego the Met today. Instead, I'll catch a taxi down to Washington Square Park where some good bands are said to be playing. It's the kind of distraction I need.

Gertrude Stein in Bryant Park

The Letter

Temple of Dendur

I've snuck right up against the wall of the inner room of the sandstone temple of Dendur, situated in the airy and open Sackler Wing. It's the most visited site in the museum and I had to wait a while before I could creep into the holy chamber without being spotted. Earlier on I scouted around the Egyptian section for quite some time searching for a place to write and almost settled on the tomb of Perneb, but it was too much of a thoroughfare and I abandoned it quickly. What I really wanted was to lie in an empty sarcophagus.

A late afternoon thunderstorm is raging outside, and the crowd has thinned considerably. I welcome the added wall of sound from the wind-whipped rain lashing against the massive glass panes of the atrium. The embalming clouds have shut out most of the indirect light, but that's no deterrent; even if I were locked up in the darkness of the King's Chamber of the Great Pyramid, I'd still manage to write. Leastways, I should be safe from any intrusion for a while, and it shouldn't take long either. I've just got to get a few things down on paper, and then – oudda here.

O

Carrie has her little daughter back. Victory! At first the in-laws refused to give Indra up. They claimed she was visiting with relatives in the north. The police suspected otherwise, searched the house, and found the little girl locked up in a closet, undernourished, bruised and shivering with fear. Carrie was ecstatic to be reunited with her daughter. However, she postponed her return trip to the States, wanting to get reacquainted with Indra before undertaking any further steps. They are now both staying at the Madras women's shelter, and in exchange Carrie is volunteering her services. Though I've e-mailed almost daily, her replies have become less frequent and increasingly brief. To my inquiries she's apologized, promising to communicate more often, explaining that between spending time with Indra and volunteering at the shelter she is left with little down time. Then they stopped completely.

In the middle of July I went on a camping trip to Saranac Lake up in the Adirondacks with Alicia and one of her friends. On my return I found a letter from Carrie. At long last – I was so happy. Included were photos of her and Indra. Both were dressed in flowing saris, and I barely recognized Carrie. Her complexion was much darker and Indra's was almost black. Little Indra, a girl of about three, was laughing in every photograph, and Carrie was smiling. Both looked beautiful, and I was happy for them. There were also photos of the shelter, and I was glad to note that it was located in a park-like setting, and not stuck in the middle of the city, surrounded by filthy buildings, as I'd imagined.

After enjoying the photos, I read the letter. My heart sank. Carrie had resolved to stay in India for at least the next six months. The shelter had asked her to stay, and she'd accepted. They were in desperate need of qualified social workers. *...how could I refuse?*

O

I stop writing and take out the letter again and carefully unfold it. Though I've read it dozens of times and almost know it by heart, I always hoped to read something new – to glean something I'd not picked up on before – anything.

Dear Clarence,

At long last I have the peace of mind and the time to write the kind of letter I've been meaning to write to you for a while. It's just past noon and right now I'm sitting under a shady neem tree. Indra is sleeping on a string cot close by. It's hot, but there's a slight breeze which makes it bearable. I feel more at peace than I have in years. New York seems so far away, almost as if it belongs to another lifetime.

Though innocuous, that last sentence stung me when I first read it. Did she intimate that our relationship also belonged to the past? And as I'm rereading it, I feel the same slight pang in my heart. I stare absent-mindedly up at the weathered relief of the goddess Isis before continuing.

I'm so grateful that everything has turned out so well for me, but most of all that Indra is safe, and that I'm together with her again. That's all that matters.

What about me?

For Indra's sake I've decided to stay here for a few more months. She's not ready for another big change. Besides, the shelter here has offered me a job. I know you'll be upset at the news, but there are so many women who need support, counseling, medical assistance and rehabilitation. Please understand, I can't just leave. There is so much demand for trained social workers and they really need me here, so how could I refuse?

In my mind I hear her voice, see the expression on her face. Her words keep on rotating in my head. Again I stop and peer up at Isis. From here on the letter gets more formal, as if she's hiding behind her words. She's trying to justify her stay, make me understand why she has to remain in India. Though interesting, what I really want to hear is a confirmation of our love, not facts relating to women's issues in India.

I had no idea how bad the situation is, and how much suffering these women have to endure. Clarence, for many women the abuse already begins at birth. I'm talking about female infanticide: baby girls – if they're not aborted – are murdered the moment they're born, without their mother's knowledge, let alone consent. Even worse, sometimes a mother might kill her own child, or have it killed, because she knows she won't be able to feed the baby girl, let alone pay the dowry. Others are sexually abused, or sold, mostly into prostitution. The majority of women suffer in silence, just like I used to. Wives are beaten as a matter of course. My own story is just one of millions. The amount of brutal rape victims is staggering, and no age group is spared. The rate of suicides among women is growing. For many it's their only way of escape from the hell they're going through. And although outlawed, there are still innumerable dowry death cases – mostly due to burns. Some survive, but remain severely disfigured. And the irony is that the rich and educated just add to the problem. Because they uphold the dowry system it trickles down to the poorest of the poor, who then get themselves into insurmountable debt.

But as I'm rereading these lines written by the woman I love, I put myself in her situation and I am beginning to understand her. Maybe it's because I'm sitting, crouched in the corner of this temple, in the proximity of Isis that I feel her resolve.

The shelter is filled with these unfortunate women. And because of my experiences, the help I've received, and what I deal with every day, I feel it is my duty to raise consciousness about rape, domestic violence, health and sex. People need to be made aware of the atrocities committed against women, and, as I said, I'm committed in doing my share. You'd do the same if you were in my situation. I know you would. These women have no idea of their rights. Nor did I. The government needs to be pressured into upholding the laws they have passed. Under Indian law women have complete equality, but you wouldn't know it based on what's going on. It's a far cry from reality.

I admire Carrie for what she's decided to do, but it still hurts. A lump forms in my throat. I swallow it away. The next paragraph is warmer, more intimate. I can smell the jasmine of her soft skin as I read the lines, and I ache to touch her, be with her.

Clarence, you're the only man I have ever really loved. Without you I would not be here now. I have found meaning in my life, and I know that this is what I'm supposed to be doing. To leave India now would be wrong. Moreover, Indra really isn't ready for such a big change, as I've already said. It would be too much of a culture shock for her. She's shocked enough as it is. I suspect she's been sexually abused as well, but I can't say for sure. It will come out when the time's ready.

Although I never mentioned it to you, I've thought of working as a social worker in India for quite a while already. Seeing the need and the awful conditions here has only confirmed my decision.

My arms embrace you. My lips kiss you. My heart holds you warm. Love you,

Draupati

It all begins to make sense: her mood swings over the last few months, her periods of complete withdrawal or over-exuberance. She'd been mulling over her future for some time already and was deeply torn between her love for me on the one hand, and her maternal instincts, coupled with her intense vocational pull on the other. But through it all, she'd always intended to return to India. I know that now.

I'm torn. My rational mind rejoices: Carrie's reunited with her daughter and she's found her calling in life. Still, I'm devastated. I can understand Carrie's choice, but it hurts. And the more it sinks in, the more it hurts. But then again, six months is not such a long time. I can wait.

The storm is subsiding. I take out one of the photos of Carrie and Indra and prepare a ceremony. I'm emulating the figures of kings carved in sunk relief in the outer walls who are making votive offerings. I go through similar motions, my heart focused on Isis, the powerful female deity of wisdom, healing and rebirth. I have to overcome myself, though it does not come easy. My supplication is that Draupati, as I call her in my offering ceremony, will be led by the guiding spirit of her destiny, and that I can muster the strength to stand fully behind it, whatever the outcome may be. I'm standing upright now, with one leg forward, and both arms in front of me in the typical Egyptian pose. I'm holding the photo in my open palms. I imagine the goddess Isis seated right in front of me, to whom the photo is offered. I slowly turn around and look for a possible crack in the wall into which I can insert and hide my sacrifice. I take slow steps towards a likely place when I suddenly get interrupted.

"Sir, what do you think you're doing?"

I apprehend a moving shadow in the ancient portal and, to my dismay, see a guard approaching.

"It's past closing time and you're not supposed to be here. Come out of there at once, sir."

I pocket the picture and come out, stepping carefully over the low chain that's spread across the ancient entry.

"Oh, it's you again." I immediately recognize the corpulent guard who'd caught me when I was trying to pray in front of the Mihrab. "What the hell are you trying to do this time?"

"I was just imagining myself as a pharaoh about to make an offering to the goddess Isis." I figure I might as well be honest with him.

He gives me a blank look that bloats awkwardly across time until he coughs and says, "Okay, okay, but this is a museum, remember. What'cha gonna do next? Perform a ritual dance in the African section?

"If the need arises…"

"Oh, brother… well, let me know, I might just join you," and he laughed.

O

Now I'm tucked into a far corner of a coffee shop; one I used to frequent when we lived in Little Italy – in happier times, before the divorce. I've come to a resolution: tomorrow morning I'll jump in my car and drive out west. I'll leave everything behind for a while. No green notebooks. No laptop. No cell phone. Just a bag of clothes, some money – that's it. New York without the hope of Carrie's imminent return has become unbearable. Who knows if she'll ever return? I need out!

Inner Chamber of the Temple of Dendur

The Shift

Nicholas Roerich House

As soon as the Met's impressive facade came to view I changed my mind and took a taxi up to the Nicholas Roerich Museum instead. The Met still reminds me too much of Draupati's absence. I haven't been back since my visit to the temple of Dendur. I tried, of course, but always ended up at a different museum – just like today. I have made circuitous visits to the Whitney, the Jewish Museum, the Guggenheim, the Neue Galerie, and diverse galleries of modern and contemporary art; even frequenting places like Madam Tussaud's, the Cooper-Hewitt, the Rose Museum, the Goethe House and the Museum of Natural History. But I was never moved to write, not a word – except once, at the Frick, where I settled down in front of Rembrandt's *The Polish Rider*, inspired to write about my own ride through life over the last few weeks, within the bigger ride of the last few years. But the notebook landed in the trash.

Now I'm sitting on the steps outside number 319, West 107th Street, writing, waiting for the museum to open. Here in the residential area of the Upper Westside it is quiet and peaceful. It's late October, and the day is like an autumnal song. The sky is a crisp blue and the leaves on the trees are multi-hued, from scintillating yellow to saturated scarlet. In the shade it's chilly, but in the midday sun it is as warm as a brick oven. Semiconscious thoughts are stirring. I think back on the road trip that took me eight thousand miles across America and back. The outer space I traversed is becoming an interior space, still shadowed by the unsolved riddles of my life. I'm trying to direct my thoughts into this dusky terrain. The warmth of unarticulated wishes is rising inside of me; ones I dare not hope for, but hope to dare.

The journey across the country was a madness sustained by a stubborn foot on the accelerator. I drove – or was driven – day and night, napping intermittently at rest stops before moving on, fueled by grilled cheese and coffee. Three days later at the Idaho/Oregon border I finally broke down and took refuge in a cheap motel, bed-locked for one rotation of the clock.

Reaching the Pacific I slowed my pace slightly, cruising down the coast along highway 101, stopping at sites I'd visited with my mother when I was a kid: the expansive dunes south of Florence, the beaches around Bandon with the massive rock formations, the Redwood National Park with its monolithic trees instilling instant reverence and awe – primal wonderland.

Though I never lingered for long at any one of them, they triggered many childhood memories. More than a son to my mother, I'd taken the place of a partner and confidant, the one source of stability in her own troubled life. There'd been men, of course, but they were short-lived affairs. I resented every one of them, because it disturbed the intimacy my mother and I shared. Once she almost married; we even moved in with the man and his two children. They had a small suburban ranch style house in Palo Alto. I was nine at the time and just accepted the circumstances, but it never felt like home. I refused to call him dad, and his two boys were much older than I, and we rarely played together. I was glad when we moved out and settled down in Santa Cruz, where I attended a small private school.

That didn't last long either, and for two years I was home-schooled while we lived in a commune in southern Oregon. They were the happiest and most carefree days of my childhood. Numerous other children were around, and we connected through shared circumstances. Though my mother did have a relationship with one of the men on the farm, we had our own little log cabin to ourselves. We might have continued staying there indefinitely, had the police not raided the place and arrested some of the people, including my mother's partner, for planting and harvesting marijuana on the side.

Returning to Santa Cruz, I reentered school. Those years belonged to some of my most unhappy. In my senior year of high school my mother fell sick. It was a slow, gradual, but steady and unrelenting decline. She refused to see a doctor until it was too late: a large and malignant tumor was discovered in her brain. My mother declined surgery and chemotherapy, preferring alternative methods. She fought it uncomplainingly to the end, but died nine months later during my freshman year at NYU.

In all of my dreams over the years, she always appeared the way she looked during the last year of her life – emaciated, white-haired, and shockingly thin. But as I drove along the coast I could picture her again as a young, beautiful woman, her perpetual smile softly framed by her wavy, shoulder length, auburn hair. I saw her strong body, dressed in the colorful and flowing dresses she loved to wear. These vivid, rich and recurring visionary recollections were trying to tell me something, though it took me a few days to decode. As soon as I did, I took initiative.

Parking on the south side, I walked onto the Golden Gate Bridge, stopping in the middle, holding a thick bouquet of red roses I'd bought that morning. Though summer, it was cold and windy, and I could feel the gentle sway of the bridge under my feet. Twenty-two years ago I'd stood on the very same spot, looking down at the mass of water below me. Back then I'd come to grant my mother's last wish. On that day not a breeze had stirred and it was heavily overcast. Today, accompanied by an unblemished blue sky, I took my perfumed roses, kissed them, and after a moment's hesitation, flung them far into the wind, watching the little flames slowly descend, and finally land in the water. I stared after that diminishing spot of red – that tiny heart, pulsating between the ripples. I stared and stared, long after the dispersing bouquet had disappeared from sight. How different it had been, on that windless, muggy day, over two decades ago, when I'd taken the urn and poured my mother's ashes into the clammy air, feeling heavy with her loss. The ritual, long overdue, had finally reconnected me with my mother. The guilt of not adequately caring for her during her painful battle with cancer, coupled with the shame of not having given her enough credit for all she'd done for me was redeemed in that one ritual act. Immediately, as if blessed, I felt released from a burden I'd carried with me for years. I could go home again, reinvigorated. There's power in ceremony!

○

It's 2 p.m., and the doors of the museum have opened. I enter. A hushed, respectful and friendly mood reigns. I've never visited this museum before, although I've known about Nicholas Roerich's art through prints and books. His influence at the beginning of the twentieth century was immense. Together with Diaghilev, the great impresario, he brought an awareness of Russian art and culture to the West. He was a true representative of the Russian folk soul. It was, above all, Roerich who spawned the idea for *The Rite of Spring,* to which Igor Stravinsky wrote his momentous music – a sonic and revolutionary gateway into the modern age. Roerich was, in essence, its creator, designing the costumes and the set for that initial ground breaking and infamous 1913 premiere in Paris. Less known is his deep and intense involvement with the masters of the Eastern esoteric streams, which in turn has influenced the Anglo-American West more than one might suppose. With time those secrets will become ever more public; such as the immense power that the Masonic Lodges have wielded in the sociopolitical realm over the centuries.

I walk up the narrow wooden stairs. Otherworldly paintings are hanging wherever the eye wanders. The transcendental quality fascinates me. A remote and immemorial part of my being begins to resonate like a Tibetan bowl as I ponder the hermetic paintings. The alluring, entrancing and strikingly luminous use of color, the bold forms, mystical themes and powerful symbolic references, all contribute to the occult atmosphere of his works, filling me with an uncanny longing to escape the mundane here and now. Nothing is held back. I feel transported. I want to remove myself from life's humdrum existence, go on a pilgrimage to Tibet, and disappear into the reduced air of the Himalayan peaks – lose myself in Shangri-La. The pull is powerful and I ponder its source. Again, it's that spiritual abyss that the typical Westerner has to live with, that abysmal hole in the soul that most of us occidentals are cursed or blessed with (depending on how you choose to view it), so obviously reflected by the superficialities of our modern society. It's our cultural heritage. Yet, we want to return to an experience of the spirit that pulsates with life. We want intensity of fulfillment. But something fundamental, though not quite explicable, holds me back from wanting to pursue too seriously this esoteric path of rarefied light. The path, as enticing and tempting as it is, cannot be for me; it would be like climbing into thin air – ecstatic annihilation.

Every so often I sit down in one of the wooden chairs and let the paintings serve as my transporter – off to the land of *Pink Mountains*. As much as I'm mesmerized by the paintings, I sense their precipitous nature and I find myself resisting the pull of the spiritual heights into a distant and lofty past, out of fear I might thereby destroy the future, lose my individual freedom. I fear the ego's euphoric dissolution, rather than its hard earned and painful transformation. The paintings, though entrancing and beckoning, are not warmly inviting – they're almost foreboding through their over emphasis of form.

However, Roerich's involvement with cultural preservation, as presented in the 'Roerich Pact' I can fully relate to and support. It calls for the rigorous protection of art from war and neglect – the red cross of culture. It was even signed in the White House by President Franklin D. Roosevelt back in 1935. But, of course, it has not been properly 'observed,' or 'fulfilled' with good faith by the United States of America and its citizens. Almost daily the pact is betrayed. The Iraq debacle is just one more example. But today, having immersed myself in Roerich's work, I renew my pact, and avow to do my share in the protection of refined culture throughout the world as expressed through the arts, sciences and religion – the trinity which, in its unity, will guarantee the survival of a civilized world based on loving human interrelationships. *Pax Cultura*.

I descend from the cool and exalted heights, knowing something has shifted – an acceptance of my destiny, hanging in the balance between fate and free will. I can meet the Met again.

Renovation

American Wing Atrium (before the renovations)

$\mathcal{S}$omething was different. I could smell it, even before I entered from the parking garage (I've just returned from Red Hook where I dropped Alicia off). The lobby felt empty. For a moment I had to recollect... what was here before? Our memory fails us easily. For one, the shop's gone! But wasn't there a model of the Parthenon displayed in the center of the ground floor entrance hall... covered by Plexiglas? Yes, now I can visualize the whole place again. It's changed completely. What's up?

I paid my perfunctory dollar (blue admissions button), got my parking ticket validated, and climbed the stairs from the ground floor up to the bathroom on the second floor, just above the museum café. In my renewed state of awareness I noticed for the first time how worn the right side of the steps are; real indentations, the kind you'd find in a medieval European castle. I chose the urinal on the far left, as I always do, and wondered how many hundreds of thousands of people it must have taken to wear down those steps. While washing my hands and scrutinizing the touch of grey at my temples, I was suddenly filled with a premonition of loss. On my way down I noticed with a shock that the comfy couches around the massive marble column were gone. Worse, the entire restaurant area was an empty cavernous hole. I couldn't believe it. No more Piccadilly Circus! No more old style museum café! Many of the chairs and tables were still there, muddled and huddled on top of one another. What's happened? I've only been away for a couple of months.

"What's going on?" I asked a nearby guard, pointing into the desolate hall, unable to hide my consternation. "When did this happen?"

"Oh, just a few weeks ago. This is only the beginning of many renovations planned over the next few years. The Roman Court will be installed in the old cafeteria space."

"So where's the restaurant now?"

"The new cafeteria has been relocated to the ground floor right under the Medieval Hall."

"Under it?"

"Yeah, just follow the signs."

Offending marks of renovations also assaulted my sensitivities in the carpeted Africa and Oceanic wing – sections had been closed off and display cabinets had been moved around, or removed altogether. Disquieting! I knew, of course, that the Met was always staging disappearing and reappearing acts – it was part of its appeal; it kept the place alive, and I always looked forward to seeing new combinations of various artworks, seeing them in different contexts, gaining perspectives through interesting juxtapositions, or meeting works again that had been removed, sometimes for years on end. But this!

Coffee is what I needed to collect myself, and I looked forward to a quiet cup at the Petrie Court Café, but a long queue was snaking out from the concession stand – now firmly placed on the left hand side where once the beautiful statues of Camille Claudel had stood. This place was no longer the quiet little retreat frequented by the few. Disinclined to stand in line and feed my discontent I decided to check out the new cafeteria.

A short walk and I was in the medieval section. I was immediately struck by the distant, but distinct smell of fries and coffee. That did not sit well with me at all. Not here. It reminded me of the time I went to Dresden, Germany to view Raphael's *Madonna and Child*. (When I was a child my mother had hung a framed print of it over my bed, and I'd always wanted to see it 'live.') The large and impressive painting was indeed prominently displayed, but unfortunately it hung right next to the sparse cafeteria, where the reek of sausages and sauerkraut was allowed to waft over the entire gallery in such an overbearing manner that I could hardly stomach it. Now I was similarly annoyed. Though not as bad, it was still distracting. Besides, the entire traffic flow was modified because of the change in location. Whole streams of people were using this hallowed space as a thoroughfare to the new museum cafeteria. The medieval hall, number four, used to be a quiet, contemplative domain, and I'm peeved at the noisy intrusion.

I asked a guard with a blond mullet, "Are many more people going through here since the opening of the new cafeteria?"

"You bet'cha. Man, you wouldn't believe the difference… s'cuse me –" and he scurried off, shouting to a group of students, who were talking and laughing too loudly, touching one of the Virgins.

Vexed, I followed the signs and made for the Robert Lehman Wing, plodding down the stairs to the lower level. The disparate smells of paint, cement, varnish and other obnoxious toxins lingered in the air, fusing with odors of baked, cooked and fried foods – all anathema to anybody wanting to focus seriously on art. The actual cafeteria was, as expected, a low-ceilinged, cheapo-diner affair. "Ain't never gonna feast my beak in this place, that's for sure," I snarled, after my speedy reconnaissance.

For a few minutes I rested on a bench by the Pazzi Fountain to gather my wits. Not long and I heard a cash register clinking right above me. "Oh no, now the Moloch has even invaded this quiet sanctuary! What's happened to the Met?"

Rudderless, I let my legs take me wherever they pleased, while my head was pouting – playing the blame game. I'd looked forward to returning to the Met, to drink up the artwork, let myself be inspired, and to write. Ridiculous really, to think that a few outer changes in the museum would result in such a pathetic emotional setback. How easily I'm derailed. I like to think I'm so spontaneous, flexible, and resilient, but I've got this sclerotic, stubborn, immutable side to me that's like non biodegradable plastic. It highlights why it's so hard for me to come to terms with my undigested past, my blindness and my blunders.

With turbid thoughts carousing through my head I stumbled into the American Wing Courtyard, and lo and behold, it too had changed; it now housed a café with the same kind of laid back feel to it that the Petrie Café used to have, except the sitting area was more expansive. This, in contrast, was a pleasant surprise and I immediately got myself some coffee and a blueberry muffin.

O

For over an hour I've been sitting here, filling pages in my notebook. And while writing, something else began taking place: my discontent from the morning was gradually giving way, or should I say, metamorphosing. I started seeing the projected renovations of the Met in a positive light, simultaneously experiencing the Met as a metaphor for my own life, one that was in need of reconstruction and major renovation. My discontent was based on my reluctance to accept and inaugurate change in myself. Even if there's a sacrifice – like the museum café becoming a subterranean diner – I needed to become someone other than my present self.

Getting up, I stroll over to the fountain – the one into which I'd thrown all my pennies – and stare at the rather human depiction of Pan – sans horns and hoofs – playing his double reed pipe. I can almost hear the flowing but shrill melody issuing from the unusually long pipes, accompanied by the tender and soft splash of the water. Taking a found penny from my pocket I flip it into the water and whisper, "So be it."

American Wing Atrium (after the renovations)

Skirt

Near Eastern Robe

In my rush to get here I forgot my wallet in the inside pocket of my jacket, still hanging over a chair in the teacher's lounge. What to do when you've got the empty pocket blues? Two options: hunt around for an admission button that's inevitably lying around outside on the front steps of the Met, or just sneak in. I chose the latter (with the intention of paying double next time I came). Walking through the gift shop I exited on the far side, into the medieval section. As simple as that. There wasn't a guard in sight. It cost me a three minute detour before I came to the stairs leading down from the Egyptian section to the Costume Institute. I hadn't frequented this part of the museum since the Rock Style exhibition in 2000. I descended the first fourteen steps, and paused for a moment, remembering the huge Day-Glo poster of the Beatles that had hung on the wall above the landing. Turning the corner I quickly skipped down the next fifteen steps to the ground floor. The Bravehearts: Men in Skirts exhibit was in its last week and I wanted to get at least a peak at it, intrigued by the concept.

Here in America there is something radical and bohemian about men wearing 'skirts'; I know, for I chose to wear a caftan intermittently in the early eighties while attending NYU. It was liberating – simply throwing a caftan over my head on hot summer mornings. At the time the rebel in me enjoyed pushing the envelope of social norms. Skirts, in the wider sense of the concept, are archetypal, exemplified by the colorful sarongs worn by the beautiful Balinese men and women; after all, it is the predominant attire and nobody is permitted to enter any of the Hindu temples without one. There is nothing emasculate about it, as demonstrated by the flowing Roman toga, the otherworldly dignity of the Chinese Robe, or the rugged virility of the Scottish kilt. It has universal appeal and transcends sex (or becomes sexless as with monks or priests).

After looking around I chose the alcove on the far left of the entrance to settle down. Just as expected – I could sit comfortably on the carpet with legs outstretched, and write without disturbance. Not much traffic down here. I'd skirted the big crowds up above me. I've got good news to relate. And bad.

First the good: On my return home from my last cathartic visit to the Met I actually acted on the sudden impulse to remodel and rejuvenate my own life. My first deed was to clear up my small allotted corner in the basement and assemble my trap set. Once set up and cleaned, I tightened the vellums, got out my battered old drum sticks, sat down and played for two hours straight. I hadn't done that in years and I still had rhythm.

But, more consequentially, I reread and made some incisive changes to my long neglected novel *Tough Triage* (which follows the lives of five individualities – their fates interwoven with one another – over three incarnations), wrote some query letters, and sent them to various agents. Against all expectations one of them showed interest. I immediately sent her a copy of the revised book. She wrote back within days, agreeing to take me on. That alone was cause for celebration. I wasn't expecting much since I'd received dozens of rejection slips for the very same novel a few years back. All the more my surprise when I received a letter from my agent, stating that a small, independent, but reputable press, was seriously considering my novel, thinking it a good fit. They would write up and send me a contract within the next few weeks. I reread that short missive umpteen times. I'd waited for news like this for years. I was ecstatic. It was a breakthrough and confirmation of my work, whatever the outcome.

Now for the disconcerting news (just to ensure I don't succumb to hubris). This morning I opened an e-mail from Carrie, which stated unequivocally that she'd decided to stay in India! To soften the blow she's invited me to join her.

I saw it coming, of course, though I was in denial. The letter from six months ago had prepared me for this final outcome. No surprises here. I understood. Yet, it hurt all over again, and I admit, I was upset. I'd looked forward to her return and had even scouted around for a larger apartment. As for immigrating to India? I don't know the language, culture, or country. And I'd have to start from scratch. How would I make a living? It would be so much simpler and more logical if she returned with Indra. After all, she grew up in the States. However, these initial thoughts quickly faded. Why should the woman always follow the man? Why shouldn't it be the other way round? I loved her, and she professed to love me too. Still, how can I just pack my bags and move off to India? Does she really want me to come, or is it her way of consoling me? Can I leave everything behind? Nevertheless, I'm entertaining the notion. The thought of living in India does have its appeal. It tickles my spirit for adventure. I could become one of the men wearing skirts – and I picture myself clad in a lungi or a jamah.

Not Quite Yet

Aristotle with a Bust of Homer, Rembrandt

Cold, gloomy and wet 'museum weather' pushed me into the Met. I'm fighting another bout of fatigue, which always borders on depression. The Roman section is still closed off and will be for a while – shut off like part of my past. I sat for the longest time in front of the magical creations of Paul Klee, eventually closing my eyes and thinking about the word *panoply*.

I'd come this morning, determined to write, but the desire has spent itself. This whole self-assigned project does *not* excite me anymore. Zero motivation. Should I just accept it and stop? Mtwanu, a conga and djembe drummer from Mali, who'd sometimes jammed with our band (the one Arietta and I played in for a couple of years when we first got together) once said, "Practice until you've reached your limit, and then practice some more – that will make all the difference. Do it and you'll see what I mean." The truth of his words has proven itself over and over again. But does it apply to this case – to my weird obsession of penning my thoughts here at the Met, of chronicling specific segments of my life? I'm no closer to finding the truth about the world and myself than when I first started. Or am I? I'd hoped for something – not quite sure what – to be revealed to me through the process of writing. I'd expected more, and I'm disappointed in myself, my journey of self-discovery. Yet, some sort of quasi-crystallization has happened and it has raised consciousness. I've become more questioning, more observant. Granted, I still don't dare to uncover the deeper layers of myself, though I've come close to prying open those obscure trapdoors hidden in the untrodden underbrush of my interior. But it's not a matter of laying bare my instinctual demoniac backwash, my emotional shlock. It's much simpler: I'm just trying to achieve calmness of mind and soul. And that's why there's nothing sensational about this journey, because the real evidence of the spirit is found in the little and evanescent details of daily events – like acknowledging someone's smile, taking a moment to listen to the birds singing, appreciating a flower, pondering why you put on a t-shirt the wrong way around, observing the way the steam rises from a cup of tea.

O

Good. I already feel much better. I just had to clarify these points to myself again. I had to give myself a reminder of why I'm doing what I'm doing. It's so easy to forget and lose sight of things.

At least I've made up my mind on one issue: I'm not going to India. The romantic in me wants to join her – badly, but my pragmatic self put a stop to that. There's no way I could forsake Alicia (more than I already have). I feel the same obligation toward her as Carrie toward Indra. Truth is – our respective responsibilities have come between us, though I prefer to see the circumstances as having sublimated our love. This was not only a tough, but a painful triage.

O

Now I'm standing in front of the 'The Million-Dollar Rembrandt' (actually it was purchased for $2,300,000 back in 1961, one Wednesday evening in November, breaking all painting purchase price records up to that time), and I'm contemplating my present predicament just as Aristotle is contemplating the bust of Homer in this painting – his good right hand gently resting on the poet's wise head. It makes me think of Odysseus, and I wish I were as skilled in navigating through the zodiacal adventures of my own destiny as Odysseus could through his. With his left hand Aristotle is touching the gold chain hanging from around his right shoulder. And almost lost in the darkness is a medallion depicting Alexander the Great, his illustrious student – as Homer was the inspiration and teacher of both. It's as if Aristotle is weighing the benefits of Homer's knowledge and wisdom with the riches and earthly power of Alexander's vast conquests. His melancholy mien shows the pull of both worlds in his soul – the spiritual and the material, the outer and the inner; it conveys the sobering knowledge that the world of the gods has retreated, that the mystery centers such as Delphi, Eleusis, and Ephesus have lost their power and become decadent; that clear thinking through philosophy must now pave the way for the new – not yet born. It's a moment of insight; consciously captured. Together, these fatefully linked figures of history form a grand triumvirate of movers and shakers: spiritually, intellectually, and physically – personified archetypes of mind body and soul from classical antiquity. The darkness that permeates the painting's background is the darkness of our age as well as my own – the one I'm endeavoring to leave behind, carried by the wings of the ample, lush and luxuriantly painted sleeves, feathering the philosopher's arms – bathed in light. I'm awed.

Reinvigorated, I slowly turn my back on Rembrandt's *Aristotle with a Bust of Homer*, and make my way from gallery to gallery, circumventing people as I gradually drain into the growing stream of humanity flooding through the Great Hall. Yes, art rejuvenates. True art is embodied spirit; and the spirit never sleeps, but always burns on and on. I feel as if my own hand has just touched Homer's head, inspiring me with the muse that once sang through him.

I will continue to write, because it's what I must do, even if it is only in short, sporadic spurts, and even if I don't fully know why. Life has its phases, some more defined than others. I'll know the moment when it's all said and done. And it's not quite yet.

PART THREE

Perseus with the Head of Medusa, Antonio Canova, Roman

Root Rift

Two Fluted Pillars outside the Museum Entrance

I pause in front of a large icon with Mary wearing tiny blood-red shoes. The blue of her garment is faded, but the gold behind her is as radiant as ever. I want to move on, but I feel faint – struck with sudden guilt – and I just keep staring at the virgin's little feet, standing in innocent suffering – two small burning embers. I'm nailed to the spot by the pounding knowledge of a resurfaced episode – a wound, left to fester for years without the necessary attention. Memories tend to return in altered states, popping up at arcane, though seemingly random moments. And when it shows itself in such stark relief we can begin to see the connections, the ongoing consequences. I see it now; there's no denying: it was the initial, infectious gash in our marital life, though it didn't seem to be of such great import at the time. I'm loath to go poking down that path, but the mnemonic punch has left me little option. I must!

Tomorrow will be Easter Sunday. This time last year Carrie had already moved in with me. Things still looked promising between us, except for the threat of Jitendra. Now he's in prison and Carrie is living in India, reunited with Indra. And now that there's clarity between us our letters and e-mails have become intimate and refreshingly free of any expectations, guilt, or blame – a rare love, based on mutual sacrifice and acceptance of reality. I want to go and visit, but wonder if that would only complicate matters and harm the delicate balance of our present relationship.

And finally I've finished what I hope will be the last editorial changes and additions to my novel *Tough Triage* (the main reason why I have not come to the Met for a while). I sent the laboriously reworked manuscript back to my publisher this morning. Now, I'm free at last to view the *Byzantine: Faith and Power* exhibit.

It's no surprise to see the Met so packed, given the scope of this exhibition and the holiday weekend. On a whim I took the escalator immediately to the left of the grand staircase and let myself be lifted lazily up to the second floor, noting marginally that I'd never done that before.

Now I am rooted in front of the large icon of the Madonna with the intriguing red shoes (one of a few with the same motif). It's uncommonly hot and sweat is dripping down my back. But the heat is of no consequence as the memory bolt hits me. I quickly seek a vacant seat to acknowledge, write and reflect on the flashback – I know that's what I have to do today. It's as if there's an invisible mind here at the Met that is steering me along a specific course, one I need to follow in my writing. Ten minutes ago I still had no idea what I would write about, and now it has become the next logical stage of my inner trip. And it is usually the works of art that whisper the directions. You never know which artwork will speak to you next. They're like beings, and as such I meet them.

O

Five months after I met Arietta on the sunny Greek island of Naxos, I found myself in a small medieval village, high up in the Swiss Alps. After checking into a rustic hotel I went for a walk. It was good to get out and move about, to breathe in the fresh alpine air after a long day of sitting in trains. Snow was lying about six feet deep on either side of the ploughed roads. I'd never seen so much snow before. Leaving the huddle of dark, old and sagging houses behind me, I felt the exhilarating silence with all of my senses, enhanced by the majesty of the mighty mountains all around. Nature was in deep slumber, though its spirit was wide awake, beckoning me. Crossing an old, shadowy covered bridge I noticed a young woman leaning against the wooden railing on the far side, staring down at the wild, fast flowing river. I stopped. She was crying, making no attempt to wipe away her tears. Approaching her, to offer some solace, she waved me away angrily, without even looking at me. Reluctantly I resumed my walk, but my mind was caught up with the unhappy girl and her pitifully abject countenance. The walk had lost its innocence and I felt the cold creeping into my bones. Clouds began covering the glacier-topped peaks and the afternoon light was becoming diffuse and fading. Thinking better of it I turned around to get back to the warm hotel. Arriving at the covered bridge I was shocked to see the weeping woman climbing up on the railing. For a while she held onto one of the supporting posts, but then she let go and began pacing slowly toward the middle of the bridge, balancing precariously. There was no doubt – she intended to jump. Instinctively I ran forward, but halted a few feet from her.

She hadn't noticed my approach. The roar of the raging river below was deafening in contrast to the snowy stillness all around. She stopped crying and was now muttering to herself, staring hypnotically down at the hurtling torrents of grey water. Ever so slowly and quietly I stepped toward her. Finally, I took hold of her left hand, clasping it tight. Her cold fingers remained limp, though I felt her body tense up at my unsolicited touch. Like two linked statues we stood frozen in eternity, before I felt her body loosen and surrender. Without a word I pulled her from the railing, catching her gently as she fell into my arms. As soon as she was down she tore herself away, staring at me with desperate eyes that showed both surprise and distress. Her matted brown hair added to the wild, abandoned look in her flushed face. I wanted to say something reassuring to her, but my German was rudimentary and my Swiss German non-existent, so I remained silent. I judged that she was still in her teens, only a few years younger than I was. However, given her derelict and almost savage look, I feared she might yet jump over the railing into the rocky depths of the swollen river below; so I continued to gaze reassuringly into her dark, piercing eyes, hoping it would serve as well as words. Never had I felt a set of eyes thrust themselves so searchingly into mine, with such raw power. Then, as if an irrevocable decision had been made, she stepped forward, grabbed my arm impulsively and pulled me along. I acquiesced, startled. Satisfied that I was following she let go of me and began running, looking behind her every now and then, making sure I kept up with her.

By now it was getting dark. After following the narrow road away from the village for a few minutes she led me up a steep narrow path to a rough-hewn wooden *Hütte* clinging precariously to the side of the mountain. Going round the side, she unlatched a barn door, and we entered into the warmth of a dark, shadowy stall. Passing closely by two hay-munching cows and a pen full of sleeping sheep she led me up three stone steps. Putting her finger to her lips she cautioned me to be quiet and opened another door that led up some rickety stairs into the living quarters. Silently we walked along the dusky and narrow passage, our steps creaking on the ancient wooden floor. Someone somewhere coughed and called out. Quickly the girl motioned me through a low door, and then disappeared.

Alone, I looked around the simple room. An abnormally high bed with four sturdy posts took up most of the space. A small, solid table stood underneath the tiny window, framed by red and white checkered curtains. A chipped, white enamel wash bowl and a jug took up most of the space on the table. A large copper crucifix hung next to the window on the right. On the left side hung an oval framed, black-and-white photograph of a wizened woman smoking a long, curved, metal-capped pipe. On the adjacent wall, facing the bed was a bulky, gold framed picture of Christ, his large red heart exposed, embraced by thorns; his sad eyes rested on me, no matter where I stepped. The sloping, beamed roof was very low and I could touch it without stretching. The coughing fit in the next room started up again, followed by muffled conversation. Peering through the window I noticed it had begun snowing. As I wondered about my peculiar predicament the strange mountain girl reentered. She closed the door, stood and watched me intently, her dark eyes still blazing with barely contained desperation, her lips slightly parted. She expected me to do something and the silence grew and became awkward. The last light of the afternoon was giving way to darkness.

What had driven her to want to kill herself? Would she attempt it again? Why? I smiled to break the tension. She did not return the smile, but continued staring back at me, expectantly, questioningly, almost pleadingly. Tears slowly filled her eyes, tears of frustrated helplessness. She was expecting me to read her. I was slow to decipher.

Breaking out of her inert stance she snatched some matches and lit an oil lamp that stood on the window sill. Her hands were trembling. The soft, ambient light lit up her rounded, young, yet fraught features. She was transformed into a primal beauty. Her long disheveled hair hung wildly about her head, shoulders and back. The skin appeared soft on her smoothed face. How long before its youthful sheen must fade in this harsh climate? She was used to hardships and it was clear by the set features of her face and muscular frame that she had never known pampering. There was little of the modern world in her countenance – a woman untouched by current conveniences, determined by circumstance, rather than choice. Her simplicity nevertheless held secrets and was mysterious like the mountains, which had shaped her as much as anything else in her life. I doubted whether she'd ever been beyond the confines of her native alpine village. I was looking at a face from another time, another age. A girl a thousand years ago might not have been raised or treated any differently in this secluded mountain valley. What prevented her from taking the tiny step across the centuries into the modern world, with all of its opportunities? Surely she must feel its lure? She was caught up in something that prevented her freedom – that much was clear. I could see it in her eyes. She wanted out – even if it meant killing herself to escape. Was I to be a catalyst in helping her to break out of the fetters that held her?

A grating coughing spasm next door caused her to quietly leave the room again. Christ, with the heart pierced by thorns, was still looking gently toward me. Next to the bed was a small, porcelain baptismal font. There was nothing of a personal nature in the stark room; nothing that would give me a clue to her character, her interests. The only book was a small, black bible on a shelf next to her bed.

When she returned she brought a flask of wine, two glasses, and some bread. After pouring the wine she took the loaf of bread, put it to her ample bosom, and deftly cut two slices. I'd never seen anybody cut bread like that before. There was no chair in the room and we stood, looking at one another drinking the wine and eating the wholesome brown bread. I observed her, how she broke off little chunks, dipped them in the wine and ate them, slowly. I did likewise, and smiled. For the first time she smiled as well, briefly. The bread and wine were welcome, tasted good, and lessened the discomfort between us. Seeing my hunger she clasped the bread to her breast again and cut another piece. And as soon as my glass was empty she filled it up again, unprompted. Throughout our simple meal I noticed that she was still on edge, nervously listening to any sounds coming from the outside.

Warmed by the wine I became acutely aware that I was alone in a room with a woman. Through the latent fear that still lingered in her eyes I could read her plainly now: she expected me to make love to her. I sensed she was almost surprised I hadn't already taken advantage of her. There was no lust in her eyes, but a dormant craving, an insistence that manifested itself in rebellious submissiveness. I did not understand the paradoxical nature of it, but it was tangible, and the thought was undeniably arousing.

Simultaneously we closed in to kiss and our tongues rolled against one another like boulders caught in a flood – her strong arms clasped around my neck like sturdy roots. Abruptly she let go and glanced up – the look of forlorn longing had given way to relief. I gently took her tousled head in my cupped hands, eliminating the last vestiges of awkwardness between us and drew her tenderly back toward me while peering deep into her glacial-blue eyes. Our lips met once more and the boulders rolled.

By now the night had set in solidly. We were both still wearing our coats. I helped her out of hers, and while I removed mine she solemnly lit three votive candles around the room, spreading the dim light more evenly. One of them she placed on the table next to the jug, and the other two in sconces above the bed, to the left and right of a beautiful small icon of the holy virgin, which I hadn't noticed before. Crossing herself in front of the Madonna she turned toward me in readiness. After another sealing embrace we slipped off our shoes and climbed into her high bed, fully clothed, pulling the sheets and blankets over us. And in the lambent light of the candles we held each other and kissed – no more.

From below I could intermittently hear the soft, low peals of the cow bells. I distinctly felt as if I were reliving a moment from a past incarnation, at one remove from my regular life. All strangeness had evaporated, and everything seemed uncannily familiar. Lying with this girl seemed as natural as if I'd been with her umpteen times. We lay, warm in each other's embrace, letting the candles burn low, until they flickered and died, leaving only the single dull light of the oil lamp on the window sill. That's when I heard the crunch of approaching footsteps out in the snow.

At once the strange, yet so familiar girl stiffened, and her heart began to palpitate right into my chest, but now with fear. We heard the latch on the barn door lift and fall, and could follow the heavy footsteps as they made their way up the stairs and along the narrow passage, the wooden floor creaking sharply. I was wide awake, every sense alert. Surely nobody would enter this room, not at this late hour. I was waiting for a cue from her, but she did not stir, though her eyes were wide open staring at the ceiling. With the advancing footsteps the coughing in the next room started up again, the frail voice calling out. It was answered by a man's guttural voice, followed by a loud thud that reverberated right through into our room. Soft sobs drenched the ensuing silence. The girl's hands searched for mine, clasping them tightly, pulling them up to her chin. I wanted to get up, but she pulled me back. Her breathing was loud, fraught with fear. For a while we heard the footsteps pace back and forth in the house and each creak sent a shiver through the ancient floorboards. Dimly I began to fathom why she'd brought me here. I now found myself inextricably entangled in this girl's problems. The door opened before I could finish my deductions.

A bearded, stocky figure stood in the shadowy doorway, obviously drunk. The girl lay still like a corpse, eyes shut, holding her breath. Incredulously, I watched the besotted man close the door, clumsily take off his shirt in the dim, unearthly light, remove his trousers – panting noisily – and approach the bed. The girl was now shivering wildly beside me. Then, for the first time that evening, I heard the girl speak. With quivering voice she pleaded in Swiss German, "No, papa. No, please, go away…" but to no avail. He came closer and I could smell the stale smoke and liquor on his breath. As he was about to lift up the bedspread he noticed me with his squinting, murky eyes. That's when I knew exactly why she'd brought me here. She wanted him to see me – to see her lying with another man. For a few unsteady seconds he gazed at me in utter disbelief, before his eyes narrowed dangerously, and he let out a roar. He tore back the covers and hit his helpless daughter with a staggering blow to the face, followed by another into her belly. The next was meant for me, but I leaped up at once, knocking my head against the low ceiling in my haste. Instinctively, I lunged at him from the bed, throwing him to the floor with a crash. Stunned, he looked up, eyes filled with hate. He grabbed one of the girl's boots and threw it at me. I ducked. It hit the flask of wine, which fell to the floor and rolled under the bed. His daughter sat up and screamed at him through her tears. Blood trickled from her nose. Though I could hardly make out a word she said, I knew she was assailing him with all of her pent up feelings, the anger and hurt she'd kept to herself for so long. The coughing started up again next door, accompanied by feeble cries. Lubberly, he pushed himself back up and I saw murder smoldering in his eyes. He was unsteady, and I didn't wait for him to get back on his feet. Furious that he'd abused his daughter for God knows how long, I seized the enamel jug from the table and knocked it hard over his head. He slumped down, cracked his head against one of the bed posts and was out cold.

I had no intention of sticking around any longer, and I persuaded her to come back to the hotel with me. Silently she packed a small leather bag which she hauled out from under her bed. Without even glancing at her collapsed father she picked up his trousers, removed his wallet and took all the money she could find. After a few quick words to the pitifully sobbing woman in the next room, presumably her mother, we left.

The next morning when I awoke she was gone. I didn't go back to the *Hütte* to find out whether she'd returned to her dismal abode, or what had happened to her father. I caught the next red alpine train and headed for Lausanne. As I changed trains in Brig and was slowly trundling out of the station I saw a woman hurrying along the platform towards a bus. It was her. Her thick brown hair was tied into a neat bun and her steps were firm. I waved to her, but she wasn't looking my way. At that moment I realized I hadn't thought of Arietta at all throughout this crazy one night stand.

○

I've been writing for over two hours. Even more people are shuffling through the nine galleries. I get up and walk back to the icon with the holy virgin that had prompted this dormant memory. It suddenly dawned on me that the Mary in the icon above the strange Swiss girl's bed had also worn little red shoes.

○

My confession to Arietta about the incident had not gone down well at all, least of all my heroic description of posing as the girl's savior. My

214

"macho rationalizations" – as she put it – reaped nothing but scorn. My argument that I was caught up in an irreversible situation, beyond my control, fared even worse. On top of that, I'd neglected to tell her until we'd moved in together, after she'd changed her whole life around for me. In hindsight I recognized how much pain could have been averted had I not ended up sleeping with the girl – once we'd arrived back at the hotel. I'd succumbed in the heat of the moment, fueled by the adrenalin rush of our escape. And the guilt weighed on me – as it does now, all over again. Arietta claimed she could have forgiven me for lying in bed with the girl, even for kissing and caressing her, but she saw nothing pardonable in what happened at the hotel. She assured me in no uncertain terms that she'd never have moved in with me had she known of my little detour. As it was, Arietta disappeared for about three days after the disclosure. We never mentioned the episode again – though snide remarks alluding to the aberration surfaced at the most inopportune moments. I'd severed something that she'd considered holy: an unwritten and unspoken promise, given freely the day we parted in Greece, a self- evident spiritual pledge. "It's a trust issue," as she had once said.

We'd never worked through this one. Something had snapped between us and we both knew it. How should we have handled the rift, lying at the root of our relationship?

O

Drained, but strangely uplifted, I walk on, fascinated by the fresco fragments, manuscript paintings, sundry liturgical objects, exquisite embroideries, the stunningly crafted miniature icons, the many painted panels and sculptures. In gallery four I make one last stop in front of the *Mosaic Icon with the Man of Sorrows* from the late 13th, early 14th century. As I'm standing in front of this icon of "utmost humiliation" I have to admit that I had surrendered to circumstance rather than mastering it.

Yes, that's it, I let myself be taken by a situation, rather than taking hold of the situation. I leave the Met – humbled.

Invocation

California, Hiram Powers

O nly because I was tired and there was an empty chair did I stare vacantly at *Washington Crossing the Delaware*. After a while I forced myself to look away, but the ice on the river pulled me back involuntarily. I hadn't been to this part of the American Wing for ages. It always made me feel like I was visiting the museum a hundred years ago, the way the paintings were crammed all over the walls, three, sometimes four rows deep. Further to the left stood *California*, smoothly sculpted in glistening white Carrara marble – the stuff of Michelangelo's sculptures. She had moderate sex appeal, despite the idealized classical style – the way she held the divining rod, covering her own secret wellspring. And the thorns concealed behind her back made me think of the consequences of lust, if the divining rod's sensuous quiver above the desired source is pursued too instinctively.

Sauntering over to her, I was struck by the Amazon's long, beautiful toes. Although she was supposed to be an allegorical representation commemorating the 1849 California gold rush, with its deceitfulness, potential for riches and fickleness of fortune, I saw it as a tantalizing admonition of the vicissitudes of love. Also, I prefer her original name, La Dorada. Not only is it more feminine and fluid in sound, but it gives her mythical status, widening the allegory. She is fascinating, more than I cared to admit to myself, and I could fully understand how she became the center of attention when she first appeared back in 1872 – the Met's first sculptural gift bestowed by William Backhouse Astor; ironically enough, one of America's wealthiest citizens.

While the guard looked elsewhere, I moved one of the chairs right up close in front of *California*. "You're my muse today, La Dorada," I whispered, clicking my pen, ready for action.

"So be it," she responded at once. "If your invocation is genuine, listen to me and take note." Hearing her voice pop up in my head startled me. "Yes, it's me talking."

"How can that be?"

"Each art work has a being attached to it. I thought you knew that."

"Well, yes, I do, but not quite so clearly articulated."

"I'm real, all right. We are manifested inspiration. An artist's inspiration isn't something abstract. Imagination doesn't come from nowhere. It has its living source."

"I've intimated as much. So what can you tell me about yourself?"

"When Hiram Powers began chiseling away at me, it was I who moved his hand; the design, as such, was mine too. You see, the commemoration of the gold rush merely served as a platform for my existence, from where I could begin to wield my invisible influence. Look into my face; what do you see? It's not sinister, as some critics have said, nor is there a hint of mockery, or maudlin melancholy. No, it's an invitation to think beyond the allegories to the realities. My expression is serious, but well-meaning, appealing to the questioning mind within everybody. Whenever people look at me with appreciation and genuine engagement, I am near. Like now; your interest called me forth."

"Do you speak to others the way you're speaking to me now?"

"Seldom. Mostly I make myself felt in a more unconscious manner. An intense relationship with art is always a conversation. That's what draws millions of people to museums. But it rarely rises to full consciousness. The result is that people feel uplifted after these discussions. Unfortunately, the analytical intellect comes between us too often, and mind games get played – clever ones that impress. In such

Above: *California*, Hiram Powers

instances no conversation can take place. It becomes a one-sided and theoretical exercise. That's when I remove myself, and nothing can be gained from me."

"What made you talk to me today?"

"You've schooled yourself by coming here and writing."

"So you know about my project?"

"Of course."

"How much do you know?"

"Everything. Even how it will end; but I won't tell you."

"Why not?"

"Because then it won't end that way."

"Will other paintings and sculptures talk to me?"

"They do, but not as plainly… they whisper, subtly. They help you to remember. They nudge you along. You know that. Some of your thoughts are really their thoughts. They are like the muses, singing through you; something you've always wished for." I glanced up, and for a second I fancied seeing a smile flit across her face. "Through my beauty I invite people to look more intensely," she continued. "And in the afterglow of the senses' reach I can impart my secrets. I have nothing to hide. I pride my nakedness. People should exult in the beauty of the human form. If there's any lust, it is not mine.

"Observe. I'm holding the divining rod, urging people to pursue the gold that lies in the knowledge of the divine. Those thorns behind my back are not concealed. You can step around me and see them at any time. I'm beautiful from behind as well. Come on, take those three steps and examine me closely."

I stood up and walked around her. "The pursuit of the divine is not easy; no path is free of prickly patches. Notice how I stand; in perfect balance, divining my way – I've taken hold of the thorns that can easily thwart one's way. That's what you should do. See how my gaze is slightly lowered and my hair is neatly combed back; it's because I'm constantly in a state of listening so that I can respond to what comes toward me – like you. As I've said, I have nothing to hide, unlike you and most other people who walk by me every day.

"Now touch me and be filled with sublime desire. Do it and I am ready to open up to your love. I can give all of myself and still remain virginal. For my name is not California, nor is it La Dorada… no, I am one of the embodiments of the American Sophia – wisdom in all of its feminine grandeur. I stand here, not as an allegory to 'illustrate the deceitfulness of riches,' as some have claimed, nor of romantic love. No, I stand for that which is noblest in every human being – the gold of the human spirit."

"Look, lastly, at the linear beauty of the crystal which is my firm foundation, enhancing through contrast the curvatures of my figure. Approach me with thoughts as chiseled and clear, and I will stand by you."

As I gently touched her smooth, marble heel, the spell was broken and the statue stood silent and mute once more. Was it just my imagination that had conjured up this conversation? Her soft, sing-song voice still echoed in my ears. As I sat down again to write, I thought I heard her whisper, "Goodbye."

○

With a quick flip of the wrist, I shut my green notebook, pocket my pen and get up. I feel encouraged as I nod farewell to California and briskly walk down to the ever-welcoming Charles Engelhard Court to get in line for a cup of coffee at the American Wing Café. Before coming to the Met today my mind was focused on the Abu Ghraib scandal – those appalling photos just released, showing American soldiers abusing naked Iraqi detainees; as well as the terrible bomb attacks on four Madrid commuter trains a couple of weeks ago, killing close to two hundred people. I thought about the genocide in the Darfur region in Sudan, where Arab militants continue to kill thousands of helpless people. It made me feel powerless. Negative news has a paralyzing effect. But now, after my impromptu meeting with California, I'm thinking how different things might be if more humans became diviners, searching for the gold within themselves and others; then people wouldn't commit violence against one another so easily. Was that a thought Sophia planted in me, so that I may hold it like a prayer? I don't know. Maybe.

"One cappuccino and a croissant, please."

Alicia

Twentieth Century Art, Lila Acheson Wallace Wing

I can face Arietta now without getting upset anymore. The awkwardness is gone, and we can be amiable. It's partly due to the inevitable course of time, my ongoing but gradual attempt to understand and accept the situation, and the fact that I'd freed myself emotionally from Arietta through my relationship with Carrie. But something has shifted in Arietta as well. Initially I assumed it was because Carrie was out of the picture, but I soon realized it had more to do with Alicia. Over the last few weeks Arietta had voiced increasing concern about her. What really surprised me was that she actually sought my help. She even invited me to stay at the house when I came up to spend time with Alicia over spring break. I declined, checking into a motel instead, even though Sylvia was out of town, working on another film. That's when I too noticed Alicia was not doing well.

I put it down to the recent breakup with her boyfriend. But it was more than that. She'd quit the basketball team, which had been her passion, ate like a bird, and was silent for long stretches at a time – very unlike her normal, effervescent self. Furthermore, according to Arietta, she'd spend hours at a time, locked up in her room, appearing only at mealtimes, simply to sit there moodily, pecking away at a few morsels. Alicia had always had an assertive and confident personality, and it was disconcerting to see her retreat into herself. What was more disturbing were the self-deprecating remarks, especially in regard to her appearance, uttered with caustic nonchalance.

However, she did find a new passion: drawing. She'd fill many pages with well-executed sketches, some of them stunningly good, with an eye for detail, though I questioned some of the content – sci-fi landscapes, the animals and humanoids, born from a chaotic, dark, dreamlike and tortured fantasy world. But the mastery of her stroke was undeniable. Still, Arietta and I were confident that she'd come round soon enough if we both gave her more attention and care.

But it only got worse. She became obsessed with her body, which expressed itself in diverse ways, such as different hair colors, provocative fashions and body piercing. After her ears became metal heavy, she moved on to her nose and lip. That's when Arietta and I joined forces and tried to put a stop to it. Even with all of our dialogue, appeals and threats, another blinking stud appeared in her tongue. Enjoying our mutual consternation, she promised there wouldn't be any more surprises, though in the same breath she mentioned something about getting a tattoo. That's when we threatened to revoke her driving privileges.

I still hadn't taken Alicia's state too seriously until she came down to the city one weekend and I truly saw how shockingly thin she was. The skimpy clothes only highlighted her skinny form. Even her tightest jeans sagged, and the scrimpy tank tops exposed the severity of her bony shoulders and ribs; her chest was sunken, and she slouched around as if she were perpetually cold. And when she wore her favorite leather miniskirt, I saw how pitifully bony and spindly her legs were. She must have lost about forty pounds over the last few months. It alarmed me that she had no awareness of her own emaciated state – no comprehension whatsoever. Alicia would soon be seventeen, but she looked like a scrawny twelve year old.

There are always a few cases of girls suffering from eating disorders in our high school, but they get referred to specialists who work with them. I knew little about the symptoms. I felt stupid, ignorant, and helpless, though it was obvious that the popular images of women – as expressed in the media – had something to do with it. Moreover, my observation that girls who suffer from anorexia or bulimia often fail to live up to their potential had me worried.

I called Arietta, voiced my latest concerns, and was glad to hear that she'd already scheduled an appointment with a doctor. She'd also spoken with the school counselor who recommended that Alicia get professional help. Arietta had bought books on the subject and promised to pass them on to me. All in all she was way ahead of me – as always. We conversed for over an hour, and afterwards I realized we hadn't talked on the phone that long since the divorce. Nor had we argued – not once – and the entire discussion revolved around Alicia. Something was being done and I felt reassured.

O

I'm sitting in front of Rothko's *Black on Black*. It's been three weeks since that lengthy telephone exchange. I'm writing and Alicia is nearby doing a charcoal sketch of Egon Shiele's *Seated Woman*. I'm glad she accompanied me to the Met this morning. As she pointed out though, she only allowed herself to be persuaded because of her love for drawing.

O

Last night, when she arrived, I was upset again by her sunken appearance, exacerbated by heavy makeup. I'd naively thought that our proactive approach would bring swift improvements. Arietta has kept me posted on Alicia's condition, but we have been warned not to expect too much too soon. Alicia has by now had a few sessions with a professional counselor, but she "hates" him, claims he's "useless," that he'll do "nothing" for her, and that he's "creepy." (I've heard that one before). She still insists she's fine and is angry with us for making such a big deal out of it all. However, she responded more positively to the doctor, who relayed her physical condition in a very objective and matter of fact manner. As Alicia said, "At least I can take it from her, because what she says is logical and makes perfect sense; but I can't stand all the psycho-analytical shit that the counselor throws at me. What does he know anyway?"

It's obvious that she's still locked up in herself. She used to share everything with Arietta or me; even just half a year ago she was bubbling over with stories about her friends, school, and sports. That's come to a full stop. Now the slightest query is interpreted as prying. The dark cloud around her is tangible. On top of that she's started smoking (not in front of us), and her coffee intake is on par with mine. At least she claims not to take any drugs and never drinks more than a beer or two at parties. I want to believe her. Yet, it's obvious that she needs and craves human contact more than ever.

O

But here she comes now, smiling. While walking toward me she holds up her drawing. It's a perfect copy. I can see she's happy. Her face is smudged with charcoal. "Do you like it, Dad?" My eyes wet up.

Inimitable Dome

Storm King Wall (located in Storm King Art Center), Andy Goldsworthy

Plans for the summer had to be changed. Instead of flying to Greece I'm back to reworking my novel, hoping to make the new August 30th deadline. Thank God teachers get summers off. The publishers still wanted some more changes made – a whole list, in fact, some of which tested my patience. Should have known. Even so, I most likely would have cancelled the trip, anyway. At least I won't go into debt. Alicia's condition still hasn't shown any signs of improvement. On the upside – it's not any worse. Arietta and I have made a point of staying in touch regularly. There's comfort in that. Alicia's well-being has become our priority. I like our conversations, and sometimes we talk about other things.

I'm enjoying the *Andy Goldsworthy on the Roof* exhibition, though I'm not feeling exactly on top of the world. But I love his work, the way he works with nature – or to be more precise: his work *is* nature with a few contextual changes. With his ephemeral sculptures he takes nature a step beyond herself, and helps us see the beauty of momentary manifestations. Goldsworthy's mind intuits nature's potential, then builds on it and shapes it. His transient works made from natural materials such as ice, flowers, mud, snow, sand, water and rocks successfully bridge the gap between Mensch and nature, time and space, visible and invisible, life and death – by aesthetically juxtaposing them, creating and recreating landscapes, getting us to see nature with new eyes. His art is a refreshing balance to the clever and brilliant installations and techno-driven art we see burgeoning around us, some with the intention to merely shock, provoke or sensationalize.

It's a beautifully sunny and mild June day, and his two monumental, organic domes of wood, eighteen feet high and twenty-four feet in diameter, dominate the 10,000 square foot rooftop like nothing I've ever seen up here before. Their primal quality casts a devotional, reverential mood, similar to viewing cromlechs, standing stones, beehive cells of the early Irish Christian monks, or sacred buildings from other ancient sites. Yet, there's nothing antiquated about them – more like modernity metamorphosed straight from antiquity. While contemplating the inimitable setting, I'm most intrigued by the thirteen-and-a-half stone spires sheltered within each split rail structure, looking almost fragile, the way each stone is perched upon the other. It reminds me of how delicate we all are on the inside, even though we like to think we're as tough as granite. These two columns in their uprightness are mirrors of ourselves, our continuous, step for step, or stone for stone striving, each graduation making us more vulnerable, more likely to collapse, the lighter and loftier we get.

The two protective domes contrast well with Manhattan's skyline, while blending naturally with Central Park's gently undulating landscape. The domes are connected, yet acutely separated.

O

I stop writing to ponder the elemental power of this creative and erect formation. My thoughts dissolve as I give myself over to the unique architecture. I squat down on my haunches and lean against the sun warmed wall. I close my eyes and in my daydream see the dome shapes begin to move; I see them melt and merge until finally they stand *re-erected* as one large, octagonal dome, with both stone columns standing in the center, tall and close together – their unity well-protected against any outside forces. I'm taken by the new construction, the new creation;

so much so that I get up, turn around and leave before opening my eyes, so as to keep my vision intact: two stone columns, tall and close together, no longer separated.

I take out my cell and give Arietta a call.

Met Monday not MoMA

Virgin and Child, Medieval Court

I should have known better. Hundreds of people are already queuing up patiently outside the Museum of Modern Art, all wanting to check out these refurbished halls. And hundreds more are inside, waiting to sardine through the glass doors into the hyped up heaven of contemporary art – what a tight shuffle of a run. The sight angers me. I don't know why. It shouldn't, but it does – I just want to walk right in and get my ticket. No standing in line out in the cold. I could have gone earlier; after all, it's been reopened since November 20th. But I kept on putting it off, because – ironically enough – I was rehearsing the play *Museum* by Tina Howe – a comedic play with a satiric tone that cleverly explores how people view works of modern art (all the more reason to have gone). Be that as it may, I'm curious to find out what $850 million on renovations has achieved. It's supposed to be twice the size of the original museum: a space to breathe and view the art from an optimum distance; a space for the soul and senses to stretch, to yawn, to be at ease. Temples need space and true art needs worthy structures to house and home it. 630,000 square feet of redesigned spaces. More room for more paying people to pace or space around in. The excuse – the 75th anniversary of the MoMA. Cynicism is still coloring my mood, but only because I'm bothered that I can't just jaunt in, pay admission, and peruse the place. But I do want to see it – today! I have a need to know, to give my two-penny bit on the Mecca of modern. Artspeak on the subject is flourishing in all the intellectual circles; and both my higher and nether nature is vying for the *MoMAment* to add my thoughts to the rest of them.

But after a restless thirty minutes in the ever-growing line, and foreseeing at least another hour in the cold before I can get in, I think otherwise. Of course, if it weren't Monday I'd go to the Met instead. That's when I realize that the Monday after Christmas is one of the 'Holiday Mondays.' In other words: *The Met should be open today!*

Well, the MoMA's not going anywhere. With renewed élan and a definite dose of schadenfreude, I walk away from the languid line toward Fifth Avenue, hail a taxi, and speed along Madison up to 82nd in predictable fits and starts.

There's still a crowd. I reckoned that most of the tourists would be at the MoMA, or think (like me) that the Met would be closed today. I was wrong. The Met is, after all, the most visited site in New York City, with up to six million visitors a year. But it's bearable – nothing compared to the MoMA. In sedate elation I walk through the halls and chambers to where I know there'll only be a modicum of people. My mood has already changed and the cynic is subsiding. But as I gradually relax, I suddenly think about this morning's terrible news. How could those apocalyptic reports – even for a moment –have escaped me? Images of the devastating tsunami, which struck the coastlines of Sri Lanka, Indonesia, India, Thailand, and Bangladesh, inundate my mind. Tens of thousands have been killed, and it is projected that the final number will be well above one hundred thousand. The giant waves reached all the way to Somalia, Africa. In empathy with all the tsunami victims I walk to the Rockefeller Wing with the intent to sit midst the art of Africa and Oceania, but it's still closed off.

Now I'm in the medieval section slowly walking around the giant Christmas tree and the extensive crèche that's always erected at this time of the year. That's when I'm reminded of Alicia's offhand remark from yesterday. I sit down on the wooden bench in front of the wool and silk tapestry of the *Shepherd and Shepherdess Making Music* from 1500-1550. After jotting down a few notes summarizing the morning thus far, I try to recall the conversation with Alicia.

O

We'd opened Christmas presents, had breakfast, and were enjoying our last cup of coffee before her departure to spend the rest of Christmas day with Arietta. Casually Alicia mentioned that Sylvia had moved out.

"Moved out!" I gasped.

"Yeah, I thought you knew," she said, sucking absent mindedly on a candy cane.

"No, when did that happen?" I asked, shocked at the disclosure.

"Oh, I don't exactly know. She's been landing these film parts over the last two years which kept her away a lot." Alicia bit off a small chunk of the candy cane and chewed it noisily. "I don't really care."

"But why did she leave? Were they fighting? What happened? I mean, when did it become official that she was moving out?"

"There weren't any fights... not when I was around, anyway... well, come to think of it, there were a few disagreements. Anyway, apparently she met another woman," and Alicia shrugged her shoulders. "Whatever... that's all I know. I'm glad she's gone. Speaking of which... I have to go. I almost missed the train last time."

I don't even remember what prompted that noteworthy revelation. I couldn't get any more information out of Alicia, and I was surprised how indifferent she seemed about the whole affair. Arietta herself had never alluded to any of these new developments – not that we ever spoke about her relationship with Sylvia – a taboo topic.

Arietta downplayed their split-up when I called her that evening, and I couldn't tell whether she was suffering under it or not. Like Alicia, she didn't want to talk about it and quickly changed the subject. But I wondered whether our improved communications over the last few months had something to do with their eroding relationship, and not just our mutual concern over Alicia.

○

The cynical mood of the morning has totally evaporated. Though I didn't make it into the MoMA, as originally planned, I am filled with a feeling of thankfulness – knowing how many people are suffering right now. Maybe it's the latent Christmas, Hanukkah, Kwanzaa spirit, I don't know, but my mood, as I leave the Met, is imbued with inner peace.

I buy a metro card and feel some nostalgia for the era of tokens that's finally expired. I get on the 6, southbound. I find a seat next to a stocky man wearing a Yankees hat and reading *The Da Vinci Code*. Opposite me an obese woman wearing green slacks is eating curried chicken. Her lips are greasy, and it mixes with her bright red lipstick, giving the appearance of blood. Further up, a grungy, homeless man who looks like he has stepped out of the cover of Jethro Tull's *Aqualung* album, is playing a slow blues on the harmonica, while unconsciously grabbing his crotch. A young mother stuffs her left mammilla into her baby's mouth. Next to Mother Mary is a full bearded Hasidic Jew, wearing a black skullcap and long earlocks. On his knees he has a bouquet of red roses that are framed by the long fringes of his zizith. Two beautiful black girls wearing intricate cornrows are giggling and sharing an iPod between them, moving their tight, blue-jeaned hips to the music. At this moment I love them all, even the voice behind, "Stand clear of closing doors, please," that cautions all people at all stations, at all times.

2004 is trundling to a close.

New Year

Courtyard of the MoMA

I woke up early, but continued to lie in bed, trying to think back on the year and look ahead. Like every year, the New Year coincides with my birthday – all the more reason for some retrospection. I'd tried last night already, but it didn't work. I'd consciously avoided the Time's Square bash – the crowds, the noise, the hype, the loneliness of it all; I could do without the greatest party in the world. Instead, I went home, lit a candle, drank some homemade punch, lay back on my futon and tried to review the year. I didn't get very far. Inevitably my thoughts turned to the beautiful image of Draupati (as I always thought of her now). I sometimes wondered whether I shouldn't just have packed my bags and moved out to her – at least for a visit. I almost did after running into my neighbor, down in the basement, during a workout on the drums.

"Hey, bro, I haven't seen your pretty woman for months. I thought you two were for real, man… no longer around, huh?" he asked, leaning against the wall, stroking his tiny Chihuahua, which he cradled in his arms. He was a tall, thin Jamaican in his late twenties, with dreadlocks bulging out from under his ill-fitting do-rag and falling down to his waist; a barbed wire tattoo covered half his face. He always wore sandals, and had toe rings on every toe.

"She's moved back to India to be with her daughter. She left after her husband's arrest, you know."

"Ugly story, man" he said, nodding and sliding his almost seven-foot frame down to his haunches. "I heard you put up quite a fight," and he laughed, gently scratching his snuggling toy dog behind the ears.

"So you heard about it?"

"Ja mon!" He giggled. "Everybody around here knows. That rumor mill keeps on grinding, mon," and he chuckled again. "So, you'll see her sometime?"

"I wish, but it's better that I don't."

"Why?"

"Well, you know… work… obligations…"

"Hey, just tell me one thing – do you love her?"

"Of course I do."

"Then go out there and see her, you dumb-ass!"

And I almost did. I booked a ticket to Madras for over the Christmas break and sent her an e-mail that I was coming. Her reply, however, confirmed my hunch: another man had entered the equation – a lawyer who was helping women fight for their rights. She'd gotten to know him through the shelter. Though the news left me despondent for a few days, I was overcome with an inexplicable feeling of relief once I'd cancelled the flight. Strange, but her memory has become almost like a lost dream. A comforting, pleasant one… a dream I could embrace at will, leaving me contented or sweetly melancholic, depending on the moment.

My thoughts turned to Alicia and what she was going through. She still looked awfully thin, but her attitude had shifted, and she was dutifully adhering to doctor's orders (though she did quit seeing the counselor).

The next thing I knew it was morning. I'd drifted off and slept right through the cacophony of New Year's Eve. My renewed efforts to resume my retrospection fared no better. For a while I fantasized a bit about my book becoming a best seller, based on a smattering of positive reviews from the advance reading copy. But I'll have to wait for the March 1st publication date to find out. Other than that and a vague wish that the year would bring something good, my mind couldn't wrap itself around anything. Eventually a phone call from Alicia got me to my feet.

"Happy birthday, Dad! Meet us for breakfast at the Le Gamin Café in ten minutes; me and Mom have a surprise for you." Her voice sounded excited. Their unexpected invitation made me realize what a loner I'd become – and how lonely.

They were already sipping tea when I arrived. An orange gerbera in a little blue vase was placed between the salt and pepper shakers – one of my favorite flowers. Two wrapped presents lay on my side plate. After we ordered breakfast I opened them. The one was a framed drawing of me writing at the Met. "You know the day I tagged along with you? Well, I made a quick sketch of you. It was really fun. Your posture and the way you were poring over your notebook seemed like a cool composition." Alicia paused. "Do you like it?"

"Wow, it's outstanding. Your stroke is so confident and precise. And the shading... you caught every nuance... but is that really the way I look when I write – so hunched over?"

"Yeah, totally; but it makes you look like the quintessential writer type."

"Whatever that might be," I said, smiling.

"You know what I mean... just look at your wild hair. Anyway, happy birthday, Dad." She leaned over and kissed me on the cheek.

Arietta's present came in the form of an advance family ticket to the MoMA. "I thought it would be nice for the three of us to visit the MoMA today."

"Today? Together? Really?"

"Yeah, that's the idea," said Arietta, smiling, "unless you had something else in mind."

"Sure, like going down to the basement and bashing away on my drums."

"You can still do that later," she said, tapping my hand lightly with hers. "Happy birthday, Clarence."

As expected, it was packed, and it felt good to bypass the long line with our tickets. I was impressed with the changes. They surpassed my expectations. I felt I could extend my spirit throughout the hallways, staircases, openings and windows. We decided to take the elevator up to the fifth floor and work our way down. Once on top, however, I was immediately overcome with vertigo when I stood by the glass railing and looked down at the courtyard and ground floor far below me. It took me a few conscious moments and some deep breaths to adjust. Alicia, with drawing pad in hand, was eager to race ahead. We made an arrangement to meet at Rodin's *Monument to Balzac* down by the Garden Court in two hours – and off she ran.

We spent almost an hour just viewing the two uppermost floors with all the treasures of the late 1800's and early twentieth century. It was like a reunion tour of sorts. There they were again – the well known works by Picasso, Pollock, Klee, Chagall, Monet, and Van Gogh, and many other old friends. We pointed them out to one another, exchanging views, thoughts and tidbits of information. Neither one of us had been back here since we frequented the MoMA together many years ago. I'd forgotten how knowledgeable Arietta was in all things art. Her father had been an art history professor, and even as a child she'd watched him put umpteen slide shows together for his students. She loved to go through them with him, listening to his erudite ramblings. By the time she was fourteen she knew as much as an art major in college. She was the expert. Compared to her I was a novice. I realized how much I missed walking through art museums with her, hearing all those funny and interesting stories about this or that artist, or little known details about specific works.

While examining how the art was arranged in the context of the walls, roofs, slanted ceilings, staircases, and so forth, it felt like I was being reacquainted with the Arietta I once knew, before we'd grown apart. By making each other aware of this or that detail we were simultaneously exploring who we once were and who we'd become. At the same time I was also aware of all the things that we'd never spoken about, and it felt like a widening abyss beneath us, filled with the pain we'd caused each other. Did she feel it too? Had she analyzed our relationship like I had – gone over each and every detail? The longer we walked through the MoMA the more I felt we were traversing over a precariously narrow bamboo bridge swaying in the gusts of our respective guilt – a few wrong moves and we'd plunge into the chasm.

As we were quietly standing in front of Henri Rousseau's *The Sleeping Gypsy*, Arietta said softly, "Take a look, there are six stars in the sky, but the eye of the lion is like a seventh star – the brightest one. For me the lion has always stood for courage; and the number seven, which is recognized as a spiritual number in almost every culture, I see as representative of wholeness or unity of soul. However, the lion can also kill, or be killed, which would prevent the harmonic possibilities of the seven... thus doomed to incompleteness." Arietta laughed self-deprecatingly and added, "I'm sure Rousseau didn't have that in mind when he painted this painting."

That's when I knew. It was like a sign, a clue, a prodding intimation:

"Arietta?"

"Yes?"

"You know, something in what you just said... maybe it's the thing about the six stars versus the seven... incomplete against wholeness... I don't know... or maybe what you said about the lion..."

"Clarence, come out with it. You're making no sense"

"Yeah, I know. What I really want to say is... I wish we could get together sometime and just talk."

"What do you mean?"

"There's so much that we haven't said to one another... so much that we've kept to ourselves. Okay, maybe I'm only talking for myself. But there's stuff I'd like to get off my chest. Stuff I'd like to get perspective on. It sounds silly, I know, but I need closure."

"Hold on – *hold on!* You want to talk about what?"

"All the unfinished stuff... you know the "six stars" stuff. I want us to come to a place that's finished – the lion's star."

"But we *have* talked... ad nauseam. Remember the hours we spent when things first came out into the open? It did more harm than good. You know it as well as I do."

"Yes, but we often talked past one another, or we were too emotional. I don't know about you, but it was hard for me to be objective. Over the last few years I've had time to think, and I'd feel so much better if we could talk about some of that stuff."

"I don't know. I wasn't prepared for this... it comes as a bit of a shock."

"Does it? I think we're ready for it. It's been so much better between us lately. Time has changed us. If we don't take the opportunity to talk, we

Above: *The Sleeping Gypsy*, Henri Rousseau, MoMA

might miss the chance, and then we'll have to do it in some antechamber of heaven with St. Peter gloating over us."

"Very funny." She grabbed me by the arm and pulled me along. "Maybe you're right, but at the moment I'm just happy keeping it simple and hanging out with you. And you know how important it is for Alicia."

"Sure. But is that the only reason why you invited me to the MoMA today – for Alicia's sake?"

"Of course not. But I really don't know if I'm ready to talk about old stuff. It's like stirring up old shit."

"More like getting rid of the shit, once and for all."

"Maybe." Arietta brushed her thick, red, velvety hair from her forehead. After a pause she added, "Well, to be quite honest, there've been times when I've wanted to clarify a thing or two with you."

"See! There you have it."

"It's all a state of mind," she said, stopping and pointing at Umberto Boccioni's *States of Mind*. "There's an applicable metaphor here somewhere."

"How so?"

Arietta was smiling. "Look what he calls them. *The Farewells – Those Who Go – Those Who Stay*. We've said our farewells, we've gone, but something always stays," and she flicked up her hands. "C'est la vie."

At that moment Alicia ran up, panting. "Hey, where've you been? I've been waiting for you down at the Garden Court for ages. Come on, hustle, I'm starving."

"You're starving? Well, that's good to hear," I said, laughing and giving her a tight squeeze.

"Well, you know what I mean. What I really need is some coffee."

"Me too. Let's go check out the food court."

After lunch we walked around for another hour or so before it was time to go. I saw them off at Penn Station.

◯

I've been reclining on my futon, writing on the day's events, drinking rooibos tea, nibbling on an assortment of cookies, and listening to

Shostakovich's string quartets. It's dark outside by now. Must admit, it's been a good birthday. Anyway, I think I'll go and play some drums – gently, so as not to wake up wee little baby, 2005.

Meet Me at the Met

Great Hall

I suggested she meet me at the Met at 10:30. Presently I'm sitting on the hard wooden bench left of the octagonal information desk, busy with my usual accoutrements of pen and pad, keeping a ready eye on the main entrance for Arietta. I am looking forward to seeing "The Gates" together with her. It's only 10:10 a.m.

O

Arietta did call me up about ten days after my birthday: "Okay, I'll take you up on that offer of yours. Let's get together and talk. I've thought about it and I think you're right. At least it's worth a try...." We met at the Cloisters, overlooking the Hudson River. That was three weeks ago.

It wasn't as easy as I'd imagined. For a while we just ambled around the Cloisters looking at this and that, though we weren't interested in any of the art or architecture – not today. Eventually we sat down on the bench inside the Pontact Chapter House, looking out onto the west arcade of the Cuxa Cloister. That's when I let her in on the secret of my writing project, and how it had partially led me to explore the demise of our relationship.

"So you weren't just writing poetry as Alicia presumed."

"No, that's what I used to do back in the day."

"I remember. You wrote poems and I sketched, and we used to share them with each other over coffee."

"That was fun. Do you still sketch?"

"No, I haven't for years. Alicia's taken my place." She shrugged and smiled. "So, what's on your mind?

"Well, you were right with one of your accusations."

"Which one, there were so many?" And she laughed, jabbing me with her elbow. "Just kidding."

"Well, you were right when you accused me of not understanding women. That's where I fault myself the most. And yes, I still don't, of course, but I've become more aware. Anyhow, there were many specific areas that I was just clueless about."

"Like what?"

"Well, like Alicia's eating disorder or your relationship with Sylvia. I mean, how could... oh, never mind."

"Still not quite over it, are you?"

"Yeah, okay, I'm sorry," I said, surprised at the sudden surge of emotion. "Let's go. Other people are coming." We'd gotten off to a bad start.

We climbed down the stairs to the Gothic Chapel and out into the garden of the Bonnefont Cloister, walking in silence and looking over the Hudson River, though it was overcast and foggy. Much to my disappointment the concession stand in the Trie Cloister next door was closed, but we sat down anyway at one of the tables, looking into the bare winter garden and switched off fountain. Arietta must have read my mind because she brought out a thermos. "Want some coffee?"

"You bet! That's exactly what I need. Well prepared, as always. Thanks."

"And somewhere in my bag I've also got a cranberry muffin... here you go," and she handed me the muffin and poured me a steaming cup.

Warmed up, strengthened and feeling better, I told her the thoughts that I'd kept to myself for so long. How I'd battled to come to terms with her leaving me, the anger and hate I had to overcome, the ongoing love I'd felt for her, the slow process of forging a new life for myself, and even slower realizations of my own shortcomings that had led to the split.

She was mostly silent, listening intently, only asking a few clarifying questions intermittently, or urging me to continue when I paused too long. In between, her eyes went misty.

After I'd exhausted myself she wanted to go. Instead of bringing her down to Penn Station I offered to drive her up to Red Hook. She accepted. In the car she told me details of how she got together with Sylvia. "Really, it was mostly because I needed someone to be intimate with, and you were too locked up in your own affairs. It began as a friendship and just developed from there."

"How can it just develop?" Again I sensed a fine film of blame in my voice.

"Really quite naturally." She took a quick sip from her bottled water. "It was in the summer before we separated, during the heat wave. You were constantly writing on your book and I was mostly down at the theater. We were putting on *A Taste of Honey* by Shelagh Delaney."

"Yeah, I remember."

"In between rehearsals we spent many afternoons at her place. It was terribly hot and we often lay half naked in her loft. In our sleepy, steamy state we sometimes satisfied ourselves, a bit like in Otto Dix's painting in the Neue Gallerie – you know the one – Dix's *Two Girls* on the bed, masturbating. Then, one day we did it to one another, and, yeah…." Arietta sat back, looked out of the window, unconsciously playing with her pearl earring, slowly twirling it back and forth. "You know, it really didn't feel like I was having an affair. Not at first anyway. We were more like two giggly high school girls. There was no romantic passion involved. I'd never done anything like that before; in fact, it had never even occurred to me. Nor was I really attracted to her – we were just playing around. I know you'll think it strange, but had I gone with another man I would have felt like I was cheating on you, but with her it was just an extension of our friendship… until we fell in love. Yes, then I knew it was different. And that's when I told you."

I didn't want to hear more. Not at the moment. I thought I'd be stronger. We drove on in silence. After a while she put her hand on mine and squeezed it. The gesture choked me up.

After arriving at her house we continued sitting in the car in silence. There was so much more that I'd wanted to say and ask, but I'd reached my limit for the day. I could sense my emotional vulnerability and I was beginning to hurt. Old wounds easily open, no matter how much time passes. I intuited she felt the same. Even so, I had one more question on my mind, something I was curious about, for years already.

"Remember the time you left me for those three days, after I told you about the Swiss girl?"

"Of course!"

"Where did you go?"

"Oh yes, I never did tell you…" She took a strand of her ruby hair, twirled it a moment before flicking it back. "God, I was so mad at you that day. So mad, in fact, that I went to see my ex-boyfriend. He was still studying at Carnegie Mellon at the time. If you recall, I left him because of you."

"What! You went back to that Larry Crawford guy? Oh man, how could you, after the way he treated you?" (She'd told me ghastly stories of his pathological possessiveness and his dominating and abusive nature).

"Yeah, and as it turned out, he was still an asshole. I was just reacting, you know… avenging myself for what you'd done. After an evening with him I remembered exactly why I'd dumped him. Clarence, if it makes you feel any better – you were always in my mind, even though I was so damned pissed off at you. There was no doubt in my mind that I'd return to you. The rest of the time I stayed at my sister's."

"But you did spend the night at his place?"

"Yes."

"And… did you… you know—"

"Sleep with him?" she asked, looking sharply at me. "No, I didn't… but almost." With that she opened the car door. "Okay, got to go now. Bye… and thanks." Before shutting the door she added, "It meant a lot to me… you know… talking and all." She was about to say something else, but decided against it. "Take care."

After our rendezvous I came down with a severe bout of flu: fever, runny nose, and a cough that crept right down to the depths of my chest, followed by a sinus infection. Luckily it coincided with the winter break so I only missed one week of school. But I *had* missed the unveiling of "The Gates" on February 12th. And it's a true test of my patience that I didn't take a sneak preview of them this morning before my scheduled date with Arietta. Even my first glimpse of the saffron sails from outside the park, as I walked over to the Met thirty minutes ago, moved me. This is, no doubt, the first great artistic event of the millennium, eagerly anticipated by literally millions. Thousands have come flying in from all over the world; a welcome boost to the city's economy. Years ago, in '95, I'd witnessed Christo and his wife Jean Claude's wrapping of the Reichstag in Berlin, Germany, and although it was impressive and thought provoking – given the Nazi backdrop – it wasn't that much different from seeing huge buildings in New York covered completely in plastic during construction. "The Gates," however, are an entirely different happening, on so many levels; the aesthetic allure alone is justification enough. Although many are pooh-poohing the project ("Put sugar on shit and it still tastes like shit!"), it cannot dampen my enthusiasm; so what if it cost $20 million (carried wholly by the artists).

O

There she is. Finally. It's 10:42. She looks striking in her long cashmere coat, her silky, long, bronze-red hair fluttering behind her. It'll blend well with the large swaths of bright orange fabric. "Sorry I'm late... damn traffic," she yells over to me as the guards check through her purse.

The Gates

The Gates, Christo and Jean-Claude, Central Park

We walked up the extremely crowded narrow staircase to the Met's Roof Garden, where we hoped to get a great bird's eye view of the gates meandering through Central Park. We were disappointed. It wasn't what it was made out to be. Instead of one continuous orange ribbon, it looked more like something constructed from a Meccano set. The eye was caught by the frames that appeared flimsy from this vantage point, instead of the color. Undeterred, we squeezed our way back down the congested staircase to get out into the park as quickly as possible.

It was a brilliantly blue and crisp Sunday morning and hundreds of thousands of people were milling about from one end of the park to the other – an unprecedented sight. It made perfect sense that Christo wanted people to experience the gates up close. Seeing them at ground level was a very different experience to the one we had from the Roof Garden. The processions of gates merged into one another, one orange flame after another. For a few expectant minutes we just looked at the looming sixteen foot tall gateways, a foot for each day of their existence, apprehending them with awe – this rolling and heaving saffron delight. At eye level, the colors shifted between silvery bronze and succulent ruby red, depending on how the pleated nylon caught the sun. Passing through the inaugural gate was almost a ceremonial act; I was conscious of their symbolic significance – gates and archways have always held an important place in mythologies, legends, folk tales, fables, as well as in social customs and traditions, expressing change from one state into another – inner or outer (expressions of initiation and transformation). They convey a beginning or an end, an entering and an exiting. As it is, we are continuously going through something, yet we're mostly unconscious of all these little gateways. In between there are the more obvious occasions like the first day of school, the wedding day, respective graduations, transfers, promotions, or the first home run (not to mention unforgettable disasters, accidents, firings, break-ups, and so forth). But even within each day we traverse through wide and narrow, tall and tiny gates, mostly unconsciously. Gateways demarcate one state from another, and the grandest, most mysterious ones we call birth and death.

With these thoughts in mind I took Arietta by the arm and we passed through the first gate together. We continued stepping through the next few swelling sentinels in silence and made our way past the Obelisk, then down to the Great Lawn with Turtle Pond on our right. Arietta stopped often, scrutinizing, studying and contemplating the gates from different vantage points, shooting away with her digital camera, while I philosophized and tried to get little sample pieces of the fabric from the volunteer helpers, but they'd run out of the little squares; none left, not one.

The paths with their new look and greater meaning summoned us along; an endless interweaving, crisscrossing thoroughfare, daring and urging us to pass through every single one of the gates. Obsessed, we continued on westwards to Summit Rock, the highest natural elevation of the park, marveling at the magnitude of the spectacle below us. Not lingering long we ambled north, our eyes continuously feasting on the warm undulating colors adorning this usually drab winter landscape. On and on we strolled, past the reservoir, until we came to the somewhat less populated Great Hill in the northwestern quadrant of the park. Here we rested, awed by the sight of the friendly gates marching around the crescent field below. Tired, we flopped down at a picnic table, amidst the orange glory and bleak elm trees, uttering inane comments like, "Amazing... remarkable... fantastic... wow... isn't this great?" We were catching our breaths as much as releasing exclamations.

"It seems as if these gates want to tell us something," Arietta said after a while, stretching her legs in front of her and wiggling her feet. "And I'm not talking about the gates as a symbol. What I'm feeling arises more out of the color."

"What do you mean?"

"There's power in it. A quiet, restful power… issuing from my soul… coming from inside, so to speak."

"Yup, I hear you. It has a radiant quality."

"But not forceful … more in a tender and warm kind of way." Arietta brushed the ample hair out of her face with both hands, leaving them clasped on top of her head, holding the locks in place, which highlighted her well-formed, almost classical facial features.

"Exactly. What genius to choose this color for the month of February, which is not only outwardly the dreariest month, but also inwardly. We're getting sick of winter and spring is still a long way off."

Arietta let go of her hair, leaned forward and rested her chin on the palms of her hand, staring dreamily out into the lightly billowing fleet of fabric. "I remember my father once saying – and he's studied color theory right back to Newton and Goethe – that red is the most majestic color, but that orange is the most strengthening… and I think he was right. I can feel it – just staring into this orange splendor."

"Right, it makes me yearn for something, but I don't really know for what."

"Something better—"

"Essential—"

"Hopeful," she added quietly, staring in front of her for a while longer, before standing up and saying decisively, "Okay, let's go and follow the call of the maze again."

And we did, through the North Woods, along wide and narrow paths, up and down bluffs, and along the quiet shores of Harlem Meer. The Gates began to walk with us, clambering, jumping, skipping, sometimes just standing together in gossiping clusters. It was New York's greatest open air party, a Feb fest of unparalleled proportions – with total strangers getting into conversation, laughing, exchanging trifles, or pointing things out to one another.

"I don't think this could have happened anywhere else in the world… or let's put it this way: Central Park is the perfect setting for this project, especially since 9/11."

"Definitely. It's almost as if "The Gates" are redeeming 9/11," Arietta responded. "If you think of all the people from different nationalities who were killed in the World Trade Center, and then compare it to this peaceful gathering of people from all around the world, brought together through art... yeah, it's an act of redemption."

"In a way, all true art is," I added. "Anyway, I've never loved Central Park as much as now."

"Amen."

"You know, as you were talking, I suddenly got this vision of a gigantic saffron sail fluttering between the twin towers... can't you just see it?"

"Absolutely," she said and laughed, linking her arm through mine. "Clarence, it's really good to be doing this with you today."

Three and a half hours later we arrived back at the Met, our starting point, spent and hungry.

At Arietta's suggestion we went to Café Sabarsky, on 5th and 86th , for coffee and a bite to eat. I always loved going there. It was like entering a Viennese café of the early twenties or thirties. The Austrian newspapers in wooden clamps on racks in the corner, the coat stand, the baby grand, the mirrors, the high ceilings and chandeliers – all very old school European.

It felt good coming in from the cold, as we were. Arietta's face was glowing from the long walk, looking relaxed and young. I couldn't remember the last time I'd seen her so at ease, so carefree.

We ordered soup, Viennese coffee and a Sacher Torte to share.

O

Now I'm sitting in exactly the same place as this morning, but the bench doesn't seem quit as hard. After we parted (she had to meet one of her backers who she hoped would help bankroll her next theater project), I couldn't face going back home quite yet. So here I am again, in the safe anonymity of the Met's Great Hall, strangely comforted by the familiar drone of the throng all around – writing and rereading what I've written. Every now and then I look up from my notebook and eye the entrance, half expecting to see her coming through those doors again. We had a good day. I'd forgotten how compatible we were.

I'm looking forward to tomorrow. We'd arranged to meet at the Plaza Hotel for breakfast, after which we planned to go for one more walk through The Gates. This time the invitation came from her. "And I have a surprise for you," she said, as she stepped into the taxi.

The Gates in Central Park

Imagine

The Imagine Mosaic in Central Park

Usually it's the cooing of the pigeons that wakes me up at five-thirty in the morning, but the sound of snow shovels in my ears told me it was going to be a different kind of day. Satisfied, I went back to sleep for another two hours.

I walked up St. Marks to Cooper Square through the slush and snow, catching the almost empty subway up to 57th. A man in pin stripes with an attaché case on his lap was reading a newspaper. The heading, *Gonzo Journalist Thompson Kills Self*, caught my eye. Fear and loathing leads to a bad end, in Las Vegas or anywhere else.

Walking at a fast clip toward the Plaza I wondered with anticipation what The Gates would look like on this powdered morning. As soon as I got my first glimpse of them – these giant peace flags, gently undulating in the wind – I knew that the walk through the park would be a good one.

She was already waiting for me, sitting at a table near the classical guitarist who was entertaining the guests. "You look well rested," I said, brushing off the chill and trying to warm up.

"Of course, the Plaza has really comfortable rooms," she answered.

"What do you mean?" I asked. In the way of an answer she tilted her head slightly and smiled. "Don't tell me you stayed here!"

"Uh-huh," she said, enjoying my disbelief.

"How can you afford it? I mean… why didn't you tell me?"

"Well, you never asked. And besides – I'm not paying. The sponsor of our theater, who I had to see yesterday, finagled it for me. I am, after all, staging a play for one of her friends."

"You lucky thing. I've always wanted to spend a night in this opulent landmark, with Central Park as its front lawn, as they say. Just think of all the celebrities who've stayed here… I mean, Led Zeppelin and the Beatles used to hang out here!" I looked around. Though elegant, it felt crowded. "So, does it meet your expectations? It kinda feels a bit like the Grand Central of chic."

"Actually, it's great. Now, what will you have?"

We hurried through our breakfast, and even with the excellent guitar player offering sweet and dulcet background music, we couldn't wait to get outside to walk more "gate miles."

Sounds trite, but it was magical. We entered through Artists' Gate, which today, we took as a tribute to the artists Christo and Claude. What a contrast to yesterday. We were almost alone and the snow lay untouched all around us, above and below. The snow on the elm trees accentuated the beauty of the tapering multitude of branches, lending them softness within the polyrhythm of their interweaving complex contours. The expression 'winter wonderland' had regained its meaning. The silence that only newly fallen snow can emit enshrouded us in a mood of rare serenity. And ablaze within this heightened white whoosh, along the entire twenty-three miles of pathways, were the saffron hung gates, all 7,500 of them, warming our hearts, eliciting secrets from nobler sources. The beauty was further enhanced along the Literary Walk. The vista of trees and gates topped with snow had us stopping every few feet, taking in the spectacle. Shakespeare, what sonnet would this scene have sparked in your mind? I wondered, as we walked by his statue – bald pate patched white. The volunteers with their long poles capped with tennis balls (to put the swaths back in place in case they got muddled up) were well stocked with the little square samples, and we got some for ourselves and for Alicia.

Beyond the Mall we walked down the magnificent stairs by Bethesda Terrace, along the lake, passed Cherry Hill back up to Strawberry Fields, where the golden Gates were particularly striking. On a whim we chose to follow separate ways: Arietta walked along one path and I along the other, though we both paced consciously underneath the densely placed, free-standing portals. We met up again at the *Imagine Mosaic*, dedicated to John Lennon who was shot down just across the road, outside the Dakota back in December, 1980. Red and white roses, neatly arranged around the center of the "mandala" still peeked through the fluffy snow amidst charmed, mostly hidden, good luck pennies. We were back at the place where we'd decided to get married many years ago, and now, as we stood there in silence, peering down at the circle of peace, I knew she was thinking of that special moment. It had been summer then, and teeming with people. Now, with the snow, it felt like mid-winter, and we were alone.

"Come on," she said softly, and took my hand. She led me to the center of the mosaic, careful not to trample on any of the flowers. We stood close together, quietly, looking at one another. "I have something for you," she whispered.

"I've been wondering about that surprise you mentioned yesterday."

She opened up her bag, took out a small box and handed it to me. "Here you go…"

It was quite heavy. I weighed it in my hand.

"Come on, open it."

Slowly and carefully I opened the box and withdrew a small sculpture wrapped in saffron silk paper. Instantly I realized what it was – *The Seated Harp Player*, the one she'd given to me as a parting gift in Greece, and which had broken on my travels.

"I fixed it. You can still see the cracks, but it should hold. It's as good as new if you don't look too closely at the scars."

"Does this mean…?" I asked, hesitantly, looking into her dark eyes.

"Yes, it does… if you can imagine it?" she said, giggling like a girl.

"I can… even with soggy shoes."

"Well then – imagine." She slowly put her arms around me, those arms I hadn't known for years. We kissed – rekindling passion from the ashes.

O

I've been up for a while, writing. Now, the morning light is slowly filtering through. I'm sitting by the window. The view from the Plaza is even better than I thought it would be, up here from the sixteenth floor, facing Central Park. The specks of orange appearing and disappearing behind the trees are like elusive promises of the golden age yet to come.

Though we talked until two in the morning, I still woke up before sunrise. Alicia will be happy when she hears the news of us getting back together. It won't be easy. Stuff happened. Changes will have to be made. But we're willing to work at it. If we hold true to that – the rest will follow.

Now I know what drove me to the Met with such inexorable force; why I had to write. It was more than an exercise in self-development. It was more than mere journaling (though it could serve as the groundwork for a memoir). Each visit to that venerable museum was like lowering steel bases onto the walkways of my life, to support the gates through which I needed to pass on my journey back to Arietta.

I guess I won't be using these green notebooks anymore.

Replica of the *Seated Harp Player*, Martina Angela Müller (private collection)

About the Author

Eric G. Müller was born in Durban, South Africa, and studied literature and history at the University of Witwatersrand, Johannesburg. After a few years working at a variety of jobs, playing and performing music, and traveling around Europe, he attended Emerson College in Sussex, England and the Waldorf Institute in Witten-Annen, Germany, where he specialized in music education. Together with his family he moved to Eugene, Oregon, where he taught for eight years. Currently he is living in upstate New York, teaching music, drama, English literature and creative writing. He is a founding member of the Alkion Center and is the director of the Education department. He has taught at Simon's Rock College of Bard as an adjunct teacher and summer courses at Sunbridge College. His novel *Rites of Rock* (Adonis 2005) is a fast-moving and riveting saga that examines the phenomenon of rock music. In *Coffee on the Piano for You*, Eric Müller presents old and new poetry written mostly while traveling or drinking coffee. *Meet Me at the Met* is his second novel.

www.ericgmuller.com

Photo by Martina Angela Müller

CPSIA information can be obtained at www.ICGtesting.com
Printed in the USA
BVOW03s0926210813

329114BV00006B/13/P

9 781935 514497